Killing Budd
phony love a
world and th
    The heroin   M000191329
imperfect, as well as funny as hell, scathing, snarky, and
ultimately totally authentic.
Seekers and cynics will equally enjoy the trip.
~ Arielle Ford author, *The Soulmate Secret*

"Warning: Don't read this book if you are a prude or
aren't willing to flip your sacred beliefs upside down in
the pursuit of Truth (with a capital 'T'). This story is not
for the faint of heart, but for those who sincerely desire
a deeply grounded approach to spiritual growth and
evolution. Killing Buddha is a skeptic's guide to higher
consciousness that will entertain you, make you laugh,
cry and wake the bleep up."
~ Kelly Sullivan Walden, Bestselling author of
It's All In Your Dreams and *Luminous Humanness*

"Killing Buddha is a much-needed tonic to the
sometimes-toxic beliefs that have seeped into the New
Age / Spiritual movement. By poking fun at the all-
too-common potholes of posing, preaching, fixing, and
bypassing Chasse's book reminds us that authenticity and
healing are at best a messy, funny, awkward affair. This
book will help you gain the most important spiritual tool
for the journey: the ability to laugh at yourself and love
the gift of being fully, flawed human."
~HeatherAsh Amara, author of *Warrior Goddess Training*
and *The Warrior Heart Practice*

Killing Buddha
Author: Betsy Chasse
Publisher: Rampant Feline Media
www.rampantfelinemedia.com
Editor: Cate Montana
Book Cover: Suzette Maffi
Interior Design by: Andrea Scholz
ISBN: 978-0-9998354-8-7
ISBN Ebook: 978-0-9998354-1-8

Embrace Nothing:
If you meet the Buddha, kill the Buddha.
Live your life as it is, not bound to anything

~ Linji

Killing Buddha

By Betsy Chasse

CHAPTER 1

beep beep beep beep …

Is it my phone alarm or the oven timer ringing in another batch of my now famous, all-organic, gluten-free and even in vegan flavors, gourmet dog treats—Zak's Super Snacks—available worldwide at all of the finest retailers?

Either way, I'm standing in my kitchen, my sweet baby girl balanced on my hip, giggling happily, wearing Hannah Andersen from head to toe. My three St. Bernards, Manny, Moe and Jack, are crowding around me as I lovingly scoop freshly baked dog treats from the cookie sheet into my vintage McCoy Owl Cookie Jar—the one I bought at auction after my company went global.

beep beep beep …

Wait a minute. If I've got the cookie sheet in my hand, it can't be the oven.

I scan my kitchen searching for my phone, taking in my beautiful California Craftsman home—a real one, not one of those new-builds with the fake laminate wood floors. Mine is situated on a private cliffside road with a view of the San Francisco Bay, all shabby chic, white and soft pastels filling each room, a touch of modern with a smidgen of kitsch. My kitchen is stunningly white with stainless steel, of course, because that's how I roll.

I relish the perfection my life has turned out to be. A beautiful home surrounded by other millionaire entrepreneurs. (I may not be in tech, but all rich tech people love their dogs, and my dog treats are now a national must-have status symbol.) A ridiculously handsome, equally successful husband, a gorgeous angel of a child, my three St. Bernards (all from the same mother with impeccable pedigrees), and a Maine Coon cat, the fluffiest and biggest cat of them all, round out my picture-perfect life. A soulful Norah Jones plays as I dance around the kitchen.

Beep beep beep beep beep …

Jesus Christ! Alright already, let me just get a look at my shoes before I wake up …

My eyes pop open. That is not the oven or my phone alarm, it's my car. Someone is stealing my car! In a flash, I am transported back to reality and leap from my bed in Los Angeles, CA—Fairfax and 3rd to be exact—no stunning view, no stainless steel and pastels, no Saint Bernards, just my duplex in an apparently now crime-ridden neighborhood. As I tear towards my bedroom door, sans glasses, which makes me almost blind, I miss the door and my small toe connects with the door jam. Crack! *OMG! How is it that something so useless can cause so much pain?*

But that's something to ponder after too much wine as I sit alone on a Saturday night. Right now, I've got to keep moving.

"Piggy Toes, Piggy Toes, Piggy Toes," I curse-mutter—a useless something my mother taught me to say when I was six to take away pain that doesn't really work but hey, when knives are piercing the arteries in your leg and running is paramount to your car's survival, it'll do. It's also better than the alternative F-bomb I usually drop because I've been trying to sound less like a drunken sailor and more like my vision of what a successful Female Entrepreneur of The Year would sound like. I don't want to find myself screaming, "Get The fuck out of the way Karen" at school drop-off one day when I'm late for a board meeting and Chloe (my yet-to-be-born angel of a daughter) needs to be first in line at preschool so she can get yet another gold star and once again beat out all the other kids for Star Student of the Month, getting a leg up on acceptance into Harvard. You've got to start kids on the success train early.

As they say: fake it till you make it … right?

I hear my car engine roar to life and the sound pierces my heart. *Do not rev her that hard!* I think, panicked. *She's a woman who needs time to purr.* Typical asshole man, hops in and gets pounding. Men don't realize it takes the average woman 40 minutes to even get close to an orgasm. I read this somewhere and I'm sure it's true. I imagine my ex, screaming, "Are you going to cum?" *No asshat, not even close. But you go ahead. That's why you're here, isn't it?*

"Fuck!!"

Sometimes it's the only word that heals. Someone is stealing my car, I can't find my fucking glasses or my fucking shoes, and my dog Zak is howling like a rabies-infected hyena. I try to steady myself on the wall of my hallway as I hobble-run, managing to hit and shatter one of the last remaining pictures hanging on my once love-filled walls—a daily reminder that I am now single and on the other side of 35. Even Norah Jones couldn't get a woman's engine purring coming from the cheap-ass portable speaker I was left in the break-up. *Who am I kidding? Norah hasn't been around this place in a long time.* Norah is my go-to "I'm blissfully having orgasms" soundtrack, not my "I hate all men and the world sucks" soundtrack.

I sometimes regret my emotional, wine-fueled, blasting Icona Pop's "I Love It" outburst where I decided not to keep anything we bought together and, channeling my inner voodoo priestess, cursed it all as I, all by myself at two a.m., piled all his junk and our once jointly owned stuff out on the curb and then left about seven drunken messages letting my ex know about it. My original plan was to leave pieces of our stuff at all of our favorite spots around LA. But I soon realized that would take too much time and energy and, while I'm an excellent rager (Look out when I'm mad! I really do need to work on that), my anger that night had its limits. So, I only got our stuff to the curb.

By the time I woke up filled with rager's remorse, it was gone. I have no idea if my ex came and got it or the guy who trolls my neighborhood for recyclables thought he'd won the lottery. Either way, my house currently looks like an estate sale is in progress, or a drug addict lives here and is slowly pawning all his/her stuff for continued fixes.

It's probably true that having a good sound system would make my break-up soundtrack sting a whole lot more. There is something almost comforting in listening to Adele sing "Send my love to your next lover" all tinny and muffled, as if it's not really happening to me but somewhere far, far away in a distant universe and I just happen to be able to catch the sound as it blows by. Unfortunately, it never blows on by. The distant wails of heartbreak and betrayal linger in the air like the smell of rank weed. The portable speaker is waterproof though, which helps since I spend most of my time crying and singing depressing songs about unrequited love, cowardly men, and "I'm a fucking unicorn and you'll regret it when I'm gone" in the shower. I think my rendition of "Roar" rivals Katy Perry's version, although I'm pretty sure my dog doesn't.

My car has a great sound system. *Oh wait. Shit.* Yes, the car which is currently being stolen.

Death and emergencies. They both happen in slow motion with way too much time to think.

I finally make it to the front door in time to see my beautiful baby blue BMW convertible peel out of the driveway. I stand, still reeling from the pain in my piggy toe, looking out into my now empty driveway. Everything is blurry, almost like one of those bad Instagram filters you use when you don't like how you look in the picture and you're hoping blurry will make you look younger and happier. It never does. It just tells anyone who sees it you're probably looking like crap or you're hiding something. For me, it's usually my soul. I'm hiding my soul—or what's left of it—behind a fuzzy Instagram filter.

As I stand there in a tank top and thong, I notice my elderly neighbor waving to me from his yard. I swear that guy is single-handedly the cause of California's drought. I tried once to explain to him that watering his lawn and the sidewalk for two hours twice a day was excessive. I mean, we've been having a drought in California. And he proceeded to lecture me on his time in the war and how he'd survived D-Day and he damn well was going to water whatever the hell he wanted, whenever he wanted. Anyway, he keeps waving and so I just smile and wave back, figuring he probably hasn't seen a woman in her underwear in a good 20 years and hey, he's a veteran after all. It's my civic duty to honor those men. He damn well earned the right to ogle my butt cheeks. Then I notice he is pointing towards my driveway.

"Yes, I know! Someone just stole my car," I shout.

He shouts back, "They left something in your driveway."

I squint my eyes. Why do people with bad eyesight think this will help? But in this case, it does. I notice a small rock sitting in the center of my now carless driveway with what looks like a piece of paper underneath it. I hobble over, knowing full well that at this point the entire neighborhood is getting a TMI view of my ass. Well, screw it. After my two a.m. I-am-a-woman-scorned-dragging-my-lover's-shit-to-the-curb, one woman, off-off-off-Broadway performance art piece, I should just start selling tickets to my shit show of a life.

Sure enough, my car thieves left me a note. How thoughtful of them. But of course, I live in LA. We only have conscientious car thieves.

I retrieve my love note left by the Robin Hood of LA and, since I don't have my glasses, I can't read it. I make my way back into the house, trying to convince my dog that, no, this is not walk time or play time. It is, however, apparently pee time, and I wait impatiently as he does his thing on the magnolia tree in my front yard. Finally, I head back down the hall with the broken glass and empty nails where my cinematic past once hung with pride. The only pictures left are my old movie posters. The one that took the hit is *Zombie Strippers*, the crowning achievement in my 15-year career as a Hollywood movie producer. What had started out as a promising career as an award-winning producer of artful, profound film festival favorite indie films ended as the go-to producer of anything blood, gore and boobs . . . lots and lots of boobs.

Producing horror is akin to becoming a crack addict. Indie film is great and, of course, important and fulfilling. But it doesn't pay well, and being a proper Valley girl princess, I have expensive tastes—like my BMW and normally crime-free, hip, two-bedroom duplex in the Melrose district. So, a few years back, I swallowed my pride and decided to take on a shlocky gore film with a solid paycheck and a back-end deal that might actually be worth something. I figured I'd make some money and *then* work to find the perfect film to take the indie film festival circuit by storm, thus launching me toward Hollywood blockbusters à la Kathleen Kennedy. Well, flash forward ten years. Zombies. Alien monsters. Zombie alien monsters. (All of them with ginormous boobs, by the way.) And my pièce de résistance, *Zombie Strippers*.

Yes, I had money. But I lost my soul, hence the fuzzy Instagram photos.

I manage to make it back to my bedroom without further injury, find my glasses on my one remaining nightstand (it's fine, they didn't match anyway), put them on and read the big bold letters "YOU HAVE BEEN VISITED BY REPO DUDE." Seriously? Repo Dude? *I swear to God, I should start a business charging dipshits like this tons of money to brand themselves as something that doesn't sound like they spent the last few days high and lost in the Malibu canyons.*

I shrink down onto my bed, overwhelmed, wondering if this is what Meghan Markle went through before she married her prince, and suddenly hear my real alarm—I mean my phone alarm—ringing. Still in fight or flight mode, I grab it. It's 7:00 a.m. and flashing across my screen is a calendar reminder "Super Snacks sales pitch 9 a.m."

Fuck.

CHAPTER 2

Behind my apartment sits a preposterously tiny garage with the same door they installed when they built the building, which I think was around the 1930s or 40s. I thought the cars from the 40s were bigger? What the hell parked in here? Half a Studebaker? I unlock the door and gingerly open it, the wood so rotted pieces of it are literally falling off as it rises. There, behind the old film production boxes I'm told I have to keep for seven years for tax purposes and my collection of childhood memorabilia is the one thing I forgot to throw out on that I'm-gonna-drink-all-of-our-expensive-wine-club-membership-wine-in-one-night binge: my bike—a red beach cruiser with one of those adorable little wicker baskets on the handle and a gift from my ex.

I should probably name him so I don't have to keep referring to him as "the ex" and I can stop sounding like a bitter old man hater, even though I am bitter. His name is Tom. He's an actor and I met him on the set of a horror flick I produced, back when I was a Big Hollywood Producer—okay, maybe more like a producer of really bad, shlock B horror movies that paid well as opposed to a desperate, broke, female entrepreneur with the greatest new product to hit the pet market since scoopable kitty litter. Anyway.

He was a day player. (He had a small part, which meant he only worked one day.) I know we're not supposed to screw the help, but he was really hot and charming and funny, which gets me every time. He ended up in the crew hotel. (Usually the actors get nicer digs than the help.) But he seemed to prefer it, and we had an interesting evening chat. All he ever wanted to do was be an actor, and when we got serious about our relationship, I got him a much bigger part in yet another mediocre movie I was producing (I just kept cashing those checks.). This, in turn, helped him become a working actor in a town full of people desperately wanting to be that.

For Tom it didn't really matter that he was becoming the Rutger Hauer of the new millennium. (That Dutch actor would take just about any role as long as they paid his rate.) He just wanted to work, and it made me feel needed and appreciated and fulfilled my need for approval. In turn, he loved me for delivering his dream. We moved in together and all was just peachy . . . well, for him anyway. He had a career, money, a modicum of fame, and got to have sex in his very own dressing room. (I assumed only with me.) Life should have been good.

But it wasn't. I hated the soul-crushing crappy films I was making. I felt guilty wasting my time and talent. I wanted my name in lights, not in the B-movie bargain bin section at Wal-Mart. I had big dreams—you know, the house on the cliffs, waves crashing as I enjoyed a glass of Napa Valley's finest on the deck outside my amazing kitchen. I believed

Tom and I could live that life. Okay, he wasn't Brad Pitt famous. But he was building a career and it's not impossible for a B-horror flick actor to make it big. He would be my King and I his Dog Treat Queen living a charmed life.

Then there was the fact that on a daily basis while filming, I got to have the extra pleasure of watching the man I loved have all sorts of fun all over the set with all those gorgeous women with their ginormous boobs. It was too much! Way too much! And so, after a particularly grueling shoot day in the middle of the summer, somewhere in Death Valley (aptly named for my impending Hollywood demise), after hours of watching my man's face planted between two silicone-stuffed hooters while dealing with a diva director who somehow forgot we were making something just shy of a snuff film and not *Lawrence of Arabia* (okay, both films were filmed in the desert. They did have that in common), I lost my shit and quit.

I went home, sat in my kitchen with my dog and tried to figure out what to do next. When Tom made it back from the set, he, in his infinite male wisdom, figured I just needed a vacation. Because isn't that what all girls want? For their man to whisk them off their feet for a romantic getaway when they become hysterical?

It's true I needed a vacation. I'd done two films back-to-back. For the record, making movies isn't as glamorous as one might be led to believe. I mean maybe multi-million dollar movies, but making low budget movies is grueling, often 16-18 hour days, six days a week, and nary a five-star resort in sight. *People* magazine might show Tom Cruise on set in a doublewide trailer decked out with quartz counter tops and big screen TV's, but my set life was spent in something more like an old VW bus with the seats taken out and a plastic folding table. I was exhausted and ashamed, and my love for filmmaking utterly devasted. My passion project, the script I'd been peddling around Hollywood for a couple years had gotten nowhere, and it seemed I was destined to be the Hollywood shlock queen for eternity. To say I was depressed would be an understatement. So, he booked us a weekend in Ojai, an hour's drive outside of LA, because that's what Hollywood people do. They either go to rehab or to Ojai.

What was my passion project? It was a female-driven story of love and betrayal, featuring two society wives who end up having a love affair which rocks their small, strict, religious community. Hollywood wasn't quite ready, I guess, to deal with my gender-bending romcom. At that point LGBTQ didn't have as many letters in it and the #Metoo movement wasn't even a twinkle in Harvey Weinstein's eye.

What I didn't know was that Tom had promised my agent and the director, Joao Salvadore, that I would be back to work Monday morning, bright-eyed and bushy-tailed, ready to accept my fate, fame and fortune as the one who negotiated the contracts for the burned-out porn stars who wanted to make their way up from anal princess to Zombie Stripper.

You know, go legit. After all, Salvadore is some sort of riff on the word "savior." Maybe that's what got Joao all puffed up about his shitty movies, acting like he was saving the world one pale blue frame at a time. (Get it? "Blue movie?") Who the hell was going to save me? I had hoped that after all I did for Tom, in that moment he would be my champion, love me and support me in my dreams, or at least pretend to back me up. Sadly, he didn't.

This has been a pattern in my life; do everything I can to please those I love and wait to be rewarded with the love I so desperately want. The only difference was, this time I got tired of waiting. I had to save myself. And that's what I'd done—or was trying to do by starting my own company. For once it was going to be about my dream instead of a boyfriend or my parents living vicariously through me.

I wrestle the bike from the back wall, check the tires, shove my Luis Vuitton purse into the basket and off I ride to the 9 a.m. meeting that's been three months in preparation. West Hollywood to Santa Monica by car at rush hour can take up to an hour. By bike, who knows? All I know is I have 27 minutes to get across town and into a meeting that will hopefully make this already horrible day and my horrible life worth it.

Peddling hard, I can't keep my mind from going over the final scenes in my *Killing Your Hollywood Career*, starring Sara Wells, drama. After I didn't return to work that next Monday, most of Hollywood wrote me off as either: 1) a loser alcoholic or 2) a woman who had suddenly found her moral compass. Because why else would someone abandon a two-hundred-thousand-dollars-a-year-career unless addicted to Jack Daniels or Jesus?

Ironically, it was that weekend in Ojai that sealed my fate. We took Zak with us and found our way to a doggy bakery on Main Street. Imagine an entire store dedicated to baked goods for dogs! The place was packed with skinny, rich socialites and their chihuahuas, a ton of gay men with their malamutes, black labs and blue-eyed pit bulls, families with their dogs—the place was hoppin' like a Sunset Strip club on a Saturday night. *Hmmm… interesting.* That evening, back at our hotel, I spent hours researching the dog food and treat market and, as it turns out, the pet market was booming. It was also lacking in healthy gourmet treats for dog owners, suddenly not only interested in their own health and wellbeing but their pets' as well—specially their dogs. So, when Tom went off to the set that Monday morning, much to his chagrin, I stayed home— visions of a new business dancing in my head—and baked.

Zak loved my experimental treats and rapidly gained weight. By about week four I'd figured out some recipes and baked enough treats to hand out free samples at the local dog park. Dogs loved them and people loved them. I was onto something. I was also in my creative zone again, designing a logo and packaging, researching what I needed to do to sell to the general public and get into the stores. Unlike human food, I didn't have to bake dog treats in a commercially licensed kitchen. I got a booth at the local farmers market and soon I had repeat customers. A few local indie stores asked to carry my treats. I bought a pizza dough roller to help roll out the dough, and a prop maker I knew fashioned a cookie cutter with twelve bones on it for me so I could begin mass production.

I was working my ass off, baking all day, building a website by myself at night. And it was working. And I was happy, even though everyday Tom would come home from the set and try and share with me about his day—about how much everyone missed me and how the shoot just didn't run as smoothly without me. Joao (Mr. 'I wish I were Sir David Lean, maker of *Lawrence of Arabia* and other notable film epics') called nightly, lamenting about how dumb everyone was and how they didn't understand his art the way I did. Hell, I even got a call from our leading lady, Miss Double D's herself, begging me to come back to the set because no one treated her with respect anymore. (I love calling her the cha cha queen—well not *lovingly* anymore, since she was the reason I spent so much time alone in the shower.) I'm a nice person, really, underneath my scathing sarcasm and blunt style of communication. I actually had some respect for the cha cha queen, trying to lift herself up and out of full-on porn. Baby steps, ya know... until of course I found out my boyfriend was a rung on her ladder.

I felt for them. I really did. I may have been a sell-out to myself, but I'm a damn good film producer and always took care of my cast and crew. I fed them well and gave them enough sleep. And if we had an overnight, the hotel always had a bar and pool, even if the pool chairs were cheap and had no cushions and the top shelf tequila was more like a cheap copper than a gold … I tried. And my crew loved me for it.

But as much as I wanted to be there for Tom and everyone else, I couldn't go back. Back would kill me. This I somehow understood.

Eventually, Tom started coming home later and later, and a few times not at all. If I'm being honest, it took me a while to even notice, or I was in denial, hard to tell which. I was caught up in my new dream. I tried to involve Tom by asking him to do a voice-over for a little animation I created to market Zak's Super Snacks. Unfortunately, the time I had booked for the recording conflicted with a poster shoot with Miss Anal Princess (hereafter called the AP) for *Zombie Strippers 3, Members Re-animated*, and after that shoot everyone went to the Formosa and, well, one thing led to another and I guess the AP's ass was available. And then it was two a.m. and I had plowed through two and a half bottles of Pinot Noir from our favorite winery in Paso, and half our stuff was outside on the curb.

Since Tom left, in the last year and a half I've burned through every dime I had, building my doggy treat empire. So far, I've managed to get into a boutique grocery store chain and several upscale pet stores. I've contracted a bakery in both Southern and Northern California and have a potential order pending from a national chain. What I need now is capital. Which is why I'm riding a red beach cruiser to a meeting with a plastic retro basket holding all my dreams and the results of my life savings—a bunch of perfectly dog-bone shaped dog treats and a business plan on a flash drive (producers are great at creating business plans)— praying that it will all have been worth it.

I arrive at my destination and OMG! I've actually made it all the way to Santa Monica in about twenty minutes! *Maybe this bike-riding thing isn't such a bad idea.* I find a place to lock up the bike, wipe the sweat off my brow and rip off the leggings I'd put on underneath my Nordstrom business separates collection suit—a pencil skirt and blouse—and grab one of my last remaining pairs of Jimmy Choo's out of the basket. (Sadly, I had to sell most of my Carrie-Bradshaw-would-be-proud shoe collection at a consignment store to help pay the rent.)

I gather my stuff, compose myself and enter one of those tall glass buildings on Wilshire Blvd., my Jimmys click-clacking as I make my way to the elevator. Flash drive? Check. Sample bags? Check. Zak? Ugh, No Zak to be my very enthusiastic taste tester. Made from all organic ingredients, they're actually edible for humans. Dry as hell, but the dogs love them. Hopefully someone here has a dog. It is a pet food company for God's sake. They must allow people to bring their pets.

Ding. The elevator doors open onto a large, yet

minimalistic office lobby. I introduce myself to the
receptionist who, despite the Jimmys and pencil skirt,
at first treats me like a homeless person begging for
food. This is a thing in LA. Until they know you're
legit, you're dirt. But in a really nice way, just in case.

I see a young man bounding down the hallway
toward me. It's Steven, the guy who got me this
meeting. He has a Malamute named Henry, a really
gorgeous dog. He became a regular at the Farmers
Market and when I told him I was looking for an
investor, he mentioned he worked for the largest pet
food company in the US. And here we are. "Sara,
Sara!" he calls out as if we are long lost cousins
suddenly finding each other on a train in India after
fifteen years. I, of course, respond in kind with a
gushy LA greeting.

"Steven?! Oh, Steven, hello!" smiling and hugging
and offering up those absurd European two-check
kisses cultured people do. Look, whatever it takes,
right?

He leads me down a long hallway peppered with
images of adorable pets—dogs, cats, iguanas, exotic
birds—apparently all high off of whatever pet
product they've been ingesting. *Jeez! Zak likes his food,
but what the hell are they giving these animals?* We enter
a large conference room with one of those massive
faux wood tables that makes you feel really small. I'm
already small, like short. I'm short, like 5' 2" short.
(It's a trigger, okay?) So now I'm feeling downright
insignificant. *I hope they can see me over the top of it.*

There are five other people in the room and as

they go about introducing themselves, I am trying to come up with a song to help me remember all their names. (Pitching rule #1, address everyone by name . . . except all of us were born in the 60s and 70s while our parents were high, so our names aren't like Cathy and Jim, except for the twenty-something who brought me into this acid trip. His name is Steve. *Must be from the Midwest.* But then my own name is pretty normal and I'm from California. I decide to go with Disney characters because I've got a Jasmine and an Ariel and the men . . . well, as long as I smile coyly at them, they won't care what I call them.

I set up my PowerPoint, place my product samples on the table, and launch into my pitch. I've worked on this for months, practiced in the mirror a thousand times, run the numbers, have the cute animated commercial, sans Tom's voice. But it's good.

The room is silent through my entire ten-minute presentation. They all just stare at me as I enthusiastically share about my vision to save all the dogs on the planet from poisonous ingredients the evil corporations are feeding them, never once realizing that all the people I'm pitching are the exact same people that I'm raging on about, cause' ya know, they skimp. These people skimp and put who knows WTF in their food … and I just pointed that out to them. People actually don't like you if you shove how they're screwing over the little guy into their faces... or I should say the little dog?

"Hey," I chirp. "If we're all going vegan and gluten

free, our dogs should too! Right?"

Not a sound, not a nod or a smile. I thought for sure when my 30-second animation played I'd get a laugh. Something. But no. Nothing. Just six people in a deadpan stare for ten minutes. *Jesus. These people need to eat what the pets on the walls are eating!* And then it hits me. *Oh my God, I've just alienated the whole goddamned room! I literally just called them out to their faces for making crappy dog food and* … and there's no way I can backtrack and soften some of the things I've said. After about thirty seconds of stony silence I ask, "Do you have any questions?"

Everyone looks at each other. "Not me. No. I think we've got it."

As a joke to liven things up, I ask if anyone wants to try a treat because they're, you know, really, really healthy. (I hadn't seen any live animals in the building to commandeer as test subjects.) Another awkward silence, and then my long-lost cousin Steve stands up and opens the conference room door and holds it. I guess he forgot we were cousins because not even an air kiss is blown my way as I leave.

I walk the long hallway with the taxidermy-like grinning creatures staring me down. I can almost hear them back in the conference room muttering, "Wow! She really screwed that one up. Doesn't she know we make the chemical-ridden dog food she just trashed, accusing us of poisoning America's beloved pets? Dumb ass!" I pass the patronizing receptionist who clearly already knows my fate and make my way back down the elevator to my bike.

I can't even feel. I don't know what to feel. I am numb, like literally my hands are numb and I can barely hold onto the handle of the bike as I ride toward home. All I can think as I peddle is, *I wonder when the eviction notice will come.*

*As a side note – 3 months later (I kid you not) that very same company copied my entire product line and released it into the marketplace, right down to the cute blue dog logo. I literally gave them everything and they just took it. And we wonder why we are the most litigious nation, with the highest divorce rate with a population riddled with trust issues?

CHAPTER 3

I figure now is probably a good time to properly introduce myself. My name is Sara Wells. I'm 36 years old, single, broke and a failure. So, how did I go from having an awesome career, an up-and-coming actor for a boyfriend and plenty of money, to this?

I think my road to wash up began when I was eight years old. Marching as a baton twirler in a big Christmas parade, all smiles and cute little ruffle-butt panties, leading my troop down the boulevard, I was noticed by a Hollywood talent agent who told my parents "She has the look."

Before I knew it, I was a working actor, making several hundred K a year doing commercials selling dolls, toys, French fries—anything where a cute, all-American female kid was needed, which is what I seemed to be.

At first it was really fun skipping school, working on sets, being treated as special. And my parents loved it. We finally had money to buy a house and things were going well. By age ten, I was one of the highest paid commercial actors in *The Biz*, and we moved from our small town in the desert to what's known as "The Valley:" an area near Hollywood, but "over the hill" as they say. I didn't go to school. I had a private teacher who went to work with me. All my friends were kid actors, none of them chosen by me. We were all just sort of stuck together because we all had the same life experience. No sleepovers, no junk food, just retainers and flippers to make my teeth straight and my smile bright. My blonde hair was dyed brown because when I came on the scene there was already a pretty blonde girl. What they needed was a brunette, so I became a brunette and had my hair dyed every two weeks. I couldn't get my ears pierced, and I developed an allergy to eyeliner. Every Halloween my mom would pick my costume, and instead of regular Trick or Treating, I would go by the casting directors' offices and put on a little song and dance.

All of this seemed perfectly normal to me.

It wasn't until I was much older that I realized my childhood was non-existent. Instead of school dances and awkward moments with the boys in my class, I was shoved in a limo with the geeky sidekick to the hot young TV star because my agent was hoping I could transition from commercials to a TV series, and partying with TV stars was a good way to network. So, there I am at 13, "networking" with the shorter-than-me, gawky, full-on awkward teenager with big-rimmed glasses who acts like he's as suave as Sean Connery, trying to shove his tongue down my throat as my mother laughs and says what a cute couple we make.

My parents weren't awful people; I think we all just fell into the routine. Money and success can hypnotize you, and I had both at a very early age. And it was pretty easy to do—almost too easy. Success literally chose me right off the street, like a game show contestant randomly picked from the audience. "Hey Sara Wells, come on down! We're going to make you think we've made your life better and then, when you least expect it, you're going to guess wrong and get slimed." Cue audience applause and maniacal laughter soundtrack.

One day I'm in a parade, the next day I'm in a limo with a TV star named Scout Montgomery. From a pauper to a princess … the perfect Cinderella story. All should have been well in the world.

But it wasn't. By age 13 I was tired and wanted a break. All those stories about Drew Barrymore getting drunk as a teenager—girlfriend, I feel you. When I asked my parents if I could take some time off and go to a regular school, you would have thought I'd asked to shoot heroin or something. My parents lectured me on my commitments, house payments, car payments, medical insurance. They wouldn't let me be a "quitter" just because it was hard work.

"Life is hard work, Sara. You should be grateful you have it so easy."

I didn't want to be a disappointment, so I kept going.

By the time I was 16, the work started to slow down. I wasn't an adorable little kid anymore and there were other younger, more adorable kids who could sell fries better than I could. I also wasn't tall, slim and pretty. I was short, stocky and cute. Even so, I had done a few bit parts in TV shows and was up for a series regular on a new show.

"This is 'it' Sara," my parents told me. "Get this job and your career will be solidified and your wealth secured." The producer of the show had several other successful shows on air that all went into syndication, which meant re-reruns, which meant money flowing in for a very long time. Plus, TV shows had regular shooting schedules and long breaks where I could have a more normal life. That's what I was sold. "One good TV series can make your career, kid." And wasn't that what I had been working toward all these years?

I remember when the phone rang. Mom and I rushed over. She answered and all I remember her saying is, "Well, that's disappointing." And then she hung up and stood there in silence, all the while the word *disappointing* kept reverberating in my head. She finally turned to me and said, "You didn't get it," and walked away. This was how my mom was when she was upset, she went silent and cold. I knew better than to pursue her.

That fall I was allowed to enroll in a regular high school. Work was slow. I did a couple of small parts in movies, a couple guest spots on a TV show—ironically on the show I "wasn't right" for. It was a rough time. It was becoming painfully evident that acting was not going to be my career, and I hated school. I wasn't prepared for the day-in-day-out grind, sitting in a classroom listening to a teacher drone on, uninspired about whatever they were teaching. I talked to my counselor, who told me because I had the credits to graduate and my grades were good, I should consider taking an early graduation and head to college—which would be more aligned with my previous education.

While at my "normal" high school I joined a club of students interested in making films and found I had a real knack for it. Growing up on sets proved useful, and I decided I would take all the wisdom I had gained from my childhood, go to film school, and turn it into a career as a producer.

I set my sights on USC, got all the paperwork and my transcripts together, went home and asked my parents to sign the papers. That would be that. I would use my money to pay for college, become a famous movie producer and prove to my parents and Hollywood that I was, in fact, right for something.

But what was supposed to be the start to my triumphant return to success didn't go as planned. My parents, as it turns out, had pretty much spent all my money. Between buying a house, selling that one (at a loss, I was told) and then buying another one in a nicer area, some bad investments, taxes, agent fees, expensive dentists, hair dye, manicures—plus, the last two years we'd been operating at a loss in the hopes that things would pick up again—the $3 million I'd earned was gone.

Gone. My life's work was gone. At 17.2 years old, I was already a has-been: broke, without any ability to support myself.

I lost it.

This was my first mental breakdown. I quit

speaking to my parents. I quit acting. I got a real job at a local gift shop, then a job as a nanny for a famous writer, and then just floundered about for two years not knowing what I was going to do with my life. Then, through a friend, I got a job on a movie as a production assistant. I had a car, guts, ambition, and didn't mind the low paycheck and long hours and … well, here I am today.

When I quit on Joao and started Zak's Super Snacks, I felt like I had quit on my own terms. Never again would I stay in something because I "had to." I had had enough and, for once in my life, wanted to choose something for myself, just for me. I love animals. I love Zak. I love being in the kitchen. I love doing something useful. I convinced myself my years of producing movies, my life spent in business, was enough for me to be an entrepreneur. Running a dog treat empire would be a piece of cake. It was a great idea and *of course* I could pull it off. After all, I was a nothing little kid and then I was a star (well sort of). Then I was down again and then a successful Hollywood producer. None of it I actually chose. Both times opportunity found me.

This time I would choose, and I would rise again.

A horn blows and I swerve my bike automatically. I don't think I'm rising. I'm barely peddling at this point.

CHAPTER 4

As it turns out, the way home takes me past my agent's office. It's almost lunch time and I hope maybe she doesn't have a lunch scheduled with someone not broke and epically failing at life because I need a cocktail and, in my heyday, she was always up for a martini no matter what time it was.

I enter the lobby and just walk past Jeff. *Are all the assistants in LA from the Midwest?* I don't blame them for wanting to get away from the corn fields. Those rustling leafy green stalks give me the creeps. One too many alien ship landings and zombie scenes shot at night in corn fields has permanently removed that staple from my diet. Jeff tries to do his job and intercept me, but he knows me too well and I barge into Dana's office and plop myself down on her Ethan Allen couch.

"Well, hello," she says, as if expecting me.

"I need a drink. Do you have any vodka left? I know you have a bottle in your drawer. Let's just stay here and get drunk," I whine.

She sighs, "Sara, I'm sober. I have been for six months. If you weren't so absorbed in your own self-induced downward spiral, you'd know that."

I look at her, stunned. *Why, why, why is everyone getting sober? How can anyone handle this world sober?!* She gets up from her desk and grabs what looks like a gym bag and a yoga mat from her closet. "I'm going to yoga. You should come. We'll take your car, let's go."

Forced to share how my morning went without the added benefit of a cocktail and a cigarette, I regale Dana with the quick version of how I have utterly screwed up my life. "My savings are gone," I grouse. "I'm probably going to be evicted soon, and I have no shoes." I look down at my feet. "Oh, yeah. And my car is gone."

"People who have it together do yoga and you really need to get it together." She grabs me by the arm and hauls me out her office door. "My car then. Come."

"I don't do yoga, Dana. Never have. You know that. I got this body with a very calculated balanced diet of cigarettes and Coca-Cola and my fruit comes in the form of wine."

"You're the one who came to me all hot and sweaty wearing leggings. If you want to wallow in self-pity and whine about things with someone, you'll have to come to yoga."

"Fine."

Of course, on the way I get "the talk." Agents are sort of like mothers—part therapist, part champion, part critic. Hopefully you get one with some ability to mother gracefully. Dana does. She's always been honest with me and supportive, and can deliver tough love like a skilled surgeon removing an abscessed appendix. And I, all of me, am the abscess in this conversation.

I try to dodge it by asking about Tom.

"He's doing well. Working a lot—not with Andrea you'll be glad to know. (That's HER actual name BTW. But I will always call her the AP). He's trying to figure out what went wrong with you."

This sets me off, "What went wrong?! What went wrong with me?! He was doing the chocolate cha-cha with the AP! He didn't support me or my dream. Instead he, like everyone else including you, just figured I was tired and needed a break. He didn't understand, didn't try to understand and didn't listen to me. I was just a meal ticket to him!"

"Maybe so. But you're equally responsible," she replied archly. "You were selfish, and your actions hurt a lot of people, including me. Do you think I enjoyed having to clean up after you vomited your existential crisis all over the place? Do you think that's what I get paid for? You didn't stop for one minute to think about how quitting like that impacted other people. Me. Joao. Tom. The investors. And what the hell did you expect from Tom? He's an actor, for God's sake, living his dream. And you were a part of that dream and then one day you just up and decide to blow it all up without even asking him or me!"

"It's always about taking care of everyone else isn't it?" I shoot back rebelliously. "Do a commercial, feed the family, get my boyfriend a gig, keep him happy, make another shitty movie so my agent can buy another ticket to the Bahamas. When do I get taken care of?"

We're staring at each other, neither of us sure where to go next, when I suddenly wonder if, like my parents, I was ever really part of Dana's equation. I mean, of course I was in the equation. I was the product, after all. But did Dana ever really take my dreams seriously?

"Did you even try to sell my script?"

"I did, actually; you just weren't patient enough. Sara, if you needed a break you could have taken a hiatus after the film was over. If you'd finished your contract, you would have had enough money to take a year off and make dog bones and take all the time you needed to figure yourself out. But no! As usual, your impulsiveness and anger management issues took control and that's why you're 36, single, broke and still have no idea what the hell you're doing."

"It's not Tom's fault. It's not Joao's fault. It's not my fault. It's *your* fault."

What could I say? The silence in her car was deafening. The pause lengthened and then, just when I thought the worst was over, she started in again.

"You know I love you. Hell, I've been your agent for more years than I'd like to admit. But it's time to grow up, little missy. You aren't twenty anymore, and it isn't always about what *you* want. Sure, you've had a tough life. And yes, I know what you've done for people. But you had a team and people who counted on you, and your little outburst burned a lot of bridges. Frankly, I'm not sure you or I are going to be able to salvage any of them. But I'll tell you one damn thing, if you don't start taking this seriously, you're going to end up homeless and career-less on top of being broke with no shoes."

Well *that* was a nuclear truth bomb. And damn, the truth hurts.

I've always had people who counted on me, and I guess I've always let them down. Is it *my fault?* I can see how Dana would feel that way, but I have always wondered about the people who everyone counts on. Do they have anyone they can count on? Like for real, because my life has always been about being the one, the magic little princess who finds the glass shoe and then feeds all the animals. I guess this is what happens when Cinderella has a breakdown. I know it's probably ridiculous that I compare myself to a friggin' mythical princess, but think about it: when you are the doer and you collect a group of people around you who feed off of your doing, who's responsible? Is the doer ultimately responsible for the feeders? What happens when the doer says, "I'm done?" Is it okay? Can the doer be done?

I have no idea.

We make it the rest of the way to yoga class in silence. And yep, as cliché as it sounds, the room is filled with tall lanky women in leggings and men with man buns. The teacher is an absolutely gorgeous woman with silver hair, which means she's probably in her 60's. Clearly her all-raw diet and lack of liquor and smoking habits have allowed her to age backwards, and she keeps her hair silver just to remind people like me how much we're going to suffer later in life—as if we're not suffering now.

I grab a loaner yoga mat and find a place at the back of the room. She explains this will be a "restorative" class and that we need not push too hard. And I'm like, "Honey, sitting down cross-legged is pushing it for me."

I won't bore you with a full-on story of how I suck at yoga. Just imagine a gazelle, long legs, graceful neck, effortlessly flowing across the Great Plains and then picture the opposite. There, that's me. (You might as well start practicing your visualization skills now. You're going to need them often reading this.)

The session winds down and I can barely finish the class. I'm exhausted, out of breath and sweating like a horse who just ran the Kentucky Derby and didn't win. I think they may just have to shoot me. *I thought this was supposed to be restorative?* We are all finally sitting in the lotus pose. Well, everyone else is in lotus. I'm more like criss-cross applesauce. Everyone closes their eyes and begins breathing deeply to relax even further, and it's I all I can do to avoid sounding like a wheezy Darth Vader.

"Now, let's harness the power of intention in this quiet moment," the silver-haired goddess coaches. "What are you manifesting into your life? Is it truly what you desire?"

I snort-laugh at the irony. I tend to laugh at the most inappropriate moments, so I try and play it off as a cough and the Helen Mirren look-alike yoga instructor looks me straight in the eyes and smiles and says as if she's speaking directly to me, "if it

isn't, tell the Universe what
you desire. If you don't, how can you ever get what
you want?"

In my head I think I've been telling everyone
what I want for years. Clearly, I'm not speaking their
language, or anybody's understandable language
for that matter. This is why I hate yoga and spiritual
people. Who the fuck is 'the Universe,' and why does
it have all my stuff? What do I have to do to get it to
finally give it to me?

As if she's actually in my head, Helen then says,
"Tonight when you go home, get clear on your
intentions. Write down a detailed list of everything
you desire to manifest, then add this list to your daily
meditation."

I'm supposed to meditate too?

Finally, it's over. I limp my way out of class,
smiling and nodding, hardly able to make it back to
Dana's car. I pull my bike out of the back of the
Range Rover, laughing privately at how everyone
in LA is going green, but hey, don't touch our gas-
guzzling status symbols. Thankfully, the yoga class
is only a couple of blocks from my house. Huh, who
knew? *Not like I'm ever going back!*

I get home, haul open the creaky garage door,
park my bike and let Zak out for a walk. Poor guy
has been stuck inside almost all day. One of the cool
things about Zak is that he doesn't need to walk on a
leash. He's really well-behaved like that. He doesn't
charge other dogs or people. He won't step off the
curb unless I call him. If nothing else, I got lucky in

the dog department. He loves me unconditionally. The longest-lasting man in my life, he gets me. Now if I could only find a human that did.

Walking Zak calms me. It's what I do when I need to think and strategize—apparently something I've been doing a really poor job of lately. Today was my D-Day—my do or die day—and despite working my ass off for over a year, I took a beating. And then to be told all I had to do is "ask the Universe for what you want." *Jesus, come on. I've been asking!* I just don't seem to have the hook-up needed to get this deal done. I'm truly at an impasse. No other rabbits in my hat. *Dana is right, this little missy needs to get her shit together.*

Back at my apartment, I just sit in my living room. *At least I still have something to sit on.* I scan the room trying to figure out what else I can sell, then close my eyes for a minute, taking a deep breath, hoping for a just a moment of peace ... and I realize, *this must be what meditating is.*

Huh. What the hell. I might as well give it a go.

Of course, the moment I tell myself I am meditating I can't sit still and I'm guessing smoking is a no go. What would Deepak Chopra say? I take a few more deep breaths, which feel more like exasperation and less like relaxation, and recall Ms. Yogini Mirren saying to make a list. Alright! I'm a producer. Lists I can make! Determined and grateful, there's something logical I can do. I grab an old white board I used to use for production meetings out of the hall closet and find some sharpies.

"Is there a limit to what I can ask for?" I say out

loud, as if the Universe is suddenly going to start answering me in its James Earl Jones voice.

"No, Sara, the Universe is limitless. "(You totally read that in his voice, didn't you? You did. Admit it.)

So, the Universe is limitless now, is it? Hmmm. "Well then, show me the money baby!" *Oh, that doesn't sound very spiritual.* Spiritual people don't overtly ask for money. Do they? Hell, they all probably secretly wish they were rich.

"No, Sara, the Universe is limitless and not as dogmatic or judgmental as mere humans are." (Again, you did. You know it.)

"Good! Then dammit, I want money! And I promise I'll do good stuff with it and not just spend it on shoes." (Yes, I admit I'm looking up toward the ceiling as I hold this conversation. I mean the Universe is Up There. Right?) I stare at the blank white board. *Should I write this out in complete sentences?* She did say to be clear with what I want. But maybe I should just use pictures, considering my language skills have been sorely lacking lately?

I draw a big heart in red and Zak comes and lays his head in my lap. *Wow, that was quick. I love you too, Zak.* But I want a man, a real man who will see me and appreciate me and accept my crazy and laugh with me and cry with me and not take me to Ojai when I'm having a nervous breakdown.

And I want to make a movie. I draw a really bad rendition of a movie camera. *Jesus, I have to be an artist too?* Truth is, I miss making movies. I'm a really good producer and making films has always been, if not my native passion, at least highly rewarding. Giving people a chance to escape their hum-drum lives, their sadness, their fears for two hours feels like it's as important as being a heart surgeon. I just don't want to make bad ones anymore. I want to make films that have an impact on people—a good impact that affects them, makes them think and feel and change. Change how, I'm not sure about yet. But change something, I'm sure of.

And I want to make money. There I said it. It's real and there shouldn't be anything wrong with that, so James, if you're Up There listening, don't be a hater.

I want to make Zak's Super Snacks successful. It's a great idea and I deserve the success. I've worked hard and it's a solid plan.

I want to get out of LA for a while and buy a house. Zak wants to live in the country. There's no reason he can't get in on this too. Right? Or does the Universe only handle human wants and desires?

"All creatures are deserving of love and happiness," says the Big U.

Okay then. Zak and I want *this*. I step back and examine my artwork. The heart, the lopsided camera, the dollar signs, the house in the country with smoke trickling out of the chimney and Zak running free. *All of this except, please Universe, don't be too literal because I'm a shitty artist.* I want all of this. It's not too much to ask for, is it?

I look up from my kindergarten stick figure drawings and notes and realize it's been four hours and I didn't have one cigarette or a glass of wine the entire time. *Time to change that.* I get up to go to the kitchen to pour myself a glass and notice Zak is nowhere to be found. I check the bedroom and sure enough, he's there, passed out cold, taking up most of the bed, snoring and probably farting. Yet there is something so inviting about just curling up beside him and going to sleep. So, I do. And for the first time in probably two years, I fall asleep without the help of alcohol or nicotine.

CHAPTER 5

I sleep in past 11 a.m., something I haven't done since I was with Tom and had woken up early to have sex and then gone back to sleep, covered in the sweet dew of sweaty lovemaking and snuggled up with my man. That, by far, is the best sleep anyone can have. Or so I thought until today.

This morning I wake up snuggled with probably the best love a person can have, hairy and with bad breath, but I don't care. It's true unconditional love, even if he is a dog. I feel loved and safe and I imagine that this is what I'd always wanted from Tom and every other man I have ever been with. Who knew I had it all along? He just couldn't buy me a drink.

What wakes me from this blissed-out sleep is my phone buzzing on my nightstand. I answer a groggy "Hello?" and on the other end it's Dana, speaking way too fast for my brain to keep up, sounding the way she did when she knew her commission check was going to send her on yet another trip to the Bahamas. "You're not going to believe this, but Joao called. He has another film and he only wants you. He won't do it without you, and you get to name your price and perks. But it's you or nothing. I can't even believe this. Get your ass in here."

I manage to mutter something affirmative and

she hangs up. Zak rolls over and yawns and his leg, or arm, I'm not sure, pulls me in. This might be getting weird, but beggars can't be choosers, I guess.

I hear a huge round of applause coming from somewhere and I see myself in the audience at the Kodak Theater. I'm sitting next to Helen Mirren, who is like so hot I can't even tell you and looks exactly like that yoga teacher, and everyone around me is staring at me, smiling and clapping. Tom is next to me on the other side because Helen (That's right, I can call her Helen.) is to my right. He takes my hand and pulls me up from my chair and ushers me out into the aisle and toward the stage. I'm crying and laughing with happiness.

When I arrive at the stage, I am handed a stunning golden statue. I clutch it, looking out at a sea of Hollywood elite, standing and clapping, and I realize I need to say something. So, I thank Dana, my agent, for taking me to a yoga class and something else really witty because I am quick on my feet. Of course, I thank Tom and the Anal Princess and then I'm like … wait a minute. WTF just happened?

I unravel myself from my creepy cuddle with my dog and call Dana back. "Okay. Start over. What the hell did you say?"

She repeats what she said earlier, and I am confused and, if I'm being honest, a little freaked out. I did ask for a movie, but I thought I was specific in the whole impactful, helpful part. So maybe soft-core horror porn is helping people? This doesn't sound right. But I agree to meet her in a couple of hours and figure I just need my morning coffee and nicotine to make sense of this madness.

As I'm waiting for my percolator to perk, I notice my writing on the board from the night before. It just says "movie." *Hmmm, she did say be specific.* In my head I had envisioned something other than soft-core porn, but I didn't write it down. So, I grab the sharpie and in big bold letters write "MEANINGFUL, IMPACTFUL, LIFE CHANGING!"

It's getting late so I decide to do coffee after my shower. I grab my crappy speaker and for the first time in a long time put on my power soundtrack—all chicks hellbent on living out loud without anyone, especially a man, to bring them down.

I belt out the last lines to Demi Lovato's "Confident."

> It's time to get the chains out
> Is your tongue tied up?
> 'Cause this is my ground
> And I'm dangerous
> And you can get out
> But it's all about me tonight
>
> So you say I'm complicated
> That I must be outta my mind
> But you had me underrated
> Rated, rated
> What's wrong with being, what's wrong with being
> What's wrong with being confident?
> What's wrong with being, what's wrong with being
> What's wrong with being confident?
> What's wrong with being, what's wrong with being
> What's wrong with being confident?

What's wrong with being, what's wrong with being
What's wrong with being confident?

Feeling downright uplifted, I get out of the shower
still humming, towel off, throw on my robe and grab
my coffee and a smoke. A little air dry is good for the
skin, they say.

As I'm sitting on my little back patio, aka smoking
pit, scrolling face crack and the advice columns, a
notification pops up on my phone. Voicemail Jeremy:
Warner Bros. Development.

Hmmm. *How did I miss this?* Clearly, it's been a busy
morning. I check the message, dump coffee all over
myself, get dressed as fast as I can, grab my Red
Devil and peddle my ass as fast as I can to Dana's
office. *Holy Moly this stuff actually works! Jesus!*

As I enter the office, Midwest Jeff is standing there
with my nonfat, no whip mocha, which indicates I'm
back on the "it girl" list, at least temporarily. I burst
into Dana's office. "Did he call you? Can you believe
it?!"

She smiles that weird shut-the-fuck-up-but-I-love-
you smile of hers and says, "Sara, look who's here!"

I follow her bulging eyes and circle around to see
Joao moving toward me, arms open like he's RuPaul
greeting Diana Ross, except he's short, Indian,
and, while totally gay, somehow missed the class
on hygiene and fashion. "Saaarrrraaaa, Saaarrraa,
Saaarrrra," as if saying my name in threes opens up
his personal portal to hell.

(Here's the deal. In case you haven't noticed, I am
a very visual person and I tend to use metaphors way

too much. Sometimes—a lot of the time, especially in moments like this—my imagination tends to take over. Which is actually good because it helps me stop my mouth from saying things I probably shouldn't say out loud. (Not all the time, mind you; I hope you enjoy these as much as I do.)

So as Joao is rushing in for his drag queen diva hug, I see myself back on stage at the Kodak Theater, crying, laughing, smiling, and as I look out into the sea of what earlier had been famous celebrities' faces, I notice they have all now turned into the Who's Who of porn, horror and everything C, D, and E movies. I can't even get a B movie actor's face to appear.

"Helen? Helen? Where are you?" The once golden statue I'm holding in my hand has morphed into a smaller version of the famed Le Genie Du Mal (The Genie of Evil by Guillaume Geefs), his wings spreading as he leaps at me, his chained ankles the only thing stopping him from devouring my face. Instead he simply spews blood all over my Valentino vintage dress.

As this is happening in my head, I hear Joao, who has now made contact with my stone-like body, say, "I am so excited to be doing *Satan's Handbags* with you! You are the only person who have truly seen me for the artist I am!"

Yes, he said "have," not has. And he was born in Ohio for fuck sake.

Blood splatter, vomit in my mouth . . . *breathe Sara, breathe.*

Dana is aware of my penchant for dropping out of reality when shit gets weird, so she jumps in with, "We love it Joao and you're right, Sara is a genius. We'll have the contract signed by the end of the day." And with that, like Tinkerbell herself, he vanishes. I'm not even sure he was really there. Maybe I have lost my marbles and none of this is real.

"Sara, Sara, this is amazing," Dana squeals and shakes/hugs me. There is entirely too much human contact happening right now for my comfort zone. I am not a hugger normally, especially when my agent/best friend just sold my soul, yet again, literally to the Devil.

"Dana, what the flying hell! Did you talk to Jeremy? I quit making movies to get AWAY from Joao, not so I could sign a lifetime blood contract with him!"

"It's shocking to me how good a producer you are when you're so terrible at keeping your own life on track," she says. "Sara, this is where a plan is useful. It's called Make Some Money, Get Back On Your Feet, Don't Get Evicted, Buy Some Shoes."

I interrupt her lecture. "But did you talk to Jeremy? *That's* the film I want to do. It sounds interesting and relevant, it's about modern spirituality …"

"Sara, you are the last person on Earth who should make a film on any type of spirituality. You'd make a complete fool of yourself—even more than you have already. Yes, when he couldn't reach you, he called me. And his offer sucks. So, I told him you had just booked something else. And you have—or at least will if you have any sense left."

Okay, I'm trying to stay calm and avoid envisioning my dear agent Dana as Ursula from *The Little Mermaid* and has stolen my voice. And it's not working—she's totally turned into Ursula.

"Dana you cannot turn down a project without asking me first."

"The offer was a joke. And since you can't seem to make any rational decisions, I decided to step in and drag you kicking and screaming out of your slow and painful death spiral."

"You're the one who took me to a yoga class! You heard Helen say, 'Make a list.' Well, I made a list. I wrote down that I wanted to make a movie—a meaningful movie—and in less than twelve hours shit started showing up! It's destiny!"

"Destiny? Oh, my God, do you hear yourself? You really are delusional. It's a *coincidence* Sara. And you haven't even read their script. I had Jeremy send me over the outline and it's awful—a bunch of New Age talking heads. And who the hell is Helen?"

"You can't judge destiny from a one pager!" I practically shout. "So, you're just going to piss on magic when it happens?"

"Honey, magic is when the paycheck clears and you go to the Bahamas. Jeremy's film is called *Killing Buddha* and I'm sure that's not going to go over well with the Buddhists, which, by the way, half of Hollywood now thinks they are. That or Kabbalists." Hands on hips, she glares at me. "You're not considering the follow-up to this spiritual masterpiece being *Killing*

Jesus are you?"

"Dana, Jews don't believe in Jesus. See? I think I know maybe just a little bit more than you do about spirituality! Look what I did without knowing anything about baking dog treats!"

"Who the hell mentioned the Jews?" She shakes her head in disbelief. "And they actually do believe in Jesus. Just not as a messiah. And what's any of this got to do with dog treats? Like that brilliant idea has panned out so great for you!"

"But ... "

"For Christs sake Sara, Satan is paying two hundred grand—or more if you insist—plus a very sexy backend package."

Did she really just say that? Is this really happening to me right now? I am for real having to choose between heaven and hell? Is *Satan's Handbags* really to be my redemption for that preposterously hot day in Death Valley? D-Day I like to call it. Despite myself and the crazy heat of the moment, the memories come flooding in.

Joao had been particularly unruly that day. The zombie make-up kept melting all over Tom's face, which kept ruining every take. Which meant a shot of the lovelorn small-town sheriff whose newly wedded, well-endowed wife has succumbed to the rabid bite of a zombie and her only chance for survival is to orgasm under the ministrations of her husband . . . (Sigh. If only *that* were the solution to all our problems!) a scene that normally would have taken about an hour to shoot, took five hours of excruciating do-overs, while my director tempter-tantrumed like a small child in the checkout aisle at Walmart lamenting that they were fresh out of Sour Gummies. And why was it that I, as his producer, could not have done something about the weather, or single handedly developed un-meltable make-up and I needed to fix it. And all the while Tom and the AP think it's hilarious, and she keeps rubbing her silicon-engorged mammary glands in his face and anywhere else she can reach.

Meanwhile, the caterer has decided sushi is a good idea to serve in 110 degree weather and has nothing else to feed us but rotten fish, and the production assistant I sent off to Subway for a replacement lunch has run out of gas because we're in the middle of the damn Paran desert. I am hot, and we have no ice, and Tom is enjoying himself way too much and I have clearly left my falcon feathers, saber-tooth tiger teeth, and rattles at home that day, because no matter how hard I dance the rain will not come. And *this* is what finally sets me off: Joao curled up in the sand in a fetal position screaming while the poor make-up team is literally using fans and even blowing and using their hands, their scripts, anything to keep the "actors" (yes, intentionally in quotes) cool and stop the makeup from running. The image is as real in my mind as when it happened.

Tom is laughing hysterically, as if this moment will make his blooper reel epic, and out of nowhere I scream, "SHUT THE FUCK UP!!" And everyone stops and stares at me.

I grab my director's chair (even producers get a chair) and I throw it. I take what's left of my bottled water and I pour it all over Tom and Miss AP, which at first they think is funny, until I slap the bitch in the face and scream, "If you ever shove your genetically-modified melons in my man's face again I'm going to cut you," which in hindsight might have been a bit violent. (I did say I need to work on my anger issues.)

I then make my way over to Joao, who, at this point is out of the fetal position and cowering behind a day-player grip I don't even know or care about. With the strength of a mother lifting a car from atop her newborn baby, I throw the guy about seven feet and then I pick Joao up by his shirt collar (who the hell wears a collar shirt while filming in the desert in the summer when it's 110 degrees?) and I pull him close and snarl, "I hate you. I hate you with the white-hot intensity of a thousand suns. I hate you and you are a fucking idiot."

His mouth is gaping from shock and I grab his sides (4x4 paper versions of the script handed out for the day's scenes. They are small so they can fit in your pocket.) I find them like a pickpocket on the subway in Paris stealing your wallet, and I shove them in his mouth as he falls to his knees choking on his version of *Citizen Kane*. I then storm off to a waiting passenger van, because the only sane person on the set that day is the transpo guy, who clearly knows when someone needs to make a quick getaway. He drives me nervously to my car and I leave in a cloud of desert dust.

Did I mention that our asshole diva director of photography filmed the whole thing? By Saturday morning every director, producer and studio executive in Hollywood had this whole scene playing at the head of their dailies.

I should have been nominated for an Oscar. The golden statue is back in my hand and I . . .

"Jeremy's film is only paying eighty grand, which, I suspect, won't even put a dent in your credit card debt."

Huh? Dana is speaking in the here and now and blurrily I shake off the vision and try to tune in.

"The terms are really bizarre—you can't meet with the financier, you only work with their accountant, they've already hired the crew and you have no say in any of that. It's crazy."

I'm doing the math in my head on the eighty grand and miss most of what she says. "I think eighty grand could work. Maybe."

At this point Dana starts doing this deep breathing thing and I'm worried she may hyperventilate and that her head might explode. Apparently, she's played patient mother long enough today and I may have just pushed her over the edge. She finally speaks in that false calm voice people put on when they really want to punch you in the face. "Sara, do the movie with Joao. Get back on your feet. Hit the reset button when it's over. Then you can do whatever you want. Seriously, you really ought to try the Bahamas."

I'm a little afraid of her in that way we all are when our mothers have lost their shit and start cleaning anything they can find, rubbing the counter so hard they almost burn a hole in it. But I get the words out. "Dana, I can't."

"It's easy, you just book a plane ticket and you're there." She says this, I think, because she's trying to lighten the space. She's really good like that. She knows exactly when to go ape shit crazy and when to pull it back. She's going to make a really good mom one day.

Her timing is impeccable, and I can't help but laugh. But then my laugh almost turns into a sob, which is not something that comes easy to me unless I'm already wet and in the shower and I'm sure no one is watching. "Dana, I c-can't go back to making sleazy shlock films. I just *can't!*"

We sit in silence for a few moments, my lower lip quivering. I stare out her window. In all of my years as Dana's client, I don't think I ever looked out her window. It's a nice view—trees, fancy brand shops crammed with absurdly rich people buying over-priced shoes. I used to be one of those people, buying those shoes. I fumble in my bag, pull out a cigarette and light it. She's about to stop me when I think she realizes if I don't smoke it's going to get really bad, really quick.

Once again, she jumps in to save me from a downward spiral. "Sara, please listen to me. I'm trying to help you." Her voice is quiet now. Calm. "You are a really good producer. You had a meltdown. It happens to the best of us. But unbeknownst to you, I have spent the last six months working every room

I could, saying "no" to my favorite martini at Happy Hours all over town trying to convince people you just needed a break and that you're sane and solid. This is why Jeremy called. This is why Joao called."

She pauses. "The reality is, if you weren't broke and desperate, I might consider Jeremy's film. But you are. You need money and you need credibility, neither of which this whacko doc is offering. Plus, you know nothing about the subject matter. It has disaster written all over it." She pauses again for effect. "Do the *Handbag* flick. Get some stability and I'll keep my eyes out for something meaningful for you later."

It's always later isn't it? "Tom wasn't around for later," I mutter, sniffing.

"Don't make this about Tom. This is about you making a wise choice to take care of yourself. Don't blow your comeback by taking something that isn't even comeback material."

"You always have been wiser than I am," I admit.

"But you always look better in Jimmy Choo's." Dana winks and does that love sigh because she knows she's won this battle.

"Okay. Draw it up and I'll sign." I whisper because I can't seem to find my voice. Ursula has been very convincing.

CHAPTER 6

After doing the deed I ride my bike home, because even when you sell your soul to the devil it still takes time for the check to clear. I think about stopping at my favorite wine shop on the way, a perfect Band-Aid for the prick in my finger producing the blood needed to sign my contract with Lucifer. The place always has the best Zinfandels, and right now I need something with a high alcohol count, which makes me think of Paso Robles and Tom and all the wine we drank together.

There was this one winery on the top of a hill with an amazing view of the valley. We always went there for lunch, stopping at the little cheese shop in town, getting the most decadent cheeses, bread, salami and olives. They say this is the Food of the Gods, and Tom and I were definitely living in the clouds—for a while anyway. The road to the winery was really twisty with lots of oak trees and we had usually stopped at a couple of wineries before we got there, which meant we had a good buzz going and were horny and Tom loved it when I would give him a . . .

Shit! I barely see the sign in the middle of the sidewalk in time to swerve and my front wheel bounces off the curb. I lose control and realize I have to abandon the bike or land into oncoming traffic.

Now I'm flat on the ground just over the curb, wrists hurting, knee hurting, everything hurting. And no, I'm not wearing a helmet. Who wears a helmet on a beach cruiser? Besides, helmets make my hair look flat and my head is an odd shape. *Ouch!* I have pain in places I forgot existed, but it seems as though nothing is broken—bruised and scratched—but still bending and rotating as they should. I sit up and look around. At least no one saw me.

I eye the culprit, a huge sign planted in the middle of the sidewalk, not even slightly knocked out of place. *Who allows these things on sidewalks?!* But then suddenly I realize that maybe I'm not supposed to be riding on the sidewalk in the first place? Look, it's not like I'm one of those ride-my-bike-everywhere folks. *These are desperate times people. I haven't had time to read up on all the rules.*

But then the sign catches my attention again—not so much the sign, but what's on it. There, staring at me, laughing, is a giant Buddha. *Jeez, that's mean.* I thought Buddha was all about causing no harm and loving people and stuff. And here he is pointing and laughing at me. *Hmmmpf. Not very spiritual if you ask me.* I get up off the ground with a groan, remembering what it was like to have health insurance, pull my bike fully out of the street and turn to read the sign. "The Mystic Way Book Shoppe." How cute that they spelled it in olde English. Very clever. How ironic that as I make my way home from signing my soul away to Beelzebub that I literally almost run into his nemesis, or one of them anyway.

I'm shaking from the adrenaline rush, feeling a bit wobbly, and realize I need a moment before I can ride again. *Might as well check the place out.* I park my bike and check her out first. A nice scratch across the front tire frame, but other than that, she looks good. I lock her up and walk through the large glass door.

Immediately upon entering, my nose is assaulted with the smell of incense, way too much incense. *Someone ought to just pick one scent and go with it.* Then I hear what sounds like the wailing of some sort of high-pitched guitar-like thing and suddenly feel nauseous. I wait for a moment, then move on, passing through a selection of large, absolutely stunning crystal bowls, and I'm thinking *what a waste of a salad bowl* when a guy wearing a purple sarong and yes, a man bun, walks up to me.

His skin is a perfect, even coloration, like he has a really amazing tan—a real one, not from a tanning bed. Of course, this guy would never intentionally bathe his body in cancer-causing radiation just for a good tan, would he? Nary a laugh line in sight, shiny hair, and gorgeous eye lashes. *I hate men. Why do they always get the lashes?* Anyway, I'm trying to not look drunk, because this time I am not, and he proceeds to ask, "Can I help you find something?" Which makes me laugh 'cause I want to say "My soul?" But then I know where that is. Dermogorgon, the powerful demon prince in Dungeons & Dragons, has it. (I'm trying out different names for the devil, 'cause I'm looking for a new nickname for Joao—one that he won't really understand but will think is cool. This one is Greek.) Look, I can sign away the rights to my humanity, but I don't have to be nice about it.

Tan man-bun proceeds to determine which direction to point me in. "Astrology? Alternative medicine? East Indian religions? What about Theosophy, cosmology, or Gaia philosophy? Perhaps a little Gnosticism, Neopaganism, Wicca?"

I can't even figure out what to say to him, so I mutter, "I'm just looking, thank you," and he turns like he's Mikhail Baryshnikov and proceeds to glide back to wherever he came from.

I try the deep breathing thing Dana was doing, which helps to settle my stomach. I also figure out that the farther you go into the store the less it smells like a hookah lounge. I find a water dispenser and some small glasses and, relieved, pour myself a glass and drink. Instantly I'm concerned. *What did I just drink?* I hold back on spitting it out because I've already embarrassed myself enough, and examine the container which seems to have sliced cucumbers floating in it.

Did someone do this as a joke? I hide my glass behind the jug, not wanting to appear wasteful, and proceed to an area with large shelves laden with books—thousands of them. He wasn't kidding, I'm pretty sure I could find the exact instructions to banish Belial (Greek for pure wickedness) back to the underworld and the ingredients right here in this store. *Maybe I'm a witch after all?* I wonder. *Certainly, I've been called that many times in my life.*

The store is like landing in Oz and I end up

spending about three hours poking around. By the time I get ready to leave, Mikhail, whose real name is Leonard but he goes by Ananda, and I are fast friends. I think he has some peculiar hang up about "virgins" though—which doesn't mean what you think it means. Apparently, I am in "Beginners Mind"—at least that's what he called it—a newbie just embarking on my spiritual journey, stepping my first step onto The Path, opening my first chakra. (And here I thought I overused metaphors.) I like him though, he's peaceful and Zen-like, so clearly this enlightenment thing is working for him.

I leave with about fifteen books and a maxed-out credit card. So much for a stop at the wine shop. I tried to get him to sell me an old worn-out book of curses I found on a back shelf, but he wouldn't do it, saying I wasn't ready. I probably couldn't afford it anyway. Huh. *Even cursing people is for the elite.* The rich always get the good stuff. (Side note: they put the cucumber in the water on purpose. Mikhail/Leo/Ananda hates it too. But it's very spiritual.)

Anyway, back on my bike, books in the basket, bags hanging from the handlebars, I'm home in a flash, this time without almost killing myself. I take Zak for an extra-long walk. I mean, what else am I going to do? I have no wine and even though I bought the books, that doesn't mean I'm going to read them. After all, I have a script to read. I pull the zip file out of my purse with a sigh—the bloodied electronic scroll upon which my impending descent into hell is etched.

I get comfy in bed, Zak beside me, happily tired from his extra ball time. But I can't force myself to open the file. Instead I waste a good hour Googling alternate names for Satan and I find at least 30: among them: Typhon (again Greek. They really had a knack for words.), Sedit, a Native American devil, and Mania, which is where the word maniac comes from.

Honestly, I can't even get past the title page. *What a stupid name*, Satan's Handbags. *Jesus*. As I sit there staring at the "script," my bags of books keep calling out to me. *Sara, Sara choose us! We have the answers you're looking for!*

What the hell?

Even though self-flagellation went out in the 14th century, by taking Joao's movie I'm doing it, just not with whips. Oh no. I'm doing it the good ol' American way, torturing myself by doing things I hate so I can keep up the façade and play the game and make money and buy shoes. And be loved. This is what we're all doing, I think. Anything we can do to be loved because, let's face it, the American dream isn't about following your heart and living your passion. I mean, the self-help gurus sell that—Mikhail's book shoppe was filled with "find your passion" advice. And yet at every turn we are reminded that the American dream has nothing to do with our hearts and everything to do with our bank accounts, credit score and social media engagement rate. (Ironically, I get more likes when I suffer. It's as if when I fail, I make someone else feel just a little bit better about their own life. Failure and suffering sell.)

This is where I'm at and I know it. I look back at the script. *This isn't healthy for me.*

Fuck it.

I get up and grab a book from the bag and decide to get myself a glass of water. Hydration is important I'm told. As I head back to my room, I see the white board, mocking me in big bold letters "MEANINGFUL, IMPACTFUL, LIFE CHANGING." I look down at the cover of the book I picked up: *The Seven Spiritual Laws of Success* by Deepak Chopra, and I think that signing away my life to Yen-Lo-Wang (the Chinese Ruler of Hell) is probably not one of the seven laws.

I close my eyes and take a deep breath. I see Joao, leaping from his director's chair, running toward me, arms flailing about in a fit about something. He's pointing and I turn to see Tom and The cha cha queen making out and then Dana, lying on a bed of money, laughing at them while she's throwing money in the air. How cliché.

"Come on Sara, it's fun!" she shouts.

Suddenly Joao leaps into the air and lands in the pile with her, like a St. Bernard in a pile of fall leaves. His head pops out of the pile, eyes wide and filled with joy, tongue wagging. Wait … is that Joao or is it a dog? Whatever it is, they all look so happy, but in a sort of grotesque way—like a horror movie carnival scene—calling out to me, taunting me. I can hear the organ grinder music and, way off in the distance, I see a gypsy-like tent, a glowing light of purple-blue emanating from the inside. I move toward the entrance and I see my new friend Mikhail/Leonard sitting at a small table with a crystal ball in the center. That's where the light is coming from. He looks me dead in the eye and asks, "So, what are *you* going to choose?"

And in that moment, I know. *I cannot do this.* I also know I am likely to lose my agent and probably my last friend. *But if that is what it takes to save my soul, then it's what I must do. Either that or I truly am an idiot.* Either way, I've got to start somewhere. And the bottom of the movie business alphabet is better than in the depths of hell.

I find my phone, call Dana and get her answering machine. "I'm sorry, I can't. I just can't, Dana. I know you won't understand and probably will never forgive me or maybe even speak to me again. But I can't do this. Thank you for everything."

Then I call Jeremy (who is delighted to hear from me) and take the documentary. And with that it's done, and I am now deep within the dark forest.

CHAPTER 7

The Suits want to start shooting *Killing Buddha* right away—as soon as all the paperwork is handled—paperwork I almost had to do myself because Dana was so pissed. But she came through with the contract at the last minute … having it delivered to my door because she didn't want to see me in person. *At least she's still my agent.* I'm grateful for that, and grateful that I only have a week to spend making myself sick second-guessing my decision and self-honesty before we start production.

I learned at an early age what happens when I speak up about something I don't think is right. I was 12, doing yet another Barbie commercial. I had done about 30 at that point, with the same crew and director. But this time they wanted me to do this thing with the Barbie that I knew no kid ever did. It was totally an adult manufactured, "This is what girls do with Barbies," moment. But it wasn't. It was fake and I hated it, so I spoke up.

"Ya know, we don't play this way," I said to the director. "We girls dream, but we don't dream about boys and Ken and fancy houses … some of us, most of us, girls dream about being doctors and scientists and we actually don't care what we're wearing."

The director looked at me, stunned, like I'd just

kicked him in the balls. In the two years that I'd been working with him I'd never said anything more than "Good morning" and "Yes sir." (Both my agent and mother had drilled into me the importance of keeping my mouth shut, smiling and doing what was asked. "Kids who cause trouble don't get called back," they said.) He then he turned around and looked back at this group of people sitting behind a monitor—which I now understand to be the execs—totally dumbfounded. So then this one woman comes up to me and says, "Sara, we've done market research, millions of dollars of it. Girls want to be beautiful and loved by a handsome man."

I vomited.

Like really, I just threw up right then and there. And then my social worker (a social worker has to be on the set with kids at all times) rushed in and said I needed a break. No fucking kidding, I needed a break.

That was me speaking up for what I knew to be truth. (I mean, come on girls … how many of you actually wanted to marry Ken?) And when that woman in her fancy suit and high heels informed me that everything I felt about what we were portraying was wrong because millions of other girls had said something different, right there and then I realized I was stupid and wrong and should just keep my mouth shut and do what I'm told.

How *dare* I speak?

The 12-year-old me would have begged for forgiveness if she could have—anything to stop the angst. But the 36-year-old me knows, as I lie there in my Fairfax and 3rd duplex, sweaty, dry mouthed and in tears, that this most recent choice to stand up for what I know will lead me somewhere better. I don't know where, but somehow, I know, deep within my being, that it will lead me to the peace and love I yearn for.

The week passes in a blur of angst and late night reading, highlighting passages in all the books Leo/ Ananda sold me

The morning of our first production meeting I arrive early. It's important to make a good impression with the crew and since I didn't hire any of them, today I need to set the tone for a happy, productive, well-managed shoot. Our office is in the Culver Studios, which was once the set of *Gone with The Wind*, the old plantation-looking house surrounded by big modern stages and a hip, gentrified and revitalized Culver City, sporting large sound stages. Many of my favorite sitcoms film here, along with a wayward set of indie production companies hoping to up their cool factor by having an office on an actual studio lot.

An old friend keeps an office space here, and I picked it because it was cheap and available, and appearances are everything. We wouldn't be around much; one small office was all we needed, and I wanted my team to see me as professional and well-connected. No one needed to know it's a sublet but me.

I make it past the guardians of the gate and find

my parking spot, number 23, which is an age I want
to forget. I often remind myself that I am thankful
I made it out of my twenties without a venereal
disease or a drug addiction and can still remember
most of it, although sometimes I wish I didn't. You
won't likely hear me utter, "Oh, to be twenty again."

The thing I've learned about dealing with film
crews is that you have to be both one of them and
their leader. It's a love-hate relationship most of
the time, and so far I've managed to keep my crews
happy and productive. I figure, even if I've never
met these people, never instilled a little bit of fear
in them or wowed them with my charm, I still have
the chance.

I find our office, Room 11 in Building 1. We're
in the "Mansion" on the first floor. Sadly, I don't
think they've updated the carpet since Rhett Butler's,
"Frankly my dear, I don't give a damn," and the
artwork alternates between old fake portraits of dead
people and movie posters from the 90's when the
place was owned by Sony. Once the star in the crown
of Hollywood and owned by Cecil B. DeMille, the
"Mansion" was modeled after George Washington's
Mt. Vernon and built by a famous silent movie actor.
It could use a paint job—to say the least. But it
would do.

I open the door, assuming I'm first in, and hear a
woman talking on the phone. She turns and gives me
the once-over. I immediately look at her shoes. (You
can learn much about a woman based on her shoes.)
She is wearing Birkenstocks, real ones, which means

she's going for the "I don't give a rat's ass what you think about my shoes, because I can afford not to care," look. The rest of her outfit is all black, flowing and draped in every type of bead, medallion and crystal. It's almost as if she couldn't decide which to wear, so chose them all and, annoyingly, it works. Even sitting I can tell she is tall and elegant, her legs crossed at the ankles, her long torso straight as a ballerina's, or more likely from years of yoga. Her hair is a striking silver, not gray with age, but silver with wisdom and life experience. She reminds me of The Fox Woman of the Anishinaabe and Cree tribes … I saw a poster with her image in *The Mystic Book Shoppe* and I think this woman was the model. She turns and motions me to sit.

Shit! I am supposed to be the one choosing the first chair and already I am upstaged. I went for the female 'Suit' look with crisp white-collar shirt, pencil black Audrey Hepburn pants and pearls, hoping to be in charge. Now, feeling way overdressed, I'm already being told to find a seat in the corner.

The woman finishes talking, hangs up the phone and turns to me. "I'm Brin, your spiritual consultant—not that I claim to be spiritual. I just speak their language. I have no idea what it means to be spiritual anymore," she jokes.

I start to speak and she interrupts me. "You must be Sara. Hi. I hear great things about you from Jeremy." She pulls some papers out of a file folder. "Here's a list of the people we need to interview. I've already called the ones I know, so we can split the rest."

I scan the list and the only name I recognize is Bennett, as in the singer Tony Bennett. "Why are we interviewing Tony Bennett? Wait a minute. Is he even still alive?" I ask.

Brin laughs. "Not Tony Bennett, his cousin, Marshall. He channels an alien named Lazarus." She says this matter-of-factly, as if it's as normal as saying we're interviewing Jesus, Paul and Mary about their love triangle. *Wasn't Lazarus Mary's brother?* Anyway…

The door flies open and in pop three more people: a young, chiseled Latino man who seriously belongs on the cover of a romance novel, an equally young and beautiful African American woman who looks like she's styled for an Instagram selfie, and a guy, a white guy, in an unassuming t-shirt and jeans. The one thing they all have in common is that they are young, as in their mid-twenties, except the one in the T-shirt. He might be my peer, maybe. It's so hard to tell with men. Suddenly I feel old and like I shop in the mom section at Macy's.

(Try this for your visuals: Picture Sara as Renée Zellweger circa 2001 in *Bridget Jones Diary* as me. For the rest of the merry band of traumatized humans you are about to meet, maybe go with Jamie Lee Curtis for Brin, a more brooding Channing Tatum as Jason, Marc Anthony as Fabio (except with the hair of the romance novel model Fabio), and for Michele, think Zendaya with a touch of Halle Berry. Okay, your film is cast, have at it.)

And so now you will meet them.

Oshun (The African goddess of love) speaks first. (Side note: In case you haven't noticed, I have a little habit of making up names for people. What else am I going to do with all the random information I have in my head about gods, goddesses, Satan, etcetera? I picked up this habit during my tenure as Joao's producer, changing all his character names to the names of gods and goddesses, ancient mythical creatures, and lords of the underworld as entertainment for myself. Unfortunately, it had the unintended consequence of making him look like some sort of genius, poking fun at or referencing ancient myths in his films. Sigh … doesn't that often seem to be the case? We women do all the magic and the men take the credit. Anyway, I digress.) Now, into our little crew meeting.

Interior shot: Day

THE AFRICAN QUEEN
(aka Michele)
Hi! I'm Michele, sorry I'm late.

I jump in before Brin can speak.

SARA
It's totally fine.

Arrggg. It isn't cool being late and now I've just let them all know it's okay. My nerves are getting the best of me, which is odd considering I've done this routine a million times. But I am nervous because I've been out of the game for a while and it feels a little bit like my first time running a show. I square my shoulders and rally.

SARA (Cont)
Why don't we all just get settled and introduce ourselves?

The pack pushes into our small office and gathers around a table in the corner, which is round so, of course, I can't sit at the head of it. There are an awkward few moments of everyone trying to figure out who should sit where, which are made even more awkward because the room is really too small for all of us, what with the large table, chairs and desk. The window overlooks a parking lot and people keep walking by and looking in as if we're the new cool exhibit on display. I jockey to be positioned so I can see out the window. The last thing I need is an ogling set decorator peeking over my shoulder as I try and claim leadership over this crew.

Finally, everyone is seated, and I start.

SARA (Cont)
My name is Sara, Sara Wells. I'm producing and directing.
I've been a producer for over 15 years. (Translate, I know my shit.)
I am super exited to be working on this project."

All the spiritual books I've been reading kick in and I'm on a roll. "What a powerful subject, the power of now, the seen and the unseen, spirituality and, you know, us humans. I mean, I'm no expert, that's why we have Brin. But I am thrilled to be working with all of you to bring to life a piece of cinema that will transform lives. Who knows, maybe we'll each find a little transformation for ourselves in the process! Wouldn't that be exciting!

Everyone just stares blankly at me except Brin, who laughs a tiny laugh, which I'm not sure is because I said something funny or stupid, so I go with funny and laugh with her. You know, as if I'm in the know. I turn to my right and smile at the dude in the t-shirt.

CHANNING
(AKA Jason)
Okay, I'm Jason Stroud, cameraman and I don't need any more transformation. I have everything I need right here.

With this he pulls out a small pocket Bible and drops it on the table.

BRIN
Oh, here we go.

And I'm suddenly wondering what their history is. Jason begins to protest and I, hoping to stave off a mutiny in the first five minutes, look to the Latin Adonis.

SARA
And you? (arching my eyebrows).

FABIO
(seriously that's his name)
Fabio Martinez, editor/sound man, originally from Costa Rica. Uh ... I'm Catholic.
We're not into uh, transformation.

BRIN
Just transubstantiation.

Fabio and I look at one another, baffled. I make a mental note to look that word up, hoping I'm not already in over my head. I can't help wondering why Brin is being so mean to these people. And who the hell hired a crew of people who seem so adamantly opposed to the entire concept of the film? Except me, of course. I'm open. I'm ready to be inspired. I want to be transformed. But shit, what a crew to be dealt! So far, I have a bitter Birkenstock diva who seems to despise anyone and everything, a Bible thumping Jesus freak, and a hot Catholic who should adorn every major romance novel cover. *God please, let the African Queen be normal.*

I turn and look at Michele, who doesn't seem to have been paying attention. Sitting on the table in front of her is a bling-encrusted iPhone and a small Louis Vuitton handbag. At this moment she's using the mirror on the inside to put on lip gloss. Realizing everyone is staring at her, she smacks her lips, takes a deep breath and says

OSHUN
(AKA Michele)

Hi! I'm Michele. I live in Bel-Air and graduated from Harvard-Westlake High School. I'm going to USC in the fall and my dad got me this job. It's my first official job in the film biz. I'm a PA, which means Production Assistant.

Her teeth are perfect. I often envy other people's teeth. I inherited my father's bad teeth genes and a nasty fear of dentists. Okay, yes, I smoke and drink wine, coffee, and iced tea. Really, I figure if I've already got the bad genes I might as well enjoy life. Anyway, so much for normal. But at least she seems to have some ambition. Brin has nothing to say, at least verbally. She is, however, literally glaring at this poor girl.

SARA

Brin?

I break her out of her hate trance (or she may have been casting a spell, it's hard to say). She turns and looks at me, then shrugs.

JAMIE LEE
(AKA Brin)

Brin Halloway, spiritual consultant, as in I know everything there is to know about spiritual transformation, and I mean *everything.* I'm here to guide you newbies through all the New Age spin on age old notions about life, God, the Universe and
everything.

Jason looks at her sideways when she mentions God, like she just issued a full-on duel to the death. I'm not sure what to make of these two. Do they know each other?

When Brin speaks, it's as if she is speaking to a room with a thousand people in it. She's got a grand sense about herself. She waves her hands as if they are magic wands shooting glitter and sparkling light. She also has a great manicure. I peek to see if her toes match. They do. She's probably in her mid-50's, which seems odd with this gang of Millennials and, well, me. I'm on the cusp as they say, a little bit of latchkey and a little bit of Millennial. Too old for one and not cool enough for the other.

SARA

Well, okay then. We have a tight schedule. The powers that be want this baby in the can before summer's end. Luckily, I'm well-connected and we will be traveling in style.

I reach into my briefcase and pull out the paperwork I've prepared.

SARA (cont)
Here are your production schedules, itineraries, and contact lists.
We'll be meeting up next Monday at seven a.m. at the Burbank airport to fly to Portland for our first shoot. Jason, the gear is ready at the rental house, address is in the packet I gave you. Michele, here's a list of things we need picked up and packed and ready to go for Monday.

Michele scans the list.

MICHELE
(aka Oshun aka African Queen)
I guess I'll have to get Jimmy and the Range Rover.

SARA
Who's Jimmy?

MICHELE
He's my driver. I don't drive.

SARA

(sputtering)

But you're a PA. That's the whole point of a PA … to drive, to pick up stuff and Jimmy's not on my payroll.

MICHELE

Oh, that's okay, he's on my dad's.

I can't even . . .

A sigh escapes my lips.

SARA

Okay then, does anyone have any questions?

A chorus of "nope, no" and "I got it" fills the room and with that, everyone gathers their stuff, muttering goodbyes and "see ya's" and leaves.

END SCENE

Well, that felt weird.

I'm trying to convince myself that it went well, which I can't seem to manage. My self-doubt takes over and all I can hear is Ursula (I mean Dana's) voice in my head telling me I am the last person on the planet who should be making a film about spirituality—clearly along with all the other last people who should be not making one either. Except Brin, who isn't coming across as what I expected a spiritual person to be like. I'm kind of missing Leo/Ananda, his *mmmm's* and *ohmms* and his man bun.

Brin is not love and light, and she definitely isn't

sporting any sort of bun.

I turn to my portion of Brin's list of the Who's Who of the New Thought/New Age world and pick up the phone. In the last week, since I finalized this gig, I've read every book I could on the subject, going for the ones with the most straight-forward titles, getting lost in the "void" as they call it, falling down several rabbit holes, and watching a few YouTube videos on string theory and quantum physics. I even managed to watch the entire Matrix trilogy, so I figure I'm ready to talk about consciousness, illusion and reality. I write out little scripts for each person I need to call and hope they stick to their lines.

I'm in the middle of a call with Brian Green, who wrote *The Elegant Universe*, which basically presents the idea that reality isn't real and that there is no time, which to me makes perfect sense, because in my line of business there is never enough time and I'd much prefer to think my reality isn't really happening to me most of the time anyway. "I'm really intrigued by the whole string, ya know, theory, and the bisons … oh right, bosons." I giggle nervously. "Well they are like the buffalos of the universe, aren't they? (Insert second stupid laugh here.)

"Yes, well we can discuss it in our interview. Oh, sorry, I have a call with Eckhart Tolee so I have to run. See you in a couple of weeks." As I hang up the phone, I notice Brin's horrified face across the room.

"It's Tollay," she says, "not Tolee."

"Well, Brian probably says it wrong too," I defend. She looks at me, shaking her head. "All these people know each other, Sara. It's like the knights of the round table. They all hang out together. It's a little bit like the Odd Fellows meets the Bilderbergers, only instead of One World Order domination it's the Oneness domination."

I don't even know what she just said, so I decide not to challenge her. "Hey, I have to take care of a few things before we leave." I hand her my sheet. "Can you call the last three on my list? It seems you're better equipped to handle this anyway."

Brin takes my list and smiles, maybe authentically for the first time since I've met her. I almost like her for a moment until she says. "Yes, well, we don't want to start out looking like neophytes in the desert, do we?"

I have no idea what the hell that means, so I grab my bag and head for the door. I stop before I clear the doorway and look back at Brin. "Look, I know I don't know much, if anything, about all this spiritual stuff. But I am a good producer. Thanks for hiring me."

Brin chuckles in that "do I have a story for you" kind of way. "It's actually pretty funny how I found all of you. I'll tell you one day. For now, I'll focus on the spiritual stuff. You just make sure we get it in the can."

I want to ask her to tell me now how she found us, but before I can she's already picked up the phone. "Mr. Tollay, please. Brin Halloway calling."

I quietly close the door behind me. I think we might be okay.

CHAPTER 8

I spend the week before production trying to learn everything I can about our interview list, which is sort of like trying to fit a philosophy degree into a weekend workshop. (Which, BTW, is apparently all the rage.) Who knew you could master the age-old art of energy healing or become a shaman in a weekend? It used to take twenty to thirty years of apprenticeship in the jungle. But now? You can pay $499 and get it in forty-eight hours at a swanky hotel with room service.

The people financing *Killing Buddha* pay me a huge chunk in advance, which is insane and unheard of in the movie biz. But since I am broke and on the verge of descending into hell with all of Beelzebub's latest accessories, I'm not going to argue with them. Plus, this allows me to pay off most of my debt, save myself from being evicted, buy some new shoes and rent a car. I figure I'll wait to buy a new car until after the shoot. I won't be home for a while, so no need.

There is another, very important item on my list which revolves around me not being home— Zak. He needs a place to chill and I don't just want to drop him anywhere. Zak isn't just any dog, he's basically my soulmate and seems to be the only man who sticks around. Unfortunately for me, there is only one person in the world who will love him as much as I do, so now I am driving my dog in my rental car to the house of one of those men who didn't stick around.

I haven't been to Tom's new place. I shocked even myself by not doing the late-night drive-by after my seven drunken rage-filled messages. I haven't even spoken to him. I heard through Dana that he and the AP tried to make a go at a relationship, and I didn't know what I would do if I did a drive-by and found them outside his place. So, instead of being my usual impulsive self, I baked, creating new dog treat recipes, holding on to the idea that one day I will be both an award-winning Hollywood producer and the Dog Treat Queen of the world. From my perch atop the hill above San Fran I will look back at Tom and his now hemorrhoid-ridden Anal Princess with pity and no regrets. (Okay, yes, I still have unresolved anger about that affair. Stop judging me.) I can still have the dream. I just need to replace the husband part.

Tom tried to reach out a couple of times to offer the olive branch, but I refused to believe it was because he felt bad about what he did. Men don't feel bad for cheating. They feel bad about getting caught. I assumed he called because he thought he needed us to be okay so his career wouldn't falter. Ironic to think his career was fine while mine ended up in the shitter. I know I must sound like an absolute man hater. I'm not. I am, however pointing out the obvious when it comes to what's acceptable for men and what isn't for women. A man can screw anyone he pleases, literally and figuratively, maybe cause a small scandal in public, but behind the scenes almost everyone of importance (mostly men) are congratulating him on his conquest. Guys can wait it out and everything will be just fine.

A woman, on the other hand, who has been shamed, humiliated, wronged in every way imaginable—a woman who has worked in the biz all her life, first in front of the camera and then behind the scenes working her way up from PA to producer—throws a director's chair, slaps an actress and assaults her director on film, then proceeds in a half-naked, drunken stupor to empty her house of a philandering lover's belongings while her neighbors live stream it on social media, then starts a gourmet dog treat company out of her kitchen, well, she's hysterical. She's crazy. She's psycho.

Damn right I'm hysterical. I earned the right to be. (And what is it with our new-found fascination with filming everything? Jesus! Can't a girl have a good old-fashioned meltdown anymore without it being the next day's viral video?)

I can feel myself getting worked up and what I need to be is cool as a cucumber. Tom needs to see me happy and looking awesome, wearing a super cute sundress and the newest, chicest pair of platform espadrilles. I went to Cristophe and got a haircut and color. I've been mani'd and pedi'd and waxed (not that he'll ever know, but I will, *wink wink*). My outside is ready! But my inside? It's a wreck. I can't tell if it's because I hate him with every ounce of my being, or I still love him and harbor the fantasy that he'll take one look at me looking awesome and take me into his arms, express his regret at his horrible behavior, get down on his knees and beg me to forgive him, then look me in the eyes and profess his undying love for me.

I wonder what I would say if he did that? Part of me would love nothing more than to slap him across the face, turn dramatically and walk away. But somehow, I doubt I would have the strength for that. I am a sucker for a hot man with a smooth tongue, even if it is forked. Eve, I hear you. I see you. We've been damned from the start, haven't we?

I make the final turn onto his street and I can already see him, sitting on the front steps of a pretty nice duplex. Shlock horror is still paying him well, I see. I check the mirror before he can see me—he doesn't know the car anyway, a very nondescript Camry. I'm like a female cop in one of those Dick Wolf shows, super sexy and yet totally bad ass. I take a deep breath and plant a "I'm so damn amazing and you blew it" smile on my face. Conveniently there is a spot right in front of where he's sitting, so I pull up with panache. He stands and makes his way to the passenger side door. Zak is bouncing around, panting and whining with excitement. I hate it that he loves Tom so much. What the hell Zak! Aren't you on my side? He broke your soulmate's heart. Show some balls here!

The door opens and out jumps Zak into his arms. Tom falls to his knees patting him. Huh. Who knew I was so damn psychic? Apparently, I need to work on my prophetic visions a little bit. I pop the trunk, get out of the car and begin unloading Zak's stuff, because that's what I'm here for. Tom attempts to calm an exuberant Zak, while I'm fuming, thinking *I should film this.* He could have internet gold right there—a man and his dog reunion—very viral. I hand him a tennis ball, which he throws, and Zak is off down the street in a flash.

Exterior shot: day

SARA
(hoping to get this over with quick)
Thanks for doing this for me.

TOM
No problem at all. Three years makes him part my dog anyway and it's important he spend more time with his dad.

Oooo, very smooth.

SARA
Yeah, (chuckling) I'm sure he needs to learn the ways of men from someone who's got it down.

Tom smiles and sighs.

TOM

I'm really glad to hear about your film. It sounds great. I just booked a role in an indie film directed by last year's Sundance winner!

SARA

Wow, no more chasing women with an ice pick or saving the human race one ejaculation at a time. Good for you.

I'm being sarcastic, I know. But sarcasm is where I go when I feel vulnerable, and right now my heart is breaking all over again. Shit! I've got to keep it together. The rest of my vision was wrong, too. He's not pining for me in the least. Cool as a cucumber, cool as a cucumber, I keep repeating in my head, which is not really helping because how the hell do I know how a cold cucumber feels?

TOM

I guess we've both had our fill of that, haven't we?

Zak has bounded back, tennis ball all slobbery. Tom throws it again.

TOM (Cont)

It's nice to see you back in the game. (Gives me the once over.)
It suits you. (It's always about the looks, isn't it?) Really, it's good to see the old Sara back.

Seriously dude, where's charming Tom? This isn't charming in the least.

SARA

Hmmm, I guess the new Sara wasn't such a winner, was she?

I stab back for all the moments I never got to have my say. Zak is already back and pushing for the next throw. Tom gives him a cuddle and looks at me.

TOM

Sara, I don't want to fight with you. I'm sorry. I want you to be happy. I'm happy that you got a film. And from what Dana said, you stood your ground against Joao and took something that spoke to your heart. She may be pissed right now, but she'll get over it.
She loves you Sara.

Aww, how nice of him to let me know someone still loves me. Asshole. I hate him. He keeps smiling and throws another ball for Zak.

TOM (Cont)

That's brave by the way, to do what you did. You've always been brave, Sara. I truly am happy for you. Can we leave it at that?

I can feel a rage-filled rant coming on. You see, Tom has this way about him, like he's a prince or a king speaking to his queen, convincing her that he doesn't really care about all the other women he beds, that she is the only one that matters—in that moment at least. I sometimes wondered if it was all just an act. I lost count of how many times, while watching him work, I would hear the same tone he used on me to get me in the mood or to bend to his will. It's like dark chocolate and red wine, addicting, and I can feel myself melting towards him and I can't, I won't, ever again fall for it. "Can we leave it at that…" Oh, that's safe for you Tom, isn't it? *Fucker…*

Zak is back and has dropped the ball at my feet. I can feel the tears starting to well up in my eyes and I pretend it's because I'm going to miss Zak. Tom moves back to the trunk to gather Zak's stuff and I use Zak as my prop. *I can put on a show too, dammit,* gushing about how much I'm going to miss him. I look up and Tom is standing over us, a large bag of dog food in his arms. Zak stands between us, unsure of what to do, looking at the car and then back at Tom.

SARA
Yeah, let's just leave it at that.

END SCENE

I manage to push out through a year and a half of unspoken hurt. I make my way back to the driver's side of my car and Zak starts to follow. I hear Tom call his name, and Zak turns and runs to him as he starts to climb the stairs to his apartment. How quickly they forget, don't they? I mean my dog. No, actually, I mean both of them. I don't want to look at Tom, but I want to know if he's looking at me, so I use the moment I'm getting into the car to steal a glance. He's not. His back is to me and I sit there and watch, hoping he'll turn and catch me looking at him. He doesn't, not even when he turns to open his door, which would have been a perfect chance to sneak a peek at me.

He doesn't take it. Of course he doesn't. I start the car and pull away and barely make it to the end of the block before I finally let it loose.

I surprise even myself at the level of rage and anger I still have inside me. I thought I had cried myself out of it all in shower after shower, as if the water would wash away every speck of betrayal and hurt. Clearly, it didn't. I still have more left in me, so I decide to let myself have one last cry over Tom, taking the long way home, grateful my Camry has Bluetooth, allowing myself to listen to my breakup playlist one more time, belting out every word of every song on it.

I drive around the block six times just to finish it. Thank you, Adele, and to every female singer who's been brave enough to write a song about our pain. Women are brave, aren't we? I finally park my car at my place and make myself a promise to never let anyone or anything cause me that much pain ever again. I am on a new journey now. I am going to become the master of my fate, the master of my emotions, of myself. I will be stronger than I have ever been. I will never let anyone have that type of power over me again. I finally made a choice that wasn't safe and smart and sanctioned by "my team." I finally made a choice that wasn't about somebody needing something from me. I finally did what I wanted without the need for approval and love from others. I followed my heart for me. And I know this was the right choice.

CHAPTER 9

The flight to Portland was uneventful. The best part was watching Michele's driver Jimmy unload the Range Rover at the airport in LA, commandeer a skycap's cart, and convince Jason that he could let someone else carry his camera equipment. I wondered and secretly hoped Jimmy would be traveling with us. But he wasn't and I had a hilarious time envisioning Michele on the other end of this flight.

When we land in Portland, I have to say I am impressed. Michele has every man available carrying our bags. It's amazing what beauty and naiveté will get you ... girlfriend has the art of manipulation down.

We arrive at The Portland Convention Center where the marquee reads "The Mind Body Spirit Expo" and I just can't hide my excitement. After yesterday's Tom meltdown, I felt sure I would wake up with a rage hang over. But I didn't. I didn't wake up with any hangover. I felt almost alien to myself and know I am ready for the new me.

We find our way into the expo hall, which is filled to the brim with vendors. I haven't even begun to take it all in when Brin corrals us all. "Okay, the holonomic brain lecture is in half an hour, you've gotta get footage of that."

We all just kind of stare at her for a moment because WTF, holonomic is a word no one should really understand, right? I try and play it off. "Yeah, I know, it's …"

Brin cuts me off. "It's a model of cognitive brain function based on neurological wave interference patterns and holographic gestalt perception."

"Exactly what I was going to say." Quickly, I turn to Jason and Fabio. "Get some good general b-roll footage and don't forget that holo thing in half an hour. Michele, we'll find you if anything interesting shows up for us. In the meantime, you stick with the boys and make sure the release signs are up and that you get a release from anyone you film close up." I rummage in my bag for our media passes and hand them around. "Also, everyone wear your badges. Okay?"

Michele is staring into her phone and I don't think she heard a word of what I said. I notice Fabio (seriously, even I can't come up with a name better than that for him) nudge her and they move off towards the entrance, Jason grabbing shots of the sign and the people. He's very serious about his job. Actually, he's just very serious. I grab Brin by the arm, "Come on! Let's go check out the booths!"

We make our way to the main exhibition hall. It's packed with man buns and flowy skirts, crystal everything, open midriffs and tans. I can't quite decide if I'm in the extras holding room for the newest version of "Excalibur" or at Coachella.

These people really do love mythical beings and regardless of age, all the women look like goddesses. I feel out of place, like I missed the memo on what to wear, while everyone else, including Brin, is spiritual chic. Me? I am ready to work. Jeans, white button-down shirt, silver Tiffany pen necklace, glasses, a small backpack.

Brin glances around and purrs, "Ah, yes, angels and dolphins outside their natural habitat. Faeries and unicorns can't be far away."

We walk by a booth with, no joke, faerie wind chimes, faerie lawn statues, faerie fountains. "See, They're always in front. Softens you up before you get to the back where they talk conspiracy stuff and alien rectal probes."

"Rectal probes?" I ask, shocked.

"Or brain implants. Take your pick. If we're really lucky we'll see an orb juggler." Brin gets to the next booth before she realizes she's lost me. "Sara?"

I've stopped listening. I'm like a four-year-old in Disneyland for the first time. I find a booth selling flower essences and smile reminiscently. "I used to sell dog treats next to a woman who made these at the farmers market on Fairfax."

Brin, who has found me lost in the smell of patchouli and lavender, looks at me confused. "Dog treats?"

"It's a long story. You know, woman hits 35, questions her life, her career, that annoying biological clock kicks in and I can't reconcile Hollywood shlock queen and PTA mom. So, I quit it all and became an entrepreneur, making and selling gourmet dog treats because isn't that how it is? We think because we can negotiate a solid back end deal with the AP that we should somehow be able to build a multi-million-dollar empire out of food we give our dogs to make them love us, because why else would they? And then I epically failed and so here I am, surrounded by unicorns, faeries and … oh look! An aura reader!"

I leave Brin shaking her head in confusion and run toward the next booth like an eager puppy off its leash. I'd read about auras in one of my books and I want to get a "before" picture because this is the first day on my journey to enlightenment and I think it would be cool to hang it on my fridge next to the "after" picture once I've got it. (Enlightenment)

Brin waits patiently and with some amusement. After my picture we bump into the team. Fabio looks like he's just had to have sex with a cougar and she wasn't all he had hoped for underneath the Spanx and false eye lashes (and teeth, most likely). Jason looks as serious as ever and Michele is on her phone.

"How's it going?" I ask.

"We got b-roll of the entrance, the sign and the . . . the dudes with the ponytails and shaved heads in orange robes dancing and pounding the drums," Jason is shaking his head in amazement. "We're headed over to the brain talk now."

Brin looks at Fabio and teases "Fabs, you look like you've seen the Holy Ghost."

"There is nothing holy about what is happening here," Fabio responds firmly.

Brin laughs. "Don't worry, you've got Jason here to protect you. 'Put on the full armor of God so that you can take your stand against the devil's schemes.' Isn't that right J?"

Jason scowls and looks like he's about to make a sharp comeback and I shoo everyone off and take Brin by the arm. Peacekeeping is a full-time job on some shoots. "So how did you get hired as our spiritual consultant, anyway?" I ask. "Is there like a degree for that, or a certification or weekend course?"

Brin sighs, "Nope, it's called growing up hippie with cult-following parents who, I think, invented the term non-conformist. We traveled to India, lived in an ashram and then in our car. I dropped acid for the first time when I was twelve. My parents were crazy vegans." She shrugged. "Actually, I think my parents hated eating altogether. They pretended it was because they felt sad for the plants, but it was really because all of our money went to fanatical gurus. You remember Osho?" She didn't wait for me to answer. "Yep, I was there!"

"Wow, that's rough." Brin wins the childhood trauma contest, hands down. I am suddenly concerned that our spiritual expert is as bitter as I am, except instead of hating men, I think she might just hate people—all of them.

"Look at these people, giving everything they have to the New Age merchants in the temple," she scoffs, confirming my assessment.

I can't help myself. "So, what are you? Jesus?

Am I about to witness the rage of a prophet?" I look around. "These people actually seem really happy and loving and excited to be here. Isn't that what spirituality is all about? Being positive and all about love?"

Brin stops walking and looks me straight in the eyes. "People are always happy when they think they're going to find happiness. Guru shopping is the new cocaine. You're always in a good mood when somebody's telling you there's more waiting for you. Wait until they find out the well is dry and they're stuck with what they have."

Is she talking about me? I feel slightly embarrassed about my excitement and desire to be happy, and a bit confused. I thought that's what we were supposed to be looking for. I'm trying to figure Brin out. *I mean, wow, is she bitter*! She really plays the part of New Age wise woman, but underneath … yep, bitter and angry. *Well, at least we have something in common.*

"So why did you take this job if you hate all of this?" I ask, genuinely curious.

Brin takes a moment and looks around the busy scene. We've made it to the back of the expo hall and, sure enough, it has become a little weird and dark. We journeyed from unicorns and faeries to the Zombie Apocalypse. Here the signs feature ominous figures in robes, aliens, the Earth in flames. Okay, so maybe not so positive after all.

Brin finally answers. "Like you, I need to reinvent myself." She glances around, sighs and shrugs. "Instead of carrying on the family tradition of suffering in the name of enlightenment, I went to college, got my BA and then got a really good job working as an executive for a company until I got aged out. Look, I get it. Why keep a graying ex-hippy with a six-figure salary on the payroll with a pension and a gold star health care package when there is a desperate, recently-graduated, deep-in-debt neophyte who's willing to do anything just to make their first student loan payment on time? Yay for capitalism! I tried retirement and I sucked at it. I tried traveling back to India, looking for I'm not sure what. But then this gig showed up and I figured I'd finally make some money off my in-depth knowledge of all things woo woo. Hey, I could have written a book like everyone else. This just seemed more fun."

Wow, I didn't expect that! I had built up a story about Brin—that she was going to be my expert enlightenment mentor and guide me on my path to nirvana. Certainly, she is an expert. *This woman can pull a random spiritual verse out of her ass better than the Anal Princess and her pearls.* And yet here we are, almost exactly at the same point in life, lost with a great resume, unable to figure out what to do with it, angry at the man, our parents, our circumstances.

I actually feel good about this. She's obviously searching too, which makes me feel less alone, even if she does know more than I do. So what if she's farther along on the journey? She's clearly in Dark Night of the Soul territory. (I read about that in a book called *The Different Stages of Enlightenment* and it doesn't look so bad, which is a relief.) All the same,

I'm a little uncomfortable with her sudden vulnerable confession. I'm good with a little less truth and honesty and little more mystery in a person. What we give up can and probably will be used to hurt us later. At least that's my experience.

I dodge the moment saying, "I gotta pee." Which is true. "Why don't you find the gang and let's have lunch? I'll meet you in the food court in ..." I glance at my watch. "Half an hour."

With that I take my leave of Brin. I want to have some time to myself to explore. I was given a cool bag at registration and I intend to fill it. Brin may be bitter and this may all be old hat for her, but I am ready to find the new Sara, the better and happier, more confident Sara. I am ready to expand into all that is being offered to me. What that is exactly, I don't know. But I know it's here and I know I will find it. I even wore my comfy Tommy Hilfigers, so I'm ready to mingle.

There is certainly a lot to choose from. It seems the New Age really wanted variety as opposed to the basic Methodist religion I'd been mostly stuck with. There must have been a dozen divination booths where readers divined with God, aliens, your long-lost brother or your past self. There were apps for everything, from star constellation maps to daily astrology readings. *It's nice to see the New Age embracing the new age*, I laughed, and signed up.

Past life regressions, channels who channel spirits and dead saints you've heard of or haven't, a whole row devoted to anything Lord of the Rings, things you can put into just about every orifice you have. It's all here. I politely decline the green vagina egg and am a little shocked to see women lined up around the corner to drop their panties and have a rock shoved up their va-jay-jays. But hey, if it gets you enlightenment—which seems to be the overarching theme—then so be it. Right? Never mind I'm not really clear on what enlightenment actually is. (The dictionary definition "the state of being enlightened" wasn't exactly helpful.) From what I'd read so far, apparently there is no clear path, no "one thing" that will get me enlightenment and no real consensus defining what it even is. And that's overwhelming. Some spiritual teachers offer "it" in three easy steps and others want you to spend weeks blindfolded in the forest, searching for the center of your soul. Speaking of forests, I'm totally lost in here, but determined to find myself in one of these booths.

Half an hour turns into an hour and a half and I realize it's past time to find my team and I head to the food court. I scan the room and see Fabio by a door that leads to an outdoor seating area. He's watching something and I follow his gaze and see Michele talking to a man. Beyond that I see Brin walking in a circle behind him. *Hmm that's weird.*

I head over to Fabio and see that Brin is walking some sort of temporary labyrinth with rocks and crystals organized in a giant pattern within a circle. I finally see Jason, off to the side, filming Brin, who looks like she's floating. I wonder how she will feel being caught at peace and she suddenly looks up, as if she was tapped on the shoulder and looks right at me. It's like she knew I was there, which gives me the heebie jeebies, because there are over a thousand people in this room and she literally turned, opened her eyes and looked right at me. I feel like I just got caught peeping into a window at two star crossed lovers forbidden by society. She bows, hands pressed together at her heart, scoops up her shoes and walks out of the labyrinth.

I head outside and she steers toward me. "Hey, where were you?" she asks. "Get lost in the craziness?"

And suddenly I feel guilty, spying on her like I lied to my mother about pot or something. "Yeah, what a crazy scene. I think I have something for that." I fumble around in my now overflowing bag. "It's a necklace you're supposed to wear to keep your vibrations high—a tacky something." I'm still digging in my bag and finally find the thing I'm looking for, which, now that I'm showing it to Brin, looks gawdy, made of cheap imitation gold—a little bit star of David, a little bit cereal box prize.

Jason makes his way over to us and looks at the bauble dangling from my fingers. "Hmpf," he snorts. "Another lost sheep bled by the temple merchants." People seem to love that quote.

Brin guffaws, "Yeah, like the Church would never bleed its sheep would it?"

"Make not my Father's house a house of merchandize. John 2:16," Jason is quick to retort

Brin is about to respond and I sense I am going to have to separate them when Michele arrives with a very handsome, balding older gentleman in tow. I notice Fabio perk up and he's about to say something when Michele speaks, "Hello everyone, this is my new friend Lawrence. He's an archeologist and has one of the real crystal skulls."

I'm wondering what she means, thinking of Indiana Jones, and I'm suddenly thankful for Brin because that was about to come out of my mouth. "They've been found all over the world," says Brin almost lazily. "Supposedly they hold all the information about our planet, past and future, in their crystal lattice structure."

Indiana, I mean Lawrence, speaks up with a seriously fake English accent, and I can tell he's no Indiana Jones. "Oohhh, 'Supposedly?' A skeptic? I love it."

Brin eyes him coldly and looks back at me, "They *supposedly* work like quantum computers." She fully enunciates the word and I'm not sure I have the strength for another Brin battle. Michele, who is suddenly present and focused—I mean she hasn't touched her phone in over a minute—squeals, "And guess what! Larry has invited us to film his upcoming week-long retreat where about a thousand people will be meditating with the skull. It's very exclusive!"

Larry the fake Englishman has put his arm around Michele, which makes me uncomfortable and I see Fabio move closer to her protectively. Cute, a budding set romance. "Well, it sounds really interesting," I say diplomatically. "Why don't you join us for dinner Larry, and we can talk more about it?"

"Oh, sorry Sara," Michele effuses. "Larry has invited me to a private session with the skull. Tonight. I get to sleep right up close. He says it's life altering!"

I bet it is. I look at Brin who shrugs. Fabio looks like he was just stabbed in the heart with the. sword of the witch king and Jason—well, it's clear he really couldn't care less. "Okay then," I say. "We're leaving at eight tomorrow morning. Meet us in the lobby after breakfast. I'll check it out and check our shooting schedule and see if we can fit it in."

"Cool!" Michele turns to her male Irina Spalko. "I'm just going to dash up to my room for a sec. Meet you in the lobby in fifteen minutes?"

He nods and does a slight European-looking bow which looks totally fake, but Michelle actually titters in excitement. I turn to my crew. "Time to get some rest and eat." We head to the elevators with me walking slightly behind everyone. My bag is heavy, filled with every possible cure for the lost soul, or so I'm told. And I don't feel well. I missed lunch which doesn't do well for me.

"What a zoo!" mutters Jason as we wait at the elevator. "I feel like I've been lost in a funhouse with those mirrors where nothing looks right."

"I know!" Fabio chimes in. "It's like seeking is the religion here."

Brin worms in between them and in showman style declares, "You know what they say. There's a seeker born every minute."

This stings me. Am I just a seeker, destined to be forever lost in a sea of confusing, sometimes bizarre and uncomfortable rituals, wearing crystals and bathed in rose oil, wearing a hemp skirt? I'd visited almost every booth, and nothing today made me feel any better about myself. Truth be told, it only made me feel worse, like I was wrong, broken, needing more fixing than my first car that I loved but eventually realized wasn't worth fixing. It was time to bite the bullet and buy a new one. *Is that where I am at?* I wonder. *A human being not worth fixing who should just be retired for a newer model? Does this mean I'm a total loss?*

I really am not feeling well, the competing scents from the soy, lavender and honey-infused candles and straight up patchouli incense linger even outside of the gigantic ballroom that housed the cacophony of solutions to ease human woes. As we get into the elevator, I barely make it to the back wall and grab onto the bar as the door closes and we begin to rise up. Michelle, who is crowded in next to me, whispers, "Are you okay?"

I nod. But I feel like I'm on Thunder Mountain at Disneyland. I can hear laughing and I see myself dressed in a white Valentino gown, standing in the middle of the Labyrinth. Booth owners come at me, à la a Busby Berkeley dance number, shoving their wares at me ... and I don't want to be rude. Maybe one of these people has what I'm looking for. So I try and listen as they speak to me.

"Try this miracle food allergy testing pendulum for fifty bucks!"

Another vendor crowds close. "Only two hundred dollars for a Jovian astrology chart!"

Another astrologer butts in. "I'll do it with a north/south node analysis for two-fifty!"

Somebody else pushes in, waving a chart. "Your astro-cartography analysis! Don't leave home without it!"

It's getting crowded in the elevator and the vendors are getting pushy and aggressive. I see my aura photo and someone comments, "Yellow in the aura indicates spiritual advancement."

"No, it doesn't, it means you're highly intellectual and are too much in your mind!"

"No! Yellow is the lowest frequency. You've got to get to indigo!"

"Bright colored chakras show you're spiritually evolved …"

How many people can fit in this damn elevator? They are all coming at me and I am pressed up against the back wall and I can't breathe. I hear the ding of the elevator door opening and I push past Michele, Fabio, Brin and Jason and head straight for my room where I spend about 15 minutes sitting in prayer by the porcelain altar. But since I didn't eat lunch, I have nothing to vomit. It feels like I'm wrenching out my soul, like my insides are trying to escape.

I sag to the cool floor, head resting on my hand on the seat. *I thought this would be easier.* The spiritual life is *supposed* to be easier than the soul-killing world I had built for myself based on money and status. Jesus, the yoga goddess said make a list, I made a list and boom! I manifested a movie—two movies. Like instantly!! The spiritual life is supposed to be better, more fulfilling. Leo/Ananda promised I'd find what I was looking for. Happiness, he said I would find happiness. "It's within you," he said. That's what all the books say.

Humph. If it's within me then why do I need to go broke buying ugly necklaces and putting weird rocks up my vah-jay-jay? Whatever is left in me right now wants out, that's for sure. Honestly, I don't think there is anything left. I'm empty, every piece of me, and I've only just begun my journey to enlightened Sara. *Jesus, I don't know if I'll make it.*

I get up and make my way to my bed and on the way grab my bag off the dresser and dig out my emergency food supply. *Maybe something to eat will help.* I always keep snacks in my bag because often, on set, I miss lunch. I find a semi-solid banana, a granola bar and some chocolate. *Dinner is served.* I text Brin, letting her know I'm tired and that I'll meet them downstairs in the morning. I skip the protein and go right for the chocolate, then exhausted, fall asleep.

CHAPTER 10

I have a really weird sleep. Like I'm asleep, but not. I feel like I am Carmine Carini Jr. sinking to the bottom of the Brooklyn river encased in cement. I am hot and sweaty and fighting my pillow. I hate hotel pillows. *Who chooses them?* It's like they went for quantity over quality. Seriously, I do not need six pillows, just two really good ones will do.

My alarm wakes me out of the cement I am dying in and I pull myself out of bed, shower and make my way downstairs. I need coffee, a cigarette and a blueberry muffin with those sugar crystals on top to get this show on the road. It's as if I went on a typical Sara binge and downed two bottles of wine, but I didn't. *Damn, maybe I should have.*

As I exit the elevator, I see Jason, all packed up, ready to go, sitting in the lobby reading a tiny book, probably his Bible. My mom would have liked him. Fabio is in the café and I jump in line with him, much to the chagrin of an elderly woman dressed like a wood nymph standing behind him.

"Namaste," I say as I squeeze in. Look, if you're that old and your midriff is still showing, then you can handle the love and the light. Right?

"How did you sleep" I ask Fabio. (Really, he is a Fabio, except he's not a blond. He's got long jet-black hair that curls in a way that makes women with straight hair like me jealous.)

"Okay." He answers as he glances around. "I'm worried about Michele. She's not down yet. Brin went to load her luggage into the van. I'm supposed to get her a green tea matcha His brow furrows anxiously. "Should we call Michele?"

"Hmmm, I'll call her." I ring her phone and get no answer and then I remember, *Oh wait, she's a Millennial, they don't talk.* So, I text her and she responds, "I'll be down shortly!" Well, she still has five minutes, I can't argue with that. Fabio and I get our drinks and muffins and head to the van and I light up on the way. This is one thing that I do struggle with—smoking and working—especially now that everyone has gone nicotine-free or is vaping. Vaping just doesn't do it for me. It's truly anti-climactic. There is nothing better than the click of a Bic lighter as the flame pops out to let you know your fix is on its way.

Jason follows us out and we hook up with Brin standing next to the van. "Where the hell is Michele?" she snaps, annoyed.

"It's okay," I respond, puffing away. "She has a couple minutes and I have us booked on an awesome charter, so no worry about lines, etcetera. My friend owns this plane, so we're good." I take another drag and hear a gasp and turn to see Fabio almost faint as spies Michele entangled in the arms of Dr. Evil, kissing him like it's the 1940s, leg up, lips locked, while "The Boogie Woogie Bugle Boy of Company

B" is playing in my head.

Huh. Okay. I didn't see that coming. Which is somewhat surprising because usually I can peg the "it's not love, it's location" romances and I had her bedding Fabio. As for the rest of us, I figure Jason hasn't had sex in, well, maybe ever. Brin, I think, might be a lesbian. And since I'm trying to change old bad habits, sleeping with someone I'm working with is off limits. But Fabio and Michele would have been cute. Sigh …

At this point Michele comes skipping over like she's Sallie Blair and ready to sing in the old Chicago clubs. "Hey, I hope I'm not late!" she chirps breathlessly. "Did I hold you up?"

"No, we're good" I respond. "Let's get moving."

Fabio is driving and pouting and every once in a while, I see him glancing in the rear-view mirror, hoping Michele is gazing back at him. She's not. Jason has his laptop open and is dumping cards. (Our footage is saved on little SD cards, which need to be downloaded onto portable hard drives—a time-consuming, repetitive task, but important.) He has his headphones on and is checking sound quality. He stops and shows us a frame of footage. I have to say, it looks pretty nice. I commend him on the establishing shot he took of the expo: the sun is rising and the sign for the expo is lit like it's surrounded by angels beckoning in throngs of worshippers. The people are almost silhouetted as they move towards the golden orb of light.

"Like moths to a flame," Brin sighs.

Fabio drops us at the charter flight entrance at the Portland airport and heads off to return the rental van. I park everyone in the lobby and head to the office to check us in for our flight. There is one guy in the office and as I check out the window, I see no plane waiting. "Hi, I'm Sara Wells. We have a flight booked to Montecito this morning, five passengers. Is the flight delayed?"

This guy looks at me like I'm speaking Hebrew. "I have no flight booked for this morning," he says, as if it were true.

"Um, that's a mistake," I say in my most "do not fucking mess with me this morning, I've only had one cigarette" voice. "I spoke with Sanjay last week and booked this flight."

He checks his computer and says, "I'm sorry Miss, I have nothing. Sanjay took the plane to Morocco yesterday."

I am in no mood for this shit. "What do you mean he took the plane to Morocco? I have a booking on this plane. He can't just take the plane!"

"Well, it is his plane," he responds.

Jesus. I look back and I see Michele, Brin, and Jason staring at me through the window. I smile and wave and they all quickly turn away as if they weren't spying on me. The guy rattles on. "I'm sorry. I have no booking and I have no plane until Thursday."

"What do you mean you have no plane? I helped Sanjay buy this damn plane! We go way back! When his daddy said 'Make some money, boy,' I made him money investing in films. I actually own this damn plane!"

Tattoo and I go silent in a death stare. Finally, he responds. "Many women helped him buy this plane, Miss. And he's currently with the woman who is paying for its upkeep. I guess he forgot."

"He forgot? He forgot?!" I am seriously about to lose my cookies here. I haven't had enough sleep, food, coffee or cigarettes to deal with Tattoo's bull crap right now. "So, what are you saying? That we have no plane?"

Tattoo looks me dead in the eye. "How many times do I have to repeat myself?"

And here I thought Tattoo was the magic that held the island together, making all the dreams come true. Well, clearly, he isn't. He's just another bitter human, mad that he's short and doing everything in his power to make us all as miserable as he is.

Okay, I'm sorry, that was mean, but I have to now go back to my crew and look like a loser, all thanks to Sanjay who clearly has forgotten all I did for him because I wouldn't mile high his member. Saving his inheritance wasn't enough apparently. And this, in case you were wondering, is why I hate men. I have built their careers, saved them from financial ruin, and made their dreams a reality. But it's always forgotten. Women are like squirrels to men. *There is always another one skimming up a tree, ready and willing to play hide and seek with their nuts.*

My crew, of course, has been watching this entire exchange from the lobby. I open the door, and everyone turns as if they weren't placing bets on my success. Already a mutiny and it's only day two.

"Michele, I need you to book flights on Southwest for today."

She looks up and honestly says to me, "First Class?"

"Michele, Southwest doesn't have first class. It's a discount airline."

And of course, she says, "Oh, I've never flown them." Instantly I hate her too.

Shit like this does not happen to me. I have never had something as ridiculous as a missed flight happen on my watch. Sure, sets have burned down and the occasional actress has tripped in her stilettos, sinking into the cracked earth of the desert, because who wears three-inch Manolo Blahniks or those gawdy fake ones from Frederick's of Hollywood in the desert but B-movie actresses and models? But a missed flight? Things like that are rookie mistakes and I'm not a rookie. What the hell is wrong with me?

Growing up in the film biz teaches a kid a lot of tricks. How to work a room, how to charm the right people. Your entire life is designed around getting the job—in my case, getting the job so I could support my family. The more I worked, the happier everyone was. The more successful I was, the more everybody loved me. Money and success equals happiness and love. It was that simple.

Money I can make. Pleasing people, I am good at. Convincing people to do what they probably don't want to do, but do anyway—even thinking it's what they want—is my life skill. *Maybe even a skill I have used on myself?*

I brush the insight away impatiently. These skills proved handy as I moved into my career behind the camera. After just a couple of years as a production coordinator, I hooked up with a producer (literally and professionally) and moved up to Line Producer, mostly working on seedy, soft core porn-like movies made for late night channels like Cinemax (an early version of HBO). The scripts were horrible, but the money was good, and I figured it was all the great learning experience that I'd missed by not being able to afford to go to college. They were resume-builder gigs as I searched for my breakout project.

It's all about networking in show biz and I was meeting a lot of people. One of the films I got to work on won the Audience Award at The Sundance Film Festival. I was so excited about that! (FYI, this film was an outlier in my career at the time. There weren't many female line producers, and it just so happened that there were two Sara's who did the job. I got a call about this film, went in, met the producer and director and got hired. I didn't find out until later that they actually were wanting to call the other Sara, who had already done loads of cool indie flicks. But they liked me and went with it.)

I went to the festival, met another filmmaker with a script, we hit it off and while I was mostly working in shlock, I was mining for funding to make and take MY film to Sundance. The gang that won Sundance went on to make several huge films. I had

the chance to go with them, and I was really pulled
to go that way. But since they were trying to get from
indie darlings to Hollywood blockbuster status in a
hurry, I would have had to take a pay cut and a credit
drop, and my "guy" told me that was a bad idea. He
suggested I wait it out, keep doing the steady shlock
gigs and keep trying to get my film off the ground.
Not that he was actually helping me get much off
except himself, but I listened to him. He fed my need
for approval and love. At least what I thought was
love.

Now *there* was a defining "what if" moment.
What if I hadn't listened to him and instead taken
the pay cut and dropped back down to Production
Coordinator on a huge blockbuster film? What if I'd
listened to myself? But then, what if it went nowhere?
These "what if's" are what my nightmares are made
of. They are what keep me inwardly hanging out with
self-doubt. I can fake confident empowered woman
on the outside. That's the actress in me. (And they
said I had no talent!) But on the inside, I really just
want to make people think I'm smart, funny, pretty,
and loveable. I want them to *like* me as I'm becoming
successful.

The thing about films is that it's all about who's
attached to star in the film. I didn't have many
connections to name actors, but I had a good hustle.
So, while I hustled, I worked on whatever I could,
which is how I met up with Joao. The producer I was
dating was offered the job, but he had already signed
on to another project. I was as good a producer as

he was, just twenty years younger. I spent the night at his place and when I woke up, there, sitting on the nightstand, was the script and a note that read, "This one is for you, kid. Take it and run with it." Okay, the producer was older, much older, and truth be told I never thought we'd end up married or anything. It was more like a mentor-with-benefits relationship— sort of like those college girls who sleep with their professors, except I wasn't in college and he wasn't a professor. It was probably the nicest break up note I ever received.

Joao and I worked well together and, for a while, he dangled the dream of introducing me to the right people to get my film going. It was the carrot I needed to keep dealing with him and his drama. Then one day, about six films in, I realized there was no carrot, just the lies your boss tells you about the prolonged passed-over promotions because "you're just not ready." Because the reality is you're so damned good at your job he's intimidated and yet doesn't want to lose you. And because you stupidly think you're not ready and don't have the guts to realize how good you actually are, you play "nice" and put up with it.

In reality, I should have fucked over everyone who was in my way in the same passive-aggressive, narcissistic, manly way the men do to each other and respect each other afterwards. That's The Game. But while I was bathed in hope, bubbly and Chanel, listening to father figures, I wasn't actually even in The Game. I was just being played.

I was young, naïve, optimistic, and an easy target.

All I wanted was to please and impress people enough so that they would give me a chance to really shine. I fell easily for small praise and little shows of approval. Like a puppy I lapped up all the warm milk poured in my bowl ... until the milk went sour.

Hindsight is so goddamned 20-20. I look at Michele who has gone back to texting on her phone. Brin and Fabio are staring at me. Jason is fiddling with his gear. *What the fuck am I doing here?* I started this project excited about changing all that, changing my life, feeling empowered about coming back to filmmaking on my terms. And here we are, barely 24 hours in, and it's already going haywire. I'm not myself. I don't even know who myself is. I feel like my 18-year-old production assistant self—running that red light in order to impress my boss and almost killing us both.

I give myself a mental shake. *Okay, Sara Wells, you need to chill out, slow down and stay focused.* Maybe I should throw someone under the bus. That's how it's done around here.

Maybe I should get Tattoo fired. That would impress my team and show them who's boss.

CHAPTER 11

We schlep our stuff from the charter terminal all the way to the Southwest terminal. At least Tattoo let us use his luggage cart which, of course, Fabio has to return. No wonder that dude is in such good shape. We make a flight that gets us to Monterey, California. Brin sits next to me and I bury my head in my computer most of the flight—although at one point, right before takeoff, my phone dinged with a notification. And I just had to LOL.

"So much for Madame Ling's daily reading."

Brin looks at me, confused. "Who?"

"I signed up for her daily readings at the expo. I literally spent twenty minutes filling out this whole personalized form. She said she saw all sorts of travel in my future. First class all the way." As I say this, the ginormous man behind me, who has no business booking a budget airline and sitting in budget seats, adjusts his seat, which sends his knees pushing into my back. A sweet reminder from the "Universe" that I'm at its mercy. I sigh. "I guess she got the first-class part wrong."

"What else did she tell you?"

"That I was on the upswing of a huge success curve and that new love was coming into my life."

"How very novel," Brin deadpans.

"So, you don't believe in astrology?" I ask, because I thought this was like a prerequisite to enlightenment.

"Sara, astrology is an art form and actually a science. Some people have taken the time to study it deeply and some people bought the CliffsNotes at an overpriced weekend seminar."

"Oh … I see," I respond, a little crushed. I thought it was all very scientific sounding. "So, um, Brin, what's your sign?"

"I'm a Scorpio, Sagittarius rising, Virgo Moon with Mercury in Aries." She says this as if I actually understand what this means, and I realize I probably should just pretend I do. I nod my head and go back to acting as if I have something really important I'm reading on my computer.

We rent a van and drive the rest of the way to a place called The WAI retreat center on the central coast of California. WAI is the Maori word for water, BTW. The mecca for the human potential movement in the 60s, it sits on the cliffside of the Pacific Ocean and has a spectacular view of crashing waves and passing dolphins. The place is very cottage-like, earthy; the word granola (to reference, healthy conscious hippies) was clearly invented here. The rooms are simple and sparse and often shared with people you don't know who are silent because they came here to be silent. Who shares a room with someone when they go to a place to be intentionally silent? How does being silent help? Because when I am silent … okay, let's be real, when am I ever silent?

Silence scares me.

Brin insisted we shoot here because this is the place the entire Western spiritual-personal growth movement pretty much started, so I'm trusting her judgement. Even though I've decided to become "woke" in a time when yoga requires $200 designer pants and a membership, this place seems to harken back to an era when spirituality was a simple process done alone and didn't require a black American Express Card. There is something ethereal and peaceful about the place which makes it quaint, and I don't usually do well with like, actual quaint. *Vogue* cover photo quaint, I can handle. But real quaint? Real anything makes me uncomfortable, unless it's Gucci.

As we walk down to the administration building from the parking lot, I think Jason may go apoplectic as we see a group of men and women doing yoga, naked, on the main lawn overlooking the swimming pool and ocean. "My God what is wrong with these people? They're naked!" Jason sputters. Fabio, meanwhile, is walking like a Catholic school boy who is trying desperately to avoid eye contact.

"This place invented nudity," Brin says smoothly.

"God invented nudity as something to be held sacred," Jason shoots back.

"Yeah? Well, WAI perfected it." Always the one with the quick comeback, she can't stop herself. "Ah yes, there is nothing more sacred than shavasana in the buff." She looks Jason in the eye. "Corpse pose."

We are here to work and it's time for me to take

over this conversation. "Okay, listen everyone, let's just check in and get filming. We're here for 24 hours. Boys, you're sharing a room." I look over at Michele with a twinkle in my eye like, "I saw you getting some girl." Michele, you've drawn the short straw and are sharing a room with someone we don't know. Can you try not to fall in love or dig up another crystal skull? I think our production schedule is full now. Brin, you and I are roomies."

She laughs coyly and Fabio shrinks just a little and I wonder if he'd hoped I'd room them together. We make our way to the main lobby, which is next to the dining room. Really, it's basically a mess hall, and they only have food at certain times and, as I pass by, I see about 40 people all milling about in utter silence. It's really weird. It's like we're all characters in "A Quiet Place." I'm staring, and as I open the door, it creaks, and everyone glares at me as if I've just awakened the Kraken.

I've always been awkward and loud. Look, I'm insecure. I get that and I overcompensate in the most unconscious ways. I laugh at the most inappropriate moments and, of course, my usual go-to is sarcasm. Or I might just cry. I also talk too much … like I said, silence scares me. I've often wondered if these are sociopathic tendencies or if I just wasn't fully briefed on the intricacies of respectable human behavior.

I know that silent retreats are a "thing" and, damn, I could really learn to keep my mouth shut more often. I don't mean to mock. It's a well-oiled self-defense mechanism I developed to avoid being vulnerable and truly connecting with people. At least this is what my therapist told me.

WAI is the birthplace of the Western Spiritual movement, a sacred place. I am in search of a spiritual rebirth and from what I'm told this is the place to do it, so I'm going to bite my tongue and try to get something out of this. Everyone heads to their dorm rooms. I follow Brin, who seems to have the lay of the land.

"You've been here before?" I ask.

"I lived here. Actually, I was born here." She states this jaw-dropping item matter-of-factly.

"Wait, you were *born* here? Like out of the vagina born here?"

"Yep. Like out of the vagina, born right here … well, actually down on the beach in a tent." She glances around. "I think we can see the exact spot from up ahead."

As we keep walking, I can't believe what I'm hearing.

"This place started with a guy named Jonas Elden in 1962. I was born in 1965 when my parents came here from San Francisco after leaving the People's Temple of The Disciples of Christ. You know, the Jim Jones Kool-Aid cult."

I gasp out loud. "What? The guy who had his followers kill themselves in Guyana in the 70s?"

"Yep. My parents somehow skipped that crazy train. I think it was because of me. At least I like to think so. Because my parents would have totally drunk the Kool-Aid if they'd moved down there.

Anyway, Mom got pregnant with me in 1965 and was in nesting mode, and Jimmy was predicting some sort of nuclear holocaust and things were getting a little too weird even for my parents. So they moved to a place that was more focused on human potential than total annihilation, which ended up being this place."

She stops on the narrow path and looks around. "I was born somewhere over there." She points towards a cliff and beyond to a sandy beach with a cove filled with driftwood shaped like dragons and eagles and enough seashells to fill an aquarium. As I gaze upon it, for a moment I see Brin as a newborn baby, at peace … for about five minutes.

Seriously, are we all born in blissful ignorance and then life just screws with us for fun? Are we God's cosmic joke and He really is just sitting up there LOL'ing? What else does He have to do? I mean, it only took Him six days to create the place. He must be bored and we're His only entertainment. We pop out and then we have about an hour of initial, "Wow this place is amazing" and then the suffering and torture begins. "I'm cold, hungry, I can't talk …WTF is happening?"

We find a spot on the cliffs with a mesmerizing view of the Pacific, perched above the sandy beach where she was born. "The 60's" she begins, "weren't much different than right now. Everyone knew there was something more than what we knew or were being told. They just didn't know what it was. All my parents knew, in the midst of the Vietnam War, was that hate and rage and fear weren't "the way," and that change was coming. Blacks were rising. White people with a conscience and a soul were tired of living in a world that just wanted to hate and make money. Women were realizing that they had literally been slaughtered for centuries for being women. Young people were born with this intense frequency of love and the fear that if we didn't stop the hate, we'd all die in a nuclear holocaust. The idea that love was actually more powerful than hate was palpable.

"My parents rebelled against their white-collar wealth," she continues. "They resented their whiteness and privilege and so they abandoned it. My parents could have lived truly exemplary lives, by their parents' standards—Ivy League schools, degrees, respectable careers—and they chose to forgo it all in order to try to find the path of love." She pauses. "Not that they took me into much consideration in all the love-finding efforts." She shakes her head, eyes absent. "Anyway, after living here at WAI, because of John Lennon and The White Album, they took me, age four, and went to India."

"So how ..." I'm not sure I should even ask but I'm curious. "How did they afford all that?"

Brin laughs. "My great-grandmother actually supported my parents. She was the black sheep of her family, a suffragette. My mother's mother was a prude, married to a drunk narcissist—funny how the generations often switch sides. My grandmother was a racist cunt, actually, if I'm being honest. When my great-grandmother began to fade, we came home from India, moved into her house, and took care of her. I was fourteen and had no idea how to even live in a house, let alone go to school." She shakes her head and goes silent.

I can't even fully process her story, it's so wholly different than my own. I'm no stranger to comparing myself to others, and I always feel like I'm coming up short, literally and figuratively. But as Brin continues to share, I find I can't realistically compare our stories. I was born in Cedars Sinai Hospital in West LA, and my mother had an epidural. Brin was delivered on a beach by her twenty-something dad, and I'm amazed she survived. I was born into a world of conformity that took the search for material and worldly gain for granted. Brin was born into a world of searching for God and meaning. I was raised in the Valley and my parents went to the Bob's Big Boy on Riverside Drive. Brin's parents were at the forefront of almost every major spiritual movement in the last millennium and ate Indian food with their fingers sitting on the floor of an ashram.

I guess you could say living in the Valley was cool. We did get a Tom Petty song and a movie. But Brin had an entire era. Her next words jerk me back to attention.

"It was a rough transition for me. Somehow, by twelfth grade, I had managed to do well enough to get into a good college, which my parents could pay for and I went for it and never looked back. When my great-grandmother died, she left them the house, a shit ton of money and a bunch of real estate, which I still own to this day."

I think my mouth is actually hanging open. I've never met anyone like Brin, and if I make it out of this project alive, I should make a movie about her life. If anyone has an angel looking after her, it seems to be Brin. I feel like my angels are in training or maybe in the remedial class at best.

Life is a damn trip, isn't it? I hear the waves crashing against rocks that have survived the passage of time and the comings and goings of each generation of human evolution, from hate and two World Wars to love and hippie Flower Power, back to hate and the rise of Neo-fascism and racism and sexism and the #MeToo movement. All the while, they simply stand, accepting the oncoming barrage of water as it gradually wears them down into new shapes. In comparison, I'm nauseous and feeling fragile. I can barely keep up with it all and it makes me tired. I'm tired of the struggle we humans put ourselves through, and frustrated that I haven't been given the tools to find my way out of any of the pain.

Listening to Brin's story, it seems we just keep repeating the cycle. And I don't want to do that anymore—I don't want to continue the cycle of pain. This is why I'm here. It's why everybody is here. It's why everybody reads all the books and watches the YouTube videos and goes to all the workshops. Everyone who has a product or course they're selling is selling the ending of pain. But damn, so far, after weeks of reading books and listening to videos and getting my aura cleansed, I still feel shitty.

"Where are your parents now?" I ask.

"My father died ten years ago of a heart attack, and when he died, mom signed everything over to me and headed for an ashram in India. She was disappointed I didn't follow her path into the priestess field, and with her soulmate gone she decided to spend the rest of her life in seclusion and service to others. She just turned 75 last month."

Once again I find common ground with Brin in a way I hadn't expected—not in our lifestyle philosophies and backgrounds. Hell no. But despite her exciting life, Brin obviously wishes she'd had a more "stable" life like me. And yet my life has been far from stable. I can't count the times I wished I'd had a normal upbringing. Neither of us had anything close to normal. What is normal? Later, back in our room, I ponder mothers and daughters while Brin and I unpack. We both hold onto resentment for our mothers who just weren't dependable and there for us. Even as we love them, we both want to be more than they were—different, better. I'm not sure what that looks like, and apparently Brin doesn't either. But we're trying.

Brin is eyeing a pamphlet she found on the table, "Hey, I know this place isn't your cup of tea, but it is a really powerful place for a person who's really interested in human potential and growth. They have a class on exploring anger led by one of the leading experts in emotional therapy. You should go. I'll watch the kids and keep them on track. It's about an hour. I'll meet you for dinner after."

A class exploring anger is probably exactly what I need. After all, it's my inability to control my anger that landed me in "the quiet place "after all.

Brin hands me the brochure with the schedule and info about the class. It says it will teach me tools and techniques to process and be present with emotions like anger. *Hmmm.* Brin is pretty perceptive. I haven't even had a mini-Sara rage moment around her and yet here she is being spot on about what I need to handle most.

I get to the workshop and sit on a pillow on the floor and an older, bearded man, who I'm convinced came here in the 60's and just never left, sits next to me. He's wearing a sweaty wife beater and gym shorts and really should have put on underwear. Other than that, in a really uncomfortable way, he reminds me of my dad, jovial and at ease. I'm having a hard time believing this guy has anger issues. I'm also surprised how many people showed up for this thing. A lot of people have anger issues. What surprises me is that people want to deal with them.

The teacher says we should stand up and face our neighbor, close our eyes and breathe and imagine something that makes us angry. So now I am facing my dad dude and he's breathing and I'm breathing, but he's like *really* breathing. He's getting into it, which intimidates me because my dad was a jovial dude, but when he got mad, he could be like Gandalf facing down the Balrog. So, dad dude is getting there, and my eyes are closed and I'm trying to breathe, and suddenly Gandolf is in full rage and I am his Balrog. "How DARE you think you could do that to me and get away with it?" he screams out of the blue, spit flying. "I never deserved that kind of treatment! How DARE you?!"

I am not prepared for this and I think I jumped about fifteen feet into the air. I am stunned, frozen and unsure. What I am supposed to do with his rage? *Jesus!* The teacher comes over and coaches. "Good Carl, let it out, let it out." And I'm like, "Okay, maybe you should keep some of that in." And the teacher says to me, "Sara, be present with his anger." And I'm standing there wondering how one could *not* be present with it and WTF does being present with it mean anyway?

Around the room, others in the class are embracing their rage and their partners are just standing there, looking them in the eye, taking it. Some of them are crying, but not with fear. It's like they are empathizing and trying to care for them. All around me the angry people are screaming and then some of them start to sob and, like dominos, they start to fall into the arms of their partners who hug them and talk to them and comfort them. I can't believe what's happening, and as I look around the room, mouth gaping, I'm unprepared when my partner, in full limp body mode, crashes into me, flattening us both to the ground. He is at least 6'1" and he may be a hippie, but he clearly enjoys his beer because his bulging gut is crushing mine and I think I broke something and I can't breathe.

He is full on sobbing and I am full on trying to save myself from suffocation, so I put my arms around him and push, and end up rolling on top of him in some creepy porn star move. Now he is underneath me, looking up at me, very confused as to how a 5'2" woman could have emasculated him that easily. And all I can do is thank Ivan at Krav Maga three times a week. Okay, I didn't go three times a week, I went about three times. But I learned this self-defense move and right now, I'm thinking I should go back once this film is over because dad dude's rage scared me and I don't do male rage. I immediately and unconsciously go into "I will cut you if you come at me" stance, not "I hear you and love you" when a dude is going postal on me. It's a survival skill I think most women learn at some point in their lives.

The teacher, who is still standing over us, says, "Sara, I can see you're triggered. This is normal when first beginning this work. Why don't you try and release *your* anger?" And with that, Gandalf throws me off of him and sits in the lotus flower position in front of me as if he's suddenly Buddha. So, I sit up and breathe and I try to imagine Tom and, well ... nothing. Hmmm. *Maybe my drunken, rage-filled, haul-his-shit-to-the-curb experience was a healthy purge after all?* Next, I try to imagine my Mom and Dad and the moment I realized my parents had spent all my money ... oddly, nothing. I had long ago justified their behavior as something I deserved or didn't deserve. I mean, hey they didn't really mean to fuck up my entire life. And did they really fuck it all up? Or did I somehow cause it because I was a really bad actress and if only I had been better, then none of that would have happened and …

In that moment, totally in my head, feeling nothing, I realize that my anger can't just be summoned when I feel like expressing anger. I don't have that much control over it. And isn't this why I am here? My anger is visceral. It's experiential. It's a flush of chemicals in the moment. It's when life hurts so much and part of me sees that all my blaming myself and rationalizing hasn't made the pain go away—that all I can do is make it, them, him, her, hurt more. That's what anger is to me. It's rage and pain and protection. And when it happens, I can't control it. I can't summon it. It arrives and takes over. So, to be asked to just demand its presence, especially when what I feel isn't anger but discomfort; it just isn't happening.

But I try. I try to remember moments when my heart hurt so much that I wanted to eviscerate what it was that was causing the pain and I can't find it. I mean, it's there. But I usually only have the ability to recall the actual feelings once I've had at least two glasses of wine and my guard is down. All I've had so far today is two cups of coffee and a kombucha, which has alcohol, but clearly not enough to get this party started.

I stutter a few words at Gandalf, hoping that maybe acting it out will bring it out. Fake it till I make it. Ya know? I close my eyes because the white hair and beard and beer belly are not working for my method. I picture Tom and say, "You really hurt my feelings, Tom. Why did you sleep with her?"

"Is that all you've got?" says Gandalf. "Can I prompt you?" Then he starts acting like Tom— at least I think that's what he's trying to do. "You weren't worthy of my love. I don't care about you." And I sort of chuckle at the truth in that.

"You're right about that, aren't you?" I mutter as I hear screams of rage and pain all around me. And suddenly I feel self-conscious. The last time I went full rage in public I was trending for a week.

"I can't do this. It doesn't feel right," I tell Gandalf, hoping his softer side will emerge. He grimaces and looks for the teacher and shouts, "She's not doing it!"

It feels like being told on in Pre-K art class becase I'm not coloring within the lines, and I feel even more like a failure. Then the woman next to me butts in. "She's making me uncomfortable. She keeps staring at me and it's interrupting my connection to my anger." And I'm thinking, *Really? Looks like you're pretty connected to your anger and you're aiming at me.* But the teacher looks at her and says, "I hear you Leila. Tell me how that feels."

"It feels like I'm being judged by her, like she thinks she's better than me and doesn't have any anger." Mr. Rogers (the teacher) looks at me and says, "Sara, how does that make you feel?" I have no idea what to say and she sighs. "Start by acknowledging her feelings. Validating her feelings will help her feel heard and then she can hear you."

I'm perplexed, because I wasn't even looking at her or thinking about her and yet I am supposed to validate her feelings even though they are utter bullshit. "Um, I'm sorry… um…" I look around the room and everyone is staring at me as if I really did what this woman said I did and I'm beginning to wonder if I really am an asshole. And suddenly, I can feel my anger. It happens fast, starting with a numbness in my hands and feet and then my face. It's a pulse of heat in my chest. I grit my teeth and I can feel my cheekbones tense as my teeth grind together. *Here it comes!* But I don't want to rage here. I want to leave. I feel stupid and judged and unwilling to give them what they want.

My rage is a gift I give, dammit! Because in addition to anger issues, I'm also stubborn and rebellious and I'm not going to give them anything they want or expect from me—not without a paycheck or dinner and a drink. That's how I roll. You have to fucking earn my anger.

Feeling my cheeks burning, knowing I am about to cry, I get up and storm out of the room.

CHAPTER 12

I'm hungry. I want food, not grass or something that looks like baby shit and maggots. I scour the entire mess tent. Really it feels like a tent. I don't want to make WAI sound like some horrible refugee camp, it's not. For many, this is the place for true transformation. It's me, I'm the asshole. Anyway, I finally find something way off to the side with a cute handmade sign above it that reads 'Taco Cart,' and lo and behold it has meat and cheese and sour cream, guacamole and even a really wonderful looking pico de gallo. I praise the Universe, God, Bob, whatever you want to call it, for delivering me tacos. For that I am grateful.

I pile my plate high and am even more thrilled to see they have those crunchy taco shells that stand up by themselves. *Thank the Lord someone here has a Costco card and knows how to use it.*

I scan the room and see Brin, but after my anger class fiasco I would prefer to not sit with her, so I bow my head and look the other way. Alas, she sees me anyway and comes right for me. "How did the emotional therapy session go?" As the words come out of her mouth, I know my poker face is shit and my failure is written all over my face. "That bad, huh?"

"Well, the reality is, I was unable to perform an acceptable level of anger and rage or to connect with my anger in front of a room full of people, which somehow makes me an unconscious unaware nitwit." *Oops, I said that out loud. Loudly.* It just came out, because while I was unable to perform with Gandalf, Mr. Rogers, and Fiona Goode staring me down, my rage is currently teetering on the edge and I may just paint these walls with my tacos if I don't compose myself.

"Looks like you're in touch with your anger now," Brin quips.

I sit down, because I refuse to allow my tacos to go cold. It's my only hope for redemption at the moment, because so far, I haven't found a smoking area in this place and meat may be the only thing to bring me enough satisfaction to quench my rage. "I thought being spiritual meant you transcended your anger?" I complain, like I'm smarter than most of the other kids in the room.

Brin rolls her eyes. "It's a lot more complicated than that, Sara. Spiritual evolution's a process. People have a lot of pent up negative emotions inside that have to be released before they can experience anything greater."

"Sounds like it's just an excuse to be hysterical," I grouse. "I've done hysterical and it didn't end well." As I say this, I flash back to a nightmare I have had repeatedly in which Hollywood Hotshots play my Joao meltdown at parties and act it out in Vines and memes. I'm a meme now. That's what expressing my anger has gotten me.

"No one ever said personal growth was all warm and fuzzy, you know." Brin states in her "I'm a damn guru" voice. "Maybe chasing fairies and dolphins suits you better than gut-wrenching, tear-yourself apart introspection and emotional work."

I just shake my head in the hopes that she'll leave me to my tacos and start piling up all the dairy goodness and dead cow I can fit into my ever-so-crunchy, probably GMO-laden free-standing taco shell. I finish my creation, taking a deep satisfying sniff, getting sour cream on my chin in the process. I literally think I'm salivating.

Brin laughs. Seriously, she laughs. "By the way, that's not meat or cheese or real dairy. The only thing real on that plate is the pico de gallo and guacamole, which looks amazing, can I taste?"

"What is it then?" I am about to explode.

"Well …" Brin starts.

Turns out what I thought was an authentic taco extravaganza is actually a manufactured vegan dish of soy protein and something called tem-pee and other shit I cannot even pronounce and would never eat. Basically it's just grass, beans, and maggots fashioned to look like tacos. *Jesus Christ!* And these people talk about reality as if they live it? Everything here seems fake. Even the food is in disguise, trying to make you feel like you're eating a taco but they trick you into eating something deemed healthy— by whom I don't know. I suspect it's the one with the biggest marketing budget. But maybe I'm being overly cynical. After all, it's not a secret I have trust issues, and I've been on this shoot for a week, read almost every book on enlightenment I should read and so far, nothing is working. Nothing is what it's supposed to be, not even the damn taco shells. It's as if everything is jimmied up to offer me a sense of peace without actually giving me the peace I think I need.

"Nothing in this place is real," I complain bitterly. "Especially not the food. It's a lie. It's all a lie to make me think I'm happy and peaceful when I'm just pretending I am so I can play the part of spiritual master."

"Happy? You want to be happy?" Brin asks, almost challenging. "What does happy mean to you?" Now she is challenging.

"Happy is when I see a taco stand and I get all of the yummy, artery-clogging happiness that comes in a taco and I put it on my plate and then I eat it and I don't die, because tacos aren't bad for you!"

People are starting to stare. Clearly, I have that effect on people here. Brin, who has stayed standing through this exchange, finally sits, sighs and looks at the fake sour cream on my chin, which she wipes off as if I'm that pre-K child she never had. "Sara, happiness is a state of mind. Peace is a state of mind, and tacos are a state of mind. What that sour cream is made of makes no difference. It's what you make of it that does."

Her tenderness calms me. I'm annoyed that it does, but I close my eyes and I envision my favorite taco truck, the one that parked every Tuesday around the corner from my apartment. Tom and I would go there religiously. Seriously, we did Taco Tuesday. So I suck it up and take a bite out of my taco and I almost vomit and I spit it out, because I don't have that good of an imagination and that taco tastes like baby shit. Not that I've tasted baby shit. But if I did, it would taste like that.

Brin laughs uncontrollably and everyone looks at her and for once I am not the point of ire of everyone seeking to eat fake tacos.

I wipe my mouth. "So, I get the fake dairy and meat, but the taco shell? Come on, that's the real deal isn't it?" I ask, praying for one thing to eat that will send me to my happy place.

"Sorry, cauliflower and arrow root flour," she deadpans.

Damn! These people will stop at nothing to destroy pleasure. Pleasure ... peace ... everything about this place is the opposite of what I deem pleasurable or peaceful. I feel physically ill here, confused, out of place, like I just need to grab onto something that makes me feel like Sara. The Sara I know.

Jason, Michele, and Fabio find their way into the dining hall. We wave, and I sit there, deep breathing, because all I really want to do is eat something, smoke something and drink something, like a good Pinot. I am literally in Pinot Noir Country. I watch their reactions to the buffet, walking past the food like I did with utter disdain, and I realize this is a chance to win some points. I jump up and go over to them as they're eyeing the meager offerings. "Hey, who wants a burger and a beer?" I chirp. "Let's blow this popsicle stand and get some real food!" I turn and wave at Brin, gesturing for her to join us. Everyone agrees and we head to the van and get the hell out of Dodge in search of reality—or at least our version of it.

We actually find a little taco stand about eight miles away, and this place is the real deal. And it has beer. Everyone is happy. Fabio is telling Michele about Costa Rica. Michele is uninterested and seems to be texting someone. Jason is still reeling from the day, happy he got great footage and unable to process what he shot, intellectually or emotionally. Brin is making a sport of tormenting Jason's perspective on reconciling his religious views with naked people. It seems that men and women not having sex or thinking about sex, while naked, has literally blown his mind, and I'm just enjoying the moment with everyone's utter dysfunction, feeling un-alone in my own totally flawed habits.

My phone rings and it's Dana. I've barely resurrected myself into a good space and am not sure I want to answer, but I do because I'm OCD like that.

I don't get out a hello before I hear, "Did you see *The Hollywood Reporter* today?" I haven't and so I quickly open it on my phone and the top headline screams at me a reminder that I made the wrong choice: "*Satan's Handbag's* director signs multi-picture deal worth millions."

"Yes, Dana, I see it. Yeah, okay, so I made the wrong choice and I've let you all down. It's a habit, I guess." What else can I say? She's like my mother, always reminding me of what I could have been. I get it. When my mother died, I needed to replace her with another female figure I could repeatedly disappoint but who would always pretend I was enough even though I wasn't. Dana fit the bill perfectly.

While we're on the line, I get another call from the office of the people funding the film. "Dana, I have to go, my financier is on the line." And I click over to the other call. "This is Sara," I say all business-like, while in the background Brin and Jason are about to go to blows and Fabio is moping over his third beer, still futilely trying to get Michele to even look at him and the Mariachi music has hit that moment when we're all supposed to sing along and they do. I cover the phone mic with my finger and whisper in that "Mom's gonna eat you" but not-too-loud voice. "Shhh! Everyone chill the F out! The suits are on the line!"

"Hello, this is Sara," I say again as if our connection was bad. I listen. "Yes, I know the charter ended up not working out, but not to worry, our travel is booked and in line with the budget for the rest of our shoots. A minor hiccup. All is good." I listen again. "Uh huh… no worries. Thanks for checking in, talk soon. Yes, cost report coming soon." I hang up and the article about Joao pops back on my screen. He's standing there, smiling that bullshit "I'm a foreigner" lie he loves to tell, when a notification pops up over his face from the Daily Crystal. *All doing is equal.* - Lao Tzu.

I need a smoke, so I head to the van. Lighting up, leaning on the bumper reminds me of the many nights I would hang out at Basecamp where all the trucks are parked for filming, away from the actual set. It was always like a little city where I was the mayor, but tonight there aren't any huge trucks and Klieg lights to guide me. It's dark and quiet and I miss my old team. I spent seven years working with almost the same crew. We were a family—they were *my* family. I sigh, letting out a smoky exhale.

Camera guys, a couple sound guys, makeup, half the set design crew, wardrobe ... so many of them reached out after the "event" to offer support. Even Lyle from the completion bond company. (Okay, I slept with him and his olive branch was purely professional, *wink wink.*) But I even received emails and texts from other crews I worked with on commercials and in-between films. Like stepbrothers and stepsisters, their notes were awesome, full of love and positivity. But I pushed them all away. I didn't believe they cared about me, just what I could do for them. Like maybe I might mount a comeback and they should stay on my good side. Eventually they all just slithered away.

I light another cig off the butt of the first in preparation for facing WAI's "No Smoking" rule, realizing that I don't know if I know what it means to be cared about—like in the "I'd scatter your ashes off the cliffs of Scotland in the winter" kind of cared about. I think I push everyone away, either by refusing to give them what they want or by being hurt that they are doing the same to me. Being in that room today with everyone eager and willing to expose themselves and their crap reminded me of all the times I was on location somewhere in a random, shitty lobby bar where we'd all hang out after shooting and everyone would get deep and meaningful … except for me. I was always the funny one, silly, loud, probably drunk and always hiding. I could make you feel like we were best friends, and you wouldn't know one thing about me.

Prior to the desert "event" I thought I was pretty cool. I had a splendid poker face and prided myself on being the living example of the meme "Carry on." The very few times in my life I had actually been vulnerable, I was betrayed. So yeah, fuck that shit. Care about nothing.

I take a deep, satisfying drag. The Sara Wells rule of life: Do not let anyone ever know you care about anything.

Uh oh. I feel a little Tom backstory coming on. Okay, think Ryan Gosling in *The Notebook* with like a little bit of *Drive*.

I met Tom in Twenty-Nine Palms, near Palm Springs, in a rundown hotel that could house our whole crew and the trucks. The cast stayed at The Mirage, and I could have stayed there with the "cool" people. But even though I couldn't be real with them,

I loved being around my crew. The set romances, the different cliques, the grips and electricians, the make-up and hair department, starting off all in their own corners and then eventually making their way together. The thing about a movie set is that it's a tightly run, dysfunctional family. There are fights and hurt feelings, but we're all in this together and, like many screwed up but hey, we're-stuck-together families, we always ended the day together.

Tom was a day player, so he ended up in the cheap seats. After his day of filming he found his way down to the pool area where we were all sitting, high fiving the guys, smiling coyly to the make-up girl, who was cute, but married. I sat in my usual off-to-the-side-but-still-in-the-group perch, sipping a bottle of Pinot that I had brought with me. Slowly, everyone headed back to their rooms for an early call the next day, and eventually it was just me and Tom. Damn, he was hot!

"You really have a nice vibe on this set," he says moving closer. "I've been on a lot and they don't have this same sense of camaraderie."

I laugh almost defensively, like who the hell is this guy coming in here and judging my crew? Forget that he just gave me a compliment; the defenses are armed and I am ready for battle with Mr. I'm-Not-Quite-Ryan-Gosling-but-I'll-Act-Like-I-Am. "Yeah, well, we've been together for a long time. We don't have a choice," I say in my best "you will not break me" voice. I consider that I could get laid tonight, which I rarely turn down, and did I mention that he was hot? So, I smile, cock my head and do that thing women do with their eyes that sort of says, "Fuck me, but maybe not."

Tom was smarter than the "maybe not" and so we ended up screwing that night, of course. He was amazing, hung like a damn horse and it was all as it should be. Disconnected sex from an adoring fan who won't call me. Except he did.

Remembering this, my heart hurts, like, physically hurts. I look back at the picnic table where my new family is sitting, surprisingly not killing each other, and I wonder if I could get to know them. As screwed up as this situation might feel, I have a deep sense of appreciation for them. I could have been standing next to Joao in that *Hollywood Reporter* picture, with shit tons of money in the bank and no soul. But I'm not. I'm here.

I'm not sure I have a soul right now, but if I do, I know it isn't for sale anymore.

CHAPTER 13

We start the day with a short flight to San Diego and find ourselves in the complete opposite of the earthy, natural, "no meat yet free-spirited" vibes of WAI — a just-a-tad-too-close-to-tacky- but-still-classy hotel with the fake façade columns, paisley print carpeting, and fake-looking walls that fold away to expand a room, all open to expose a ginormous ballroom with about 2000 faux leather-back ballroom chairs. At least they didn't pull out the golden wire wedding chairs. These hotels have a chair for every occasion and how many synonyms can I come up with for the word fake. On the bright side, so far at least the meat is real.

We have arrived at "Wisdom Power Week," being held by the most famous modern guru multi-millionaire—the "I read Napoleon Hill and most of these people didn't so they will pay me $7500 to attend one of my retreats" kind of guru named Ardent Taylor Jones, or RJ if you're lucky. Who names their kid Ardent? I'm sure he was bullied in school for that name. But having watched hours of his YouTube videos, I can say he is truly ardent—annoyingly ardent. But people love him.

Even if he's skirting the edges of the #MeToo movement, women flock to him and men wish they were him. He's on his second or third trophy wife. Okay, that's not fair. What rich white man isn't? Anyway, this guy is where it's at in terms of personal growth, which is different than spiritual growth, or so I am told. (Somewhere around the 1980s guys like Ardent figured out if they took the "spiritual" out of growth they could sell more tickets. They also added a huge dose of "how to get rich quick," so it became about personal transformation and growth instead of seeking spiritual enlightenment.) And yet they still mix in some of the mystical practices or rituals of the ancient wisdom/mystery schools, because cultural appropriation is apparently cool as long as it's in the name of evolution.

Ardent's cultural appropriation is the firewalk, and there are huge signs advertising it all over the hotel. It's as if everything is flaming hot. "Walk the coals to your destiny" says a huge banner hanging in the ballroom, which is ironic because, of course, we're all walking on coals to our destiny in this hell hole of human drama. At the moment, Fabio is standing in front of a big step and repeat (where celebrities or wannabe celebrities pose for all those pictures you see in People Magazine) which is covered in flames. It's a perfect Instagram moment with the hashtag #IwalkedIConqueredWPW @ATJ, because if you're going to transform and conquer your daemons, there better be a hashtag for that shit..

Jason already has his camera out and is filming the signs and banners as Fabio turns to Brin and asks, genuinely perplexed, "People walk on fire?" Sweet

Fabio, so simultaneously innocent and so porn star ready, he often reminds me of the sweet neophyte who ends up screwing the hottest girl in the campy horror flick who dies because he's stupid. I hope Fabio doesn't die at the end of this story.

Brin looks at him as if he's poor dead Abel (BTW, I've always wondered who did Cain and Abel ya know... do it with? Okay, another story). "The firewalk is one of the most ancient tools for transformation," she says.

Jason stops shooting and looks at Brin and Fabio. "Yeah. Transformation of your feet into charred stumps." He hobbles around and everyone laughs except for Brin.

"Jason. If you'd just open your mind for a minute, you'd see ..."

"Do you see a man wise in his own eyes?" he interrupts. "There is more hope for a fool than for him. Proverbs. You think this (he gestures towards the fiery sign) is wise?"

"It's an initiation," Brin argues

"To what? Hell?" Jason is now about an inch from Brin's face and she's not backing down. Michele and I observe this ping-pong battle as Fabio stands in the middle like a small child wishing his parents wouldn't argue so much.

Brin counters, "It's an initiation into your own fear and weakness ... not that you'd admit to those."

"Okay, okay, people—let's put a little water on those flames," I say, trying for a little humor. Of course, no one is buying it. I don't think Michele has kept her eyes glued to anything more intently than her phone in days.

"So, who's gonna do the firewalk?" I ask jokingly.

Fabio stares at me like a petulant child and exclaims, "I'm not doing it!" Michele actually speaks to us as if we exist, piping in with, "Me either."

"Me either," says Jason. "Why don't you do it Brin, since you're the expert?"

"I've already done it, Jason. Many times. What are you so scared of? I mean it's your loss. If you don't want to transcend the limitations of the physical body, that's your problem."

Jason gets right up in her face and I'm thinking he might actually punch her. "I have no problems. I'm just not deluded into thinking I'm Jesus, that's all."

We're starting to make a scene here in this Sharks and Jets showdown, and I'm about to cut it off when Brin decides to throw down hard. "Jesus walked on water, not fire. But maybe you missed Bible class that day?"

I edge in between them. "Can we skip the debate over who holds the bag of truth right now and ..."

Brin's not ready to be done with this dance battle. Gosh, I wish it were a dance battle. Then the people staring at us might think we were paid to do this. "Don't get me wrong," she presses on. "I like Jesus. Swarthy, middle eastern, into wine, occasional temper tantrums. I do have a tiny problem with the whole 'I died for your sins' thing, though. It's so codependent."

Jason is now sputtering and I'm hoping he's not asthmatic. "Whom hast thou reproached and blasphemed?" he finally spits out. "And against whom hast thou exalted?"

"OMG, STOP!" I scream, and the entire lobby of the San Diego Hilton is now staring at us. I wave and add in my most Valley girl voice, "This is the most awesome place for my insta selfie— Yay@ATJ!" and I strike a pose. I get a few "Woot, Woot ATJ!" shouts back and grab as many arms as I can and pull everyone in for a huddle. "Listen children, we have got to stop making asses of ourselves at these places. I get it, every button that exists within our beings is being pushed. But if we do not start acting like professionals, we're all going to be out of a job and hoping the Gem Channel is hiring. So shut the F up and go to your rooms. We have an interview with Ardent in two hours in the conference room on the third floor. Be there, be ready, have it fucking lit like he's Zeus, king of the damn gods, and let's get what we need." And with that everyone disperses.

I head straight to my room to prepare. So far, we have shot some b-roll and a couple of iffy interviews. Ardent is a big cheese in this world, and this is probably our biggest interview of the entire project. I need to be ready.

I spend the hour in my room writing down questions I think are relevant. The firewalk is an ancient rite of passage used in many cultures—like literally everyone from the ancient Britannica all the way to the Toltecs and the Mayans used it. Even

Buddha firewalked. Which is something that boggles the mind, if you think about it. Just about every cultural region has their own version of the firewalk. It's like pyramids. How did all these different cultures separated by oceans develop the same or similar architecture and create similar rituals?

I get the whole idea of some tribal culture walking across coals to prepare for actually living in a world where a lion can eat you. And I can totally see how this is a great metaphor for our own "lions" in this new civilized world where real lions are locked up but the world is still full of predators. It makes sense, philosophically. And yet I'm having a hard time seeing someone like me doing this. Fear is a powerful thing, and I'm afraid of getting burned, literally and figuratively.

None of us will have to do it, I think. We can totally just film Ardent leading the troops and get a release from someone who's an expert firewalker—sort of like a reveler, people who are hired to go to parties and get people dancing and having fun. There are expert partiers, so there must be expert firewalkers. *We'll just have to find one to showcase.*

I head down to the conference room, expecting to have about twenty minutes before Mr. Magical shows up. But, when I arrive, I see he's already there, resetting the lights and the camera angle. He's about 6'4" to my 5'2" and, as I enter the room, Fabio, Michele, and Jason all look at me with this forlorn look, begging me to stop the madness. But before I can say a word RJ comes at me full force.

"You must be Sara. So glad to meet you. I hope you don't mind, but I really know this space and what makes me look the best. But, if you have a vison, let's go for it." Of course, I don't have a vision. It's a hotel conference room I've never been in and all I really care about is getting him in frame and answering my questions.

"RJ, can I call you RJ?" I chirp brightly. "We want you to be comfortable, so we're all cool with you lighting and framing however you need to be happy with how it looks." With this RJ looks at Fabio and asks him to sit in his chair and he comes around and practically shoves Jason from behind the lens to check the frame. I look at Jason and mimic a deep breath. RJ seems happy and waves Fabio out of his chair. Fabio jumps up, grabs his boom mic and I pull up a hotel chair, setting it next to the camera so it's easy for RJ to pay attention to me while still keeping his gaze steady on the lens.

I take a deep breath. "Are we ready? Okay, let's roll."

I haven't even asked a question before RJ launches into a monologue. "The thing most people don't understand is their own power—their own magical abilities," he enthuses. "What I help people realize is that the story they have been living is made up. We make it up because we can make up whatever story we want to make up about ourselves. So, if that's the case, why aren't we living the story of empowered human, of enlightened being, of master of our own destiny? The things that have happened to you mean nothing unless you make them mean something!"

I try to get a word in as he breathes, but that ain't happening.

"The truth is, you are your own storyteller," he declares, staring forcefully into the camera. I might as well be a fly on a wall in Afghanistan. "You create your story, and so nothing can be relied upon to ensure your wellbeing except you. Nothing. And tonight, you're going to be stimulating your will and learning how to follow through on your choices; how to attack what you're afraid of. How to move forward in an instant ..."

With this he snaps his fingers, as if I am now to say something and this isn't where my notes and questions started, so I'm trying to follow and find something to go on when I remember he said something about empowerment. "Empowerment is good, right?" I stutter.

And it's as if he's that one kid in class who gets easily overly excited. Ardent jumps out of his chair like he's Tom Cruise and I'm Oprah. "Yesssssss!!!" he cries. "It's all about harnessing the power of the mind. Creating your reality."

Jason is frantically trying to keep the guy in frame as he starts to pace like a caged lion. Fortunately, I think I've caught up with what he's talking about. "Exactly," I say. "Personal manifestation. Affecting the quantum field." I'm super proud of myself because I pulled that shit right out of my ass. Meanwhile, RJ has stopped and is staring right into my non-existent soul.

There is a moment of silence and I freeze. Silence is bad on camera, so I try and hold his gaze and it's penetrating, and no one cares I am utterly alone, abandoned with Ardent who, it seems, is eating my soul with every second in this standoff. Finally, he speaks. "So, you'll do the firewalk? You know you want to, Sara. I see you, your power, your strength, your resolve to expand and become what you know in your heart you are."

And I'm like *fuck!* First off, how can he see any of that? And the truth is, this whole moment has come full circular. *Somebody* has to do the firewalk who is willing to let us get up close and personal about their journey, and everyone else has balked. If I don't do this, I really am a failure and I better hope Starbucks is hiring because no one else will after this epic failure. So, I say with a total Valley girl accent, "Dude, of *course* I will. I wouldn't have it any other way. Let's do this."

With that, RJ rips off his mic and pulls me in for a bear hug where I am suffocated, not only by him but by the reality I have just created. So much for finding a reveling expert firewalker. Nope, we're stuck with me, as usual, in over my head, unable to say "no," taking one for the team just so they'll like me.

CHAPTER 14

Lest it always be just about me, I think it's important for you to get to know a bit more about what my cohorts are up to on this journey.

This hasn't been a typical gig for me. I didn't hire any of these people, the "suits" did. (FYI- suits is a term used to describe people who pretend to be in the know about filmmaking but usually aren't. They just have the money, and money does make the film roll. Get the pun!) I didn't know anyone coming in and had no idea about my crew's background and competency. I just took the hand I was dealt and hoped that by the time production was over, we all, hopefully, would have had a growth spurt—that each of us on this journey would figure something out and make it to the end.

I also haven't even met the suits, which is even stranger. Usually, I have a ton of meetings with them up front where I explain every last detail of the budget. Which can be grueling—think mansplaining, even to women, who have no idea how a film actually gets made. (One of my best skills, BTW, is that I am good "in the room.") This time I had none of that, and it makes me uncomfortable not to have had a chance to work my mojo on the money. On top of all this, every time something goes wrong, I feel like they know about it as it's happening. It's like I'm being watched.

Anyway, back to my crew. Brin knows the financier and has respected this individual's choice to remain anonymous. She basically did my job in the beginning, and says she found me through Jeremy, who was a mutual friend of a friend. The rest of the crew she found through other contacts. Originally, she was hoping I'd be the one hiring the crew, but Jeremy had a hard time getting ahold of me. He says he called my agent and never heard back and eventually found my cell. That's annoying. (Dana never even mentioned it!) But then, it's possible if I'd heard from him sooner, I wouldn't have taken the gig because I was lost in my dog treat dream. Timing is everything, they say.

Brin, well I've shared enough about her so far. Fabio is truly a gem: sweet, kind, innocent and honest—too much of all of those things to do well in the film business, by the way. Michele seems earnest in her desire to make films but is distracted since she met Lawrence the skull whisperer. Her dad got her the gig and I know he knows Brin. And he must be connected to Banksys, my nickname for the financier. (I like that code name, since it has the word bank in it, which they are, and we don't really know their identity.) And then there is Jason. Jason is serious and seriously Christian, quiet, except when he gets triggered by Brin and, if I do say so myself, hurt about something. I'm not sure what it is, but that dude's heart is in a million pieces on the inside and his Bible might be the only thing holding him together.

He is steadfast in his faith. And as much as I'd love to judge him and all the rest, we all have that one thing that keeps us from going postal. Some of us don't and, well, isn't that why sometimes good people do bad things? As a side note, I believe we all come in good and then it's downhill from there. It's sad, really, how we treat people who are hurting. Jason is hurting. Fabio is hurting—even though he doesn't quite realize it, he is lost and looking for someone to love him, and Michele is clearly rejecting him because apparently, she just doesn't feel at all. Well, she does, she just doesn't have any idea what to do with her feelings, so clothes, gadgets and rich men who treat her like her daddy are what she uses to fill her void.

I don't judge them, even though I probably would have in the past. Look there, maybe a tiny bit of spiritual growing up is happening in me! The old Sara would have judged them, mocked them and probably never even considered hiring them. Now I feel responsible for them. I am responsible for them. And I can see we all at least have one thing in common bringing us together: we all hurt.

So, from time to time I will share what's up with them, even though technically how could I know that, since I'm not them. But hey, it's a novel right? (*wink, wink*) And readers love and deserve a good backstory. So, now you know more about the "real" them, and you've got their famous actor pictures in your head, so you can fill in the gaps and pick the one you relate to the most!

So now, back to me up in my room, attempting to talk myself into walking on burning hot coals of destruction while not smoking a cigarette or getting drunk, because that's how the old Sara would have handled this situation. Jason, Fabio, and Michele are downstairs getting b-roll and mini-interviews with people attending the event. One would think this is terrible management on my part, since, as I said, it seems none of them care about any of this stuff. But I know that Jason and Fabio are professionals. I got that vibe pretty quickly. And Michele, well, even though right now she's got a crystal skull stuck up her whatever, I think she's having fun and wants to do her job right.

They're also filming the preparations for the firewalk. Building a firewalk is a sacred ritual, and it takes hours, almost an entire day, to get the coals ready for those who would abandon their right minds and leap into the unknown and walk across burning coals in the name of higher consciousness. Usually no one is allowed to enter the perimeter as those building the fire offer their ministrations to the wood that will eventually turn into tiny little chards of burning intentions and hopefully a good amount of ash. They do this in silence or in prayer or perhaps with a sense of irony and revenge. Whoever takes on this task, I hope they have a clear heart because otherwise it could get ugly.

Jason has been watching and filming one person

who's been doing fire prep for Ardent for a long time. I call her Morgaine and the only reason I know about her is because I was on the grounds, smoking, when she finally broke her fire-building trance and looked over at the boys as they were shooting. Jason was startled. I guess women don't typically look his way, and he peeked at her from around the camera as she walked over, never once removing her gaze from the center of the lens.

"Something caught your eye?" she purrs. Jason puts the camera down and is surprisingly cool.

"Hi," he says. "I couldn't help noticing how focused you are on your task and it makes for good footage. Do you mind if we interview you? We're making a documentary about all this stuff."

"All this stuff?" Miss Morgaine teases as she waves her arms as if she's just cast a spell over them.

"Well, you know, we want to know why people risk bodily injury in the hopes of getting something out of it."

"Ahh, yes, well," she nods, "for the uninitiated it must look insane."

"Have you done it?" Jason has picked the camera back up and positioned himself to get a nice shot of the priestess in all her glory. Fabio has the boom mic up and Michele has actually looked up from her phone. Morgaine has that effect on people. She is tall, wispy thin, long flowing reddish hair, not too red, but red enough to not know whether it's natural or a really good dye job. She's not wearing the typical goddess uniform, most likely because flowing skirts probably aren't good around a fire. She's going with a Laura the Tomb Raider look, with a splash of Merida (*Brave* Disney princess) without the accent.

"I have done the firewalk twelve times, and with each passing I have come to know my true self, my power, my limitations, my fears. Ardent is a genius for bringing the ancient mystical teachings to the new world." Morgaine has spoken, and Jason is so hypnotized by her he just stands there, silent.

Fabio jumps in, "Oh, so it doesn't hurt?"

Morgaine laughs that perfect "I'm a witch, but a good witch" laugh. "Oh dear, pain is only relative to your own awakening."

Jason and Fabio have no idea where to go with this.

Michele jumps in. "Cool, can you say your name and your contact information to the camera, and I'll need you to sign a form."

Morgaine looks into the camera as if she's looking right into Jason's soul. "My name is Lyra and you can find me in the light."

Michele looks at her, "Yeah, I'm gonna need something more concrete than that."

And so it goes with my little band of wayward souls, out of their element, I out of mine, lost, confused, trying to do our normal gig in a very unnatural setting. We each keep grasping on to the known, signature here, camera there, push this button, look into the lens, spreadsheets and travel itineraries and schedules. But it's not helping any of us, really.

Standing up on the balcony looking out over

the lawn at my crew and the terrifyingly large, glowing fire pit with its fluttering attendants, I get a notification from Madame Lim which reads, "He who rides a tiger is afraid to dismount."

A tiger indeed.

CHAPTER 15

I am sitting in the back of the ballroom with about a thousand other people listening to Ardent pump us up for the firewalk. Behind him walks an endless loop of successful firewalkers who have traversed the flames of Mordor—jubilant, euphoric people who have transcended their fears and doubts. I feel like Frodo floating down a sea of volcanic sludge spewing from Mount Doom, clinging in sheer panic to a rock that will keep me from floating towards my certain death, mind racing, exploring bad ideas about how I can survive this calamity.

As a producer, problem-solving is one of my main strengths. I have evacuated an entire crew and twenty trucks from mountain wildfires and had the wherewithal to stay behind with the catering crew to feed the exhausted firemen staving off the violent and unrelenting flames of a massive California wildfire. (All of whom happened to be huge fans of the AP. I have to give it to her, she stayed too and dug out a box of promo photos and signed them for the valiant heroes. She took pictures with them and handed out autographs while the mountains around us burned.) I handed out sandwiches and water.

Sitting in the hotel ballroom, I try and find that place in me where I wasn't afraid for those three days holed up on the top of that mountain in Malibu. I felt a sense of purpose for those three days, like I wasn't just feeding into the need to escape from reality with bad porn. I was potentially saving lives with real food and water. What was my purpose now for risking bodily injury, other than saving face and maybe shifting my own fearful thoughts about myself and the world? I can handle a set on fire. I'm just not sure I can handle my feet ablaze.

"You can do so much more than your fears let you believe!" Ardent bellows from the stage and everyone around me is cheering, high on the vibes emanating from the stage and everyone around them. I read in one of my books that people feed off the energy surrounding them. It's like an invisible drug shared at a club, music pumping so loud with so much bass you can't help but move to it. The floor moves you and you just go with it.

Ardent is loud and excited, sweating and spitting as he awakens each of us to our potential. And I'm trying. I'm trying to wake up. I'm trying to get into the mindset of no fear. "All things are possible when you just stop thinking!" he bellows. But not thinking is not something I think I'm capable of. How am I supposed to not think while I'm being told what to think about? It's like when you're told as a kid, "don't do that," and then all you want to do is exactly what your mom said not to do.

"Don't think about it!" roars Ardent. "Just be in the present moment. Silence those thought monsters and trust that you have more power and strength than you can know in your thinking mind!" The music has stopped and the crowd is silent as Ardent, with passion and vulnerability, as if he's imploring me to believe in myself, looks directly into the audience. He is speaking in a softer, more loving tone now, reassuring, thoughtful, caring. "I believe in you. I really do."

I'm certainly glad he does, and I actually believe him. The pep rally is over, and people start to exit the space, giggly, jumping with anticipation. I feel jittery and decide now is not the time to quit smoking. I'm told you shouldn't just go cold turkey on everything all at once, and since I'm trying to stop thinking, I should probably not try and quit smoking. There is only so much a girl can do. And while women are the masters of multi-tasking, right now I have to figure out how to walk across about seven feet of burning hot coals while not physically scarring myself for life. Emotionally it may already be too late. A cigarette right now won't matter, or an entire pack. Whatever it takes.

I head to my room to do some of my own prep work. After all, this isn't just about me. I have a job to do. Maybe just getting into my producer mind will shut up the rest of the "Saras" in my head.

Instead, I watch YouTube videos of people doing firewalks, chain smoking and freaking out, just keepin' it real. I think people only post the triumphs on YouTube. I bet no one posts the epic failures, or at least I'm not finding any. The videos show hordes of happy, almost delirious, people chanting, singing, gallantly traipsing across a burning pit of … I'm running out of metaphors—you know, fire. They are walking on fire. Well, kind of a fire—hot ash and coals that have been cooking for twelve hours and are at the peak of their heat. The kind of fire kids imagine when they leap from the couch to the ottoman pretending the floor is lava, only these people are intentionally barefooted, stomping in it, frolicking even. They make it look like they're doing a conga line at the fifth-grade dance. Jovial, blissed out, drunk on life and possibility.

I think I'm going to vomit. I've gone through a six-pack of those mini-Cokes from the minibar and have burned through my emergency pack of smokes and am now digging through the butts in the ashtray, hoping to find a nub with enough nicotine left to fill the void of no alcohol. I gave in on the smoking, but at least I've held off on ravaging the minibar liquor stash. The wine is cheap and not enough to do the trick anyway.

I try to breathe and do some of the visualizations techniques that I've read help high performance athletes compete. It's all about seeing yourself cross the finish line, triumphantly winning!

I close my eyes and inwardly chant, "I am winning! I am winning!" I see myself in my favorite Valentino dress. (Seriously, I will wear this dress in real life one day.) I am standing in front of a pit of coals. Ardent is on the other side and there are probably millions of people watching me. I can't get a good head count because I'm like Megan Rapino in a sudden death match, focused on my prize.

I stand before the coals and shout, "I AM THE QUANTUM FIELD! I AM THE VOID! I AM THE CREATOR!" and I descend upon the coals, floating, nary a pinky toe touching the flaming pit, like I am Madame Pele herself and Ardent is flabbergasted. "I have never seen someone float across the coals like that!" he gasps. "You're like Jesus on the water!"

And I am in it. I am floating, when I hear *knock knock knock* and I fall to the ground. Literally, I'm on the floor in my hotel room with the paisley carpet, and someone keeps banging on the door I don't want to open because my room smells like the smoking pit at an AC/DC concert and this is a non-smoking hotel. *Why do they take everything from us, while simultaneously forcing us to suffer more and more?* Fuck you vegans! Why can't I just enjoy my steak without you making me feel shitty?

Seriously, all my vegan friends are sick, like all the time, and malnourished. I'm really sorry the cows suffer, but can't I eat and smoke and have some joy? Maybe this is why we're all so hurt. We have taken all the joy out of life. Like why can't I just imagine myself walking across these damn soul scorching rocks of hell unharmed in peace?

I go to my door and peak through the peep hole. It's Brin. *Arrrrg!* Now? Right now, when I am so pumped? I open the door and she barges in. (Brin is a "barger." She is perpetually barging into people's space. For someone who is supposed to be all love and light, she enters a room like a heavyweight ready to rumble.)

"Why aren't you down there with Ardent doing the warmup?" she barks. Like I need to stretch before the race or something.

"I am warming up, just in my own way," I counter her punch.

"Wait, because Ardent doesn't know how to get you ready for the walk of your life?!"

Okay, well this is helping. Like this is it—if I fail, I die? "Jesus, Brin, I did the session after our interview. I drank the Kool-Aid. Now I'm just going for extra credit. And you're not helping me right now."

She pauses and looks at me. Really looks at me. "Sara, listen, you do not have to do this. We can come up with an excuse."

"I don't want an excuse! I am tired of excuses. I want to do this!" In that moment I really do.

"Sara, these people have been coming to events for months, years even, to build up to this one moment. You just said "yes" to a paycheck two weeks ago. I'm not sure you're ready."

A part of me hears her, but that part of me that refuses to not be ready for life anymore is louder. I'm honestly not sure if this voice should be my anthem or if I should shut that shit down in order to save myself from myself. But that voice in me, my Teri Hatcher cheerleader, is pumped up. "YOU CAN DO THIS!" I hear her shout, drowning out my other voice, Jiminy Cricket, the reasonable one. "Brin, I want to do this," I say with all the seriousness I can muster.

She looks deep into me and pauses. "Sara ..." and we stand, staring at each other. I, defiantly, like I did when I told my mother I wasn't going to take any more acting gigs because I had already failed at fulfilling her unrealized dreams of being famous. It was one of the few times I actually yelled at my mother and spoke my truth. I hated my mother in that moment, and also my father, for building me up with the dream of being a rich, successful Hollywood actress living in a mansion in Beverly Hills. And then pulling the dream of being a rich, successful, college-educated Hollywood producer living in a mansion in Beverly Hills right out from underneath me.

Not succeeding as an actress and not going to college—I have been living these failures my entire life. Or rather, these failures have been driving my ambition my entire life, putting this chip on my shoulder, fueling a deep desire to prove that I am smart enough to succeed without a piece of paper telling the world that I'm worthy. That I could rise to the top in spite of my shortcomings, both in terms of education and my height. I could have the hottest guy even though I was short and had no boobs. I could be the boss even though I didn't have a degree, was a woman—and a blond one at that.

Making it in Hollywood is a bitch. I often wonder what people who don't work in Hollywood think about how it goes down. So, while I'm on a rant about my past, here's a little more detail about my rise to the top of the B-list.

My second gig in Hollywood: my car was totaled,

and I was promoted to production coordinator. On that film, which was essentially what they call B-level porn (No "pink" was shown, the saying went "The barn doors could be open, but you weren't allowed to see the tools in the shed" What tools they were referring to, I have no idea...), I met a guy who was the location manager, and his next gig needed a craft service person. Craft service is the person who creates an awesome snack smorgasbord for the crew who get bored because filming is actually boring and what else can people do but eat? We didn't have smart phones and WiFi at that time; it was all beepers and newspapers then. So, this guy gets me the gig as craft service girl on this western flick, and let's just say food—cooking or feeding a crew of hungry grips— wasn't in my repertoire. I was, however, cute and barely eighteen. The production manager on the project was mortified at my day one offerings and was about to fire me when ... wait! Did I mention this was a western, which means horses and dirt— tons of shit and dirt—and part of my duties as crafty was to help clean up the set, which meant cleaning up horse manure?

Of course, in my barely eighteen-year-old "I have no f'ing clue what I'm supposed to do" wisdom, I'm wearing a checkered black and white mini skirt and halter top to the set with black Doc Martins. Because this is what one wears to a dusty, dirt-ridden western set. Before it was burned down, it was called the Paramount Ranch.

So, there I was, scooping up horse shit in my

halter top, mini skirt and Docs, with my craft service table laden with snickers bars and M&M's because no one was really health conscious back then, and all the women were complaining and the men—well, they just stood around and watched me bending over picking up horse shit. And when they heard I was being fired, they rallied to my defense and the production manager caved. Instead of a pink slip he gave me a shopping list and told me to keep it up with the miniskirts, because it clearly helped to keep the boys happy when we went over ten hours. Lesson number one in my climb to the top (I use that term loosely): use whatever you've got to keep your crew happy and get yourself booked on the next job. I was like Anne Bonney and they were my mighty band of buccaneers. (FYI, I ended up working several years with the producer on this gig. He really did like the whole gingham look, like a lot …)

It wasn't that I was okay with shaking what my mommy gave me. It's just that this is what women back then did in order to be taken seriously. I had lost all sense of dignity a long time ago as a child actor, and to make it as a woman in film production, at that time, dignity wasn't something you should or could hold on to. If you wanted to break through the glass ceiling, you needed to be willing to hang with the dick jokes and show your tits every once in a while, regardless of their size. I even wrote off my lace panties on my tax returns because the IRS sure did make a gargantuan heaping pile of dough off those babies.

Now, back to the Sara-Brin stare down in my hotel room.

Suddenly, I am fearless. *I can do this.* I've hung on the nude side of hedonism (literally, in Jamaica with the porn stars), so what's a little hot coal to me at this point? I hear Ardent's persuasive voice in my mind: "The firewalk is about committing to yourself, to your magnificence, and your ability to transcend all doubt. It's about doing and being what you are capable of."

I am capable!!! I shout to myself. Maybe this will be good for me. I need to remind myself that I am worthy of success and happiness, that I am powerful, unshakable, a force of nature and that nothing can stop me. This is what all the experts say: Eckhart, Deepak, Brené, Ardent. This is for me, for once … right? I have come too close to the top of it all and then fallen flat too many times to quit now. First when I was sixteen, then with Joao, then with Tom, then with Zak's Super Snacks. Each time I get so close to the top I could taste it, and something held me back. Was it was me? Was Jiminy Cricket wrong? Had I been playing too safe for too long? Thousands of people have walked across the coals with nary an ember sticking to their feet. This is possible with focus and determination, and I have both of those in spades.

Brin has been silent for a long time, which is odd, because she usually has a comeback. My intensity must have thrown her. She cocks her head and takes a long deep breath, studying my defiant Tinker Bell stance. "Okay then. If you've got this, then let's do it." And with that, we leave my room and head down to the pit of fire.

The elevator ride puts a damper on my enthusiasm. It's hard to keep the rally cry going with the instrumental version of "Cats in the Cradle" playing overhead, and as we leave the hotel and approach the cathexis of hell, I'm having my doubts. Pele is wavering. On the grounds around the fire pit there are hundreds of people chanting "I AM! I AM" and I can see a large line of people waiting for their chance to cross the finish line. Faced with the reality of the blazing coals, I am starting to think that maybe both Brin and Jiminy are right.

I am not ready.

I close my eyes and just listen to the drums and the chanting and call my inner Terri the Cheerleader up front and center. I visualize myself victoriously crossing the coals with ease and grace. Ardent is cheering me on and everyone around me is shouting their approval and I am feeling ten feet tall, like I am about to finally break free of every lie I've ever told myself and ascend into the stars as one of the chosen. Finally free to be me. Living my truth.

I watch about ten people cross the coals triumphantly when Brin the Barger pushes me to the front of the line. I see Ardent on the other side of the coals, just as I imagined him. He looks me straight in the heart and soul and gives me the thumbs up. People in line make room as if I'm some sort of celebrity. Jason is shooting. People who have made it to the other side turn and watch, chanting, beckoning. The rhythm is hypnotizing. I take a deep breath. I am ready. I can feel it. It's my turn! I feel a surge of energy almost pushing me towards the coals. I have no control over my body. It has been taken over by the rhythms of my surroundings. I have lost connection with thought and my inner cheerleader screams at me, "DO IT! You are PELE!"

I scream with her and with that I throw off my flip flops and with the might of a warrior I stomp my foot onto the flaming hot coals of enlightenment. My foot touches the embers and in an instant, I recoil in shocked pain. THAT FUCKING *HURT!* And I turn and run away, my foot smoking as I try and shake off the embers sticking to my skin and to my heart. *You are a failure at everything!* my soul screams. *You are a fraud. A liar. You are nothing.*

This is what I am. Nothing. A lie. I'm not even hot anymore. I can't even rock the mini skirt and halter top and gingham is now a very bad look on me. I am fat, short and a failure. And once again it's all on film. Because ya know, the revolution will be televised. And so will all your failures.

CHAPTER 16

I make my way to the pool, which, in hindsight, probably wasn't a great idea. The chlorine didn't really help. It just added to the burn. But at least the pool deck was devoid of people—for a few moments anyway. Brin and Michele follow me, which I wish they hadn't. I hear Brin ask Michele to get an ice pack and tell the boys to just hang back. I suck it up and put on my comedy face. This is what I do when I don't want to expose the real shame I'm feeling. It's all just a big damn joke. I am Gilda Radner for fuck's sake, just here for the comedic beats—that person you can laugh at so you don't have to look at yourself. Well, at least I have some value. "Look at her and laugh. Be grateful, that could be you!" I'm a lesson in gratitude. Ah, something "spiritual" after all.

Brin sits down next to me and I take a deep breath, preparing for whatever peppy, inspiring talk she's about to throw at me. She slowly lets her breath out and just sits there, silent, staring into the pool waiting for it to warp into some vision or something. After about a minute I can't take the silence. "Well, that was hilarious, wasn't it?"

Brin chuckles a little and says nothing, which isn't at all what I expected.

"I hope Jason got it on camera. I can add it to my

blooper reel. Maybe that's what my claim to fame should be. I'm the GIF girl who's the train wreck everyone can't look away from."

Brin feigns a laugh and I'm starting to get annoyed at her. "Is that all you've got? Seriously, I thought you'd have some sage wisdom to throw down, inspire me to get up and try again, to believe in myself. I can still hear Ardent shouting at me to love myself. Isn't that what all the sages do? Spout pithy platitudes that don't mean anything but sound really good and make people think they've just be given the holy grail of wisdom?"

Brin looks at me like I'm pathetic, which I am. "Sara, I really don't know what to say. I tried to tell you not to do this, but you don't really seem interested in listening. You want to do everything your way and there isn't much room for any outside input."

"Outside input? I've got twenty different apps on my phone sending me "divine" messages all day long. I watched every video Ardent had on YouTube. I spent two hours listening to him affirm my magical abilities to walk on water, or in this case, hot coals, like I was Jesus. And I am not Jesus!"

"I visualized, dammit! I saw it. I felt it. And then I *really* felt it. What the hell am I missing?" I'm mad and try to stand up only to remember my foot is a charred piece of chicken breast and I hobble over to a chaise lounge. Brin follows.

"Sara, transformation isn't something you get from an app or a book, a video or a pep talk infused with shamanic drumbeats. Sure, you get the insight, the intellectual information, but the actual shift comes from your actions, your authenticity, your vulnerability—which only develop over *time*. Years. Decades. You've been at this what? Five minutes? You, my dear, are not vulnerable or authentic. You're all surface show, like a vaudeville act. You're approaching spirituality like some sort of prize you want to win. You're impatient. And this," she waves her hand at my charred foot, "is the price you pay."

Wow, that was mean. "So, I guess I'm a faker? Well, you're right Brin, I am a faker. I've been a faker my whole life. You know what happens when I get real? People let me down. They don't take me seriously. They laugh. They lose my money. They bang porn stars. They leave. and they die, like my father did before he could see my name in the main movie credits—alone—not squished in between ten other names in a super tiny font and probably spelled wrong, He never saw me succeed."

I suck in my breath and beat back the tears. "If I had just gone to college, got a degree and become a famous film producer and not the queen of schlock, all would have been fine. I'd be rich and married with two kids, living in a nice house, driving a damn Prius and serving as president of the PTA." I was on a roll. "Jesus, *you* got a degree. You played the part. So, please don't tell me about faking it. I've tried to live my dream, over and over again, and lost everything every time."

I hurt and I'm starting to rage and all I want to do is smoke and drink. I hate the part of me that had a dream and went for it and failed. I hate my parents. I hate any desire I ever had. I hate thinking I could move beyond middle class white girl from the Valley. I hate ideas. I hate ambition. I hate money. I hate success. I don't even know what that means anymore.

Michele arrives with the ice pack and a bottle of tequila and four shot glasses. "I thought we could all use a drink—except for Jason," she announces. "He doesn't drink." And with that the boys arrive as if on cue.

Jason has the camera to his eye and walks right up to me. "Excuse me miss, can we get your reaction to the firewalk?" I glare at him. Everyone glares at him. "Oh, come on, I'm just trying to capture the joy of victory and the agony of defeat." He laughs at himself, while no one else does. "Get it? Da Feet!" He hobble/dances around.

Brin pours the shots. "Jason you're an asshole, you know that?"

I laugh because I need to and it was actually funny. I kind of love Jason right now. Anyone who just wants to laugh and be utterly disconnected from reality is good right now. I take my shot and down it before anyone notices and quickly pour myself another.

"Well, here's to transformation, starting from the bottom up." I waggle my scorched foot and we drink. Then everyone just sort of stands there awkwardly, unsure of where to go next. "God, I could really use a cigarette," I whine.

Michele jumps up, happy, I think, to have a new task at hand. "I'll find some!" Jason and Fabio look at each other hoping one of them has a way out of this situation. I decide to rescue them. "Why don't you boys go film more of the firewalk. I'm sure you'll find someone who mastered it and wants to gloat."

Everyone leaves except for Brin. I pour myself another shot and offer her one as well. She waves it off, and I shrug and chug. "I have tried to change, Brin. But every time I try to make a change it fails. It feels like my destiny isn't to live my dream, but to live everyone else's." I take another shot, because why the hell not?

Brin slowly pulls the bottle from me and we have a short tug of war. She finally relinquishes. "Here's the thing Sara, people don't like change. Most people never follow their dreams, and when they see other people doing it, they get angry and try and force the person who's trying to change to stay the same. We're all so very co-dependent. Frankly, you're brave for even attempting it. I admire that in you."

"Yay, I'm brave!" I can't accept the compliment and I'm getting drunk and don't care. I take another huge swig, from the bottle this time. Brin is right about one thing, I'm sick of people holding me back, telling me what I should do. Calling me brave while screwing me over or screwing someone else. *I am brave dammit!* I am. How's that Ardent? Convincing enough?

"Okay missy, I think you've had enough of that." Brin once again tries to pry the tequila bottle from my hands.

"Stop it, Brin!" I glare blurrily at her. "You are not my mother or my lover and you're certainly not my boss! I am in charge here. If I wanna drink, I'll drink, an' if I wanna smoke, I'll damn well smoke."

After six or seven shots of tequila, I am slurring my words and at the mention of smoking I careen around, looking for Michele with my cigarettes. Brin grabs the bottle and looks for a hiding place. Out of the corner of my eye I see a hotel worker, maybe a waiter, off to the side of the fire pit, somewhat in the bushes, *and he's smoking!* I want it. I want what he has, and I am going to take it. That's what successful people do, right? They go after what they want and they take it, screw asking nicely. Screw doing it right or doing a good job. Successful people take what they want. Maybe this has been my problem all along. I keep asking for it instead of taking it, which is exactly what I am going to do now.

I can barely get myself out of the chaise lounge, so I close my eyes and I visualize myself crossing over to the waiter, yanking that ciggy out of his hand and taking a long, sensuous drag from it. I honestly don't even care if it's menthol.

I open my eyes to gaze at my prize, get up and start walking. In my trance all I see is that glowing cigarette tip. I see people, running and shouting, waving at me, trying to get in my way. I hear myself scream at them, "Fuck off haters!" as I pancake a large man who's jumped in my path. I am so close I can smell the nicotine. Nothing can stop me in my haze of boozy focused desire. Within moments I am on top of the poor waiter, my arm reaching out, snatching the cigarette from between his fingers like a sniper finding the mark. As I come to a stop, the butt reaches my lips and I suck on that baby like it's the oxygen mask on a plane that's going down.

Oh, my god, you have no idea how marvelous that tastes! I could have been laid by a Norse god and this still would have been better. I fall to the ground and sit, taking another drag, and see about a thousand people in utter silence staring at me. Ardent is being helped up by a throng of shocked devotees and it's all coming together for me. I can see my path from the chaise lounge to my unwitting mark and it goes straight through the fire pit, only backwards. Ardent was the offense to my defense and, well, when I am focused, nothing will stand in my way, not even a six-foot four-inch billionaire guru.

I think maybe I'm supposed to feel bad, but I don't feel bad. I feel great. Or maybe that's just the tequila talking. I jump up. "I'm okay! I'm okay! I did it! I did it backwards, but I did it! Woo Hoo!" I'm hopping around on one foot and no one is smiling or laughing ... well maybe a couple of guys in the back, they get it.

Brin comes charging at me. "Brin, I did it, I did the firewalk!"

"You did it alright ..." and with that Ardent is on us, surrounded by a sea of angry mini-me's. Of course, pretty much anyone is mini next to him. He is seething and through gritted teeth he snarls, "I am going to have to ask you and your team to leave."

Brin is holding me up and smiling, almost bowing, dragging me backwards. "We were just going to do that sir. I'm so sorry."

I'm like, "Sorry? Sorry for what? I did his damn firewalk. He's just mad that I did it my own way." I start laughing drunkenly. "Isn't that always how it is? You give men what they want and they still aren't happy." Brin literally covers my mouth with her hand as she drags me toward the hotel, and I feel like I'm crowd surfing at a Black Flag Concert. I sort of roll my head around and see Michele.

"Michele, hey Michele, did you see what I did? I did it for you and you and you …" I point to Fabio and Jason and then to Brin, "and for me. I did it my way! Maybe I'm not such a failure after all."

Michele smiles at me and it's the nicest smile anyone has ever given me. I take back everything I said about her. She's actually a really nice girl. But Brin still has hold of my arm and it feels like I'm a crash dummy as I flip and flop around in her grip as we get into the elevator and ride up to my floor.

The thing about tequila is there's a sweet spot. There is just the right amount and then there is vomit in your car or an elevator. Suddenly, I cross over into the possibly vomiting category, the elevator making me nauseous as the throbbing pain in my foot crashes back into my awareness. I have never been so grateful for a "ding" from an elevator. The doors open and I think it's Brin who pulls me out. Or maybe it's Fabio and Jason? *What are they doing* here?

Why aren't you guys shooting? And before the doors close, I hear Michele call out, "Don't let them take away your thunder, honey. You did it!"

Okay, she is Halle Berry, like for real. The doors close and Brin is looking at me like my mother did when I painted our walls with her nail polish. Once again, I think I've created something beautiful, something amazing, and I'm about to be punished for it. I float somehow to my door and Brin starts pawing through my fanny pack for my room key. Giggling, I dig the key out of my back pocket because I always lose my room keys in my bag. She snatches it from my fingers, unamused, opens the door and somehow drags me to my bed and flops me down.

I hear footsteps and whispering. I hear the door open. I vaguely see her standing in the light from the hallway. "Sara, I'm not mad at you," she says softly. "I'm frustrated, disappointed, but not angry. I don't even know what to feel or to say, which is shocking, I know …"

I hear the door close and I'm kind of impressed. I actually stunned Brin into silence. But who am I kidding? Drunk Sara has stunned many into silence. It's my superpower, actually. Drunk Sara is the Sara I want to be but am too afraid to be: ballsy, courageous, speaks her mind, stands up for herself, walks across burning coals of fire like she's the second coming of Jesus. Drunk Sara is vulnerable and has feelings. Okay, I always have feelings, it's just that when I'm drunk I share them and honestly, it usually doesn't end well. I can't figure out if it's because I'm drunk or because sharing your honest feelings with people just doesn't end well.

Think about that for a minute. It's easy to say it's because I'm drunk. But is it really just that? Or is it that true, honest, unfiltered truth from someone is too much for most of us to hear? To be present to and to take in? I'm too much to take in when I'm drunk, and when I'm sober I'm too afraid to be too much to bear.

I'm lying on my bed in my hotel room. Hotel rooms attempt to make you feel safe and comfortable, but they fail. The ceiling is too white and the walls too perfectly aligned with photos of places that look happy and warm, when in fact, you're usually alone, with too many pillows and sheets that are tucked so tightly it feels like a strait jacket set up so you don't wander the halls and scare people. I scare people, I think. I'm inconsistent. I am either the epitome of having it all together or a total hot mess. There is no in-between, and that is what I am seeking. I think. The in-between.

I hear the door open again and I crack one eye and see Brin carrying an ice bucket. My foot is throbbing, my head is throbbing and as she enters, my phone rings and my head swivels towards it. It's Banksy's … and I can't even imagine what they are calling about at this hour and once again I can't not answer. *I really need to work on that.* "Hello, this is Sara," I answer in the most professional voice I can muster in my current state. On the other end is an over-excited voice screeching something about RJ, ruining the firewalk and the entire retreat and a possible lawsuit. "It really wasn't that bad, a little mishap really. I'll handle it in the morning. I promise." They hang up, without acknowledging anything I said.

"How the fuck did they know what happened?" I slur at Brin, who says nothing as she positions me on the bed so my foot can fit into the ice bucket. As my toes hit the ice, the pain is almost unbearable. Shock shoots through my leg and into my soul. I cry out in agony and it feels like the night I waited at home for Tom to come back from his shoot. I was so excited because I'd closed a huge deal with a major organic food store chain on the west coast that day. It was big, well, sort of big. It was validation. It was only ten stores, but it was progress. I planned on opening a special bottle of wine we bought together in Paso Robles. At about seven he texted and said they were running behind and that he probably wouldn't be done until at least nine or maybe ten.

Okay, I figured. I'll eat and open another bottle and save the special one for when he gets home. At ten I got another text that said they were still working. By eleven I had finished two bottles of our cheap wine and called the studio, where I found out that they had actually wrapped at 6:30 and everyone had left by seven and headed for the Formosa. I knew the bartender there, so I called and asked if Tom was there and got my heart ripped open by a stranger. I mean, bartenders have that "I'm your friend" vibe, but you don't really know what they're into unless you go home with them. On a side note, I usually try not to sleep with my bartenders. It makes things awkward. Anyway, this particular bartender ended up being the "friend" telling me that the life I thought I was living was a lie. So, I opened the good bottle and drank it. I didn't decant it or let it breathe. I couldn't breathe, why should the damn wine? Of course, you know what happened next. So does my entire neighborhood and all of my peers who watched it live.

The pain is searing, emotionally, physically. I don't know where I am anymore. Who I am anymore. Was I ever anybody? I try to take some deep breaths and eventually I open my eyes. Brin is gone, my phone is in my hand and I see that I have called Tom and been on the line for twenty-six minutes. I hear him breathe and I hang up.

CHAPTER 17

I open my eyes. The ceiling is still ridiculously white, the pictures on the wall still have the happy beach scenes with the colored umbrellas with everything else in black and white. All perfectly aligned.

I am not aligned at all. I hurt. That's all I can say. I hurt. Why should I have to say more? And yet in this world just to say "I hurt" isn't enough. Everyone needs to know the adjectives, like on a scale of one to ten how bad is your suffering, because people need to know if your suffering is equal to, less than, or more than their own.

The ice bucket my foot was supposed to be resting in has tipped over and soaked the bottom of the bed and I'm swimming on a water-logged mattress. My phone is still clutched against my chest as if it's my life jacket. I hear a knock at my door.

Who is it?" I whimper.

"Hello Miss, I have a package for you."

OMG, what the hell? "Please just leave it by the door." I beg, checking the time and, of course, it's time to get moving. I'm not sure I even can move. My foot has blistered and is swollen. My head is blistered and swollen, so at least I'm balanced from head to toe. I move and it's ugly. I'm dizzy, fragile and yet I have been here before. I make my way to the shower and nearly drown in a deluge of frigid water. I vomit. I brush my teeth, balancing on one foot. I vomit again, and then drink the three bottles of water thankfully present in the room along with three Advil.

I grab my stuff and open my door. Sitting on the floor is a box, a shoe box actually, wrapped with a ginormous red bow with a little card tied to it. I reach down for the card and regret it. I remind myself I need to stay at one level if I'm going to survive the day, but am able to retrieve the card. It says, "No one can fill your shoes xo Joao." I kick off the lid and in it are a pair of Gucci sliders, black with red devils made of sequins on them. Included is a pair of Bombas footie socks, extra cushion.

This is my life. Men I want quit me like a gym membership in February and Joao, who I dumped, stalks me like a green anaconda slithering around for sex and then a death party (ok, I might have this backwards; I think the female Anacondas eat the males)…anyway, you get what I mean…. I can't win. This is why women love shoes. They don't leave. They don't cheat and they never lie. They speak to you the moment you slip your foot into them. They tell you, "Not with this outfit, not tonight, but I still love you." And you believe them. Why would they lie? They are yours and they just want you to be happy and the next time you reach for them, they are still there, waiting patiently in your closet.

I gingerly put on the socks and the shoes. The slider barely makes it over my swollen foot and whispers quietly "I got you." (See? shoes…). Then I grab my bag and hobble my way to the lobby where Michele is waiting for me with a mocha and a pack of yellow American Spirits. Bless her, she's really getting the hang of being a PA. The coffee and cig help the body but not my heart. I don't know about you, but for me the day after is usually filled with self-loathing and shame. I wish I had blacked out and had no memory of what happened. Unfortunately, I always remember. I have one of those memories that means I don't need to make lists. I can remember phone numbers. I can remember full sentences of what was said twenty years ago. "You're really cute, but a terrible actress. Do you know how to give a blow job?" Or "You shouldn't take a pay cut, even if it's a studio film." Or "He left hours ago with some chick." Or "I'll help you, just do this film with me and I'll connect you." And "Oh, Sara, you're so good at your job, I really need you on this one. Next time I promise you I will …"

This eidetic memory thing has made many of my more traumatic life experiences worse. Not only can I viscerally feel the pain of the experience, but I can literally replay every word, dissecting its meaning over and over again, hoping for a different outcome.

I stand outside the hotel lobby and, even though it's making me feel sick, light another cigarette off the butt of the first one. I'm tired. I'm tired of waiting my turn. I keep trying to change lanes, but people don't want you to change lanes. Didn't Brin just say so? I need to lower my expectations about myself.

Instead of trying to shine, I should just do what's expected of me. That way everyone will be happy. Others will get what they want and then they will love me and then I can be happy and have all the door prizes to show for it—the house, the car, the nice shoes.

No one actually believes in real happiness, do they?

I confess, I did. For years, I drove by all those mansions in Hollywood with my dad, listening to him telling me about all the famous people that lived in them and how one day I would too. "My girl, you are as talented and smart as they are," he'd say. "You deserve to be living among them. Put in the work, never give up and one day another little girl will be driving by *your* house dreaming." And it was all a lie. *If I ever have kids, I will never lie to them about how great they are or how fucked up this world is.* No princess movies, no knights in shining armor, no rescues. No trophies for participating for my kids, ever.

Jason pulls up and I limp toward the van. Both the smokes and the mocha have made me feel sick. I grab a bottle of water and awkwardly climb into the front seat.

The next week is a blur. We travel to several California spiritual enclaves—Northern California, Santa Barbara, Ojai. And I have succumbed to what I must do as I interview what I'm told are the Gold Standards of New Thought leaders. To my surprise, it goes extremely well. Tons of wisdom spewed and filmed, but it all still feels foreign to me. I hear what they're saying and it all sounds perfectly logical, even if it sometimes makes no sense.

"The path of the co-creator is to be awakened spiritually within, which then turns into your own deeper life purpose."

"Life is a process. A succession of Nows where we choose either to be present and awake to our condition, or we stay asleep. Only when we're present do we have choice and the opportunity to create our lives the way we want them. All true artists, whether they know it or not, create from a place of no-mind and inner stillness."

"The choiceless truth of who you are is revealed to be permanently here, permeating everything."

They all sound the same to me, speaking in roundabout sentences that lead nowhere, leaving me lost and confused. No one is addressing anger and pain in a way that makes sense to me. It's either all love and light or I should be a "master" and go within and get over it. Within where? I spend almost all my time inside my head and it's a place that's hurtful, judgmental and mean. Why would I want to go in there? And what about all the hurt and anger I feel? If that's all I find when I go within, how do I deal with that?

Maybe that's the point? To confuse you so much that you stop trying to understand and just drone on with life, wearing your crystals, sniffing your rose oil, eating bland food and calling it bliss because at a certain point you're so beaten down and exhausted from it all that you can't even get angry. Besides, anger is bad. It seems anything other than being positive is bad. Love is all you need. And you just so desperately want to belong, you just nod your head all trance-like and utter "oooohhhhhmmmmmmmm." Just love everything, even when it sucks and then you'll be happy.

So, this is me, loving the fuck out of everything.

But honestly, I'm struggling with the whole New Age concept of love. I chose this film because I thought it could help me, and so far, everything I have faced has been an assault on everything I know about life, which is work hard, never give up, do the "right" thing and sleep with whomever you need to. Frankly, it's all making me feel worse about myself. No one here is loving. They sound loving. They speak in soft tones. They look into my eyes and listen intently and nod knowingly. And yet I don't feel heard or seen. Every time I look at myself, I see another flaw, another failure, another bad habit I need to change. It's too much. I'm too far broken. This is not the love and light and joy I was expecting the spiritual path to be.

On the way back home from our road trip, the van is oddly quiet and I'm grateful. Perusing my notes, I get a text from Tom. "Hey, I think you're coming home for a few days? Want to see Zak?" This is ironic, because dogs actually do love everything unconditionally. That's all they do. Who knew I had one of the greatest spiritual teachers of all time right in front of me? Seeing Zak would be good, so I text back, "Sure." I'm hoping he doesn't remember the call the other night. As I said, I remember everything, but for some reason I don't know what happened on that call and it scares me.

Ojai is about an hour and half from LA. It's a pretty drive, if you take the back route, which we do, along the farm roads and nurseries that fill the fabulous homes of LA with fruit trees and foliage. Suddenly Michele squeals from the back seat and everyone jumps. "OMG! Daddy is buying me a car! Can you drop me at the BMW dealership in Thousand Oaks?"

I'm seriously wondering if it's appropriate to ask to be adopted.

We all sort of mumble, "Sure, yeah, okay." I watch as Fabio starts to ask Michele a question, but she's already deep into picking out colors, because I guess that's what matters. I hear her. I feel her. I've been there. My BMW was a silver-blue convertible, with black leather seats and warmers, not that you need that in LA. But I'll tell you what, there is nothing like driving the coast on a cool winter morning in LA with the top down, your ass being warmed and the wind blowing through your hair. Maybe that's what happiness is, and I just didn't get it. One of the best things about buying my BMW was that I got to take a driving course on a racetrack. I learned I love to drive fast cars. Another great thing was that for a moment, my parents were proud of me. Even without a college degree I had found success.

I look around at my mismatched band of misfits. How the hell did I become their leader? Most of the time it feels like they're leading me. I wonder about some of the skeletons in their closets. We all have them, right? I think I'm telling myself this so I don't feel so shitty about myself. *Maybe instead of making up funny stories about them in my head, I should actually talk to them?* Right now, they are the closest people I have in my life.

But now is not the time to talk. *Is it ever?*

We find the BMW dealership and Michele practically leaps from the van as it's still moving. I see Jimmy, her trusted driver, sitting at the wheel of a black Bentley. There is a man in the back seat, and Michele squeals again like a three-year-old girl meeting Micky Mouse. "Daddy!" Turning quickly, she says, "See you guys Monday! Oh, and I'm doing a weekend retreat with Lawrence and the skull at the Sheraton in Laguna Beach this weekend, so I won't be around."

Fabio gets out and unloads her bags as Jimmy takes them, then he just sort of stands there, left behind. I feel for him. He's sort of like Josh in the movie Big, a little kid in a man's body who finds love but can't take it with him.

Fabio gets back in the van and Brin announces, "Hey, I know a decent dive bar with great food close by. Let's eat." And with that we find ourselves driving through suburbia, miles and miles of boxy, all beige, tract home neighborhoods with a Wal-Mart, Target, and a place called Bob's with a parking lot lined with big trucks, motorcycles and beaters. It's noon on a Saturday. I haven't even considered drinking anything but water since my date with the Mexican devil, but greasy food does sound appealing.

We find a table, and for the record, this place really is a dive bar—old vinyl-covered cushioned chairs and thick round wood tables. The dark wood paneling keeps the place locked in an unknown hour of day as if time didn't exist in here, which, from the looks on some of the patrons faces, is probably a good thing.

Jason is earnestly trying to help Fabio with his quest for love. "Fabio, the thing is with women like that, you gotta just come out and say what you want. She's used to a daddy figure, so you need to be her daddy."

I can't believe he just said that. "Jason, where do you get your dating tips from?"

He stiffens, immediately defensive. "Men should be in charge in a relationship. They are the master of the house. It's a proven fact that women respond to men who lead them. In Corinthians, it says, 'But I want you to understand that the head of every man is Christ, the head of a wife is her husband, and the head of Christ is God. In Colossians it says …"

Brin can't hold herself back any longer. "You mean those parts of the Bible written by little boys who were so frightened by the power of a woman's intuition they literally killed them for it?!"

Jason takes one of those long deep, "I might kill you" breaths and stands up. "I left my wallet in the van," he mutters and storms off.

"Why are you so rough with him?" Fabio asks her. "He's a bit of a broken man himself, and when a man is broken, he uses what he can to ease his pain."

Who knew Fabio was a budding life coach?

My phone dings and it's a message from Madame whatever her name is: "Happiness is having a large, loving, caring, close-knit family in another city." - George Burns. Man, isn't that the truth. I look up and realize I can't sit here anymore. I'm not that hungry and I just want to go home, have a shower and sleep in my own bed. "You know what, I'm not hungry." I reach for my purse. "I'm gonna grab an Uber and go home."

I get up and walk out, leaving Fabio and Brin a little perplexed and quiet, which is actually a good thing.

People often think I'm a complete extrovert, but here's something I've learned, most extroverts are actually shy and insecure and are truly introverts who have developed coping mechanisms to deal with their fears by being loud, funny, bossy, and overly talkative. I read this in one of my books and it was probably one of the things that rang most true for me. Frankly, I hate being alone. Alone leaves me in my head listening to voices that don't like me. Being surrounded by people who don't love me feels much safer by comparison. *I need to learn to be alone.* And now seems like a good time to practice.

I make my way to the parking lot and pause to get my bearings. The restaurant door squeaks behind me and Brin and Fabio follow me out into the light. Several yards away, Jason is talking to a guy who starts to walk away and drops something on the ground. Jason rushes to pick it up and calls out to the guy who just keeps walking. Standing there with a piece of paper in his hand, he looks worse than a guy who's been rejected by the girl of his dreams.

"What was that all about?" I ask him.

"He tried to sell me some crack," Jason says, shaking his head.

"Did you buy any?" asks Brin.

Fabio and I can't believe what she just said and yet she keeps going as she takes the pamphlet from his hand, scanning it. "Calvery Christian Drug Counseling?" She bursts out laughing. "Wait, because praying is going to help a crack addict?"

Jason is fuming. "It helped me."

Finally, it's out. Well, it's been out to everyone except Brin it seems, which is really shocking because I thought she knew everything.

"So, you traded one habit for another," she snaps. "Well …"

Jason lunges at her and Fabio grabs him just in time. I don't blame him; I was about to do the same. "Oh yeah, honey?" he snarls. "Well, what sort of habit do they call going broke on rocks and oils?" He manages to rip the faux-crystal necklace off her neck, throws it to the ground and stomps on it. It crushes into an almost dust-like substance. "Here," he snarls, "snort that."

He stalks to the van and Fabio, Brin, and I just stand there looking at each other, which, I just realized, happens a lot in this story. We are stunning people—and not the kind accomplished by walking the red carpet. I grab Brin by the arm. "We're taking an Uber. Fabio, you guys go ahead and drop the gear, return the van and we'll see you on Wednesday for the next shoot."

I'm developing a headache and I'm almost out of cigs. I spy a CVS in the shopping mall across from the parking lot and head straight for it, dragging her with me. I don't say a word until we get into the store and find the aspirin section, then I let fly. "Brin, what the *hell* is wrong with you? Why are you so hard on Jason?"

She shakes her head. "It's not Jason, it's … it's everyone's need to have an easy fix. Yeah, it's true, we do replace one addiction with another. I'm no different. He just gets in the cross hairs with his damn Bible thumping self-righteousness."

At the checkout I discover CVS doesn't sell cigarettes anymore. It really sucks how everyone has decided to go against one of my favorite addictions. Personally, I think we were all a bit more chill when we could smoke, drink, eat meat and carbs and butter. No, wait, I think butter is back on the okay list now. Maybe it's egg whites?

"Jason actually looks pretty happy most of the time," I chide. "You know what I think my dear Brin? I think it annoys you that he has something that works for him." (Have you ever noticed how someone who is unhappy always wants to shit all over whatever it is that makes you happy? Like people who used to smoke like a damn chimney but have quit and become cigarette Nazis.)

"What part of blindly following a dead martyr,

controlled by fear of what might happen if he thinks for himself, works?" she says, a little bit sarcastic and a whole lotta unresolved bullshit.

"Come on Brin, sometimes people just need to hold onto something."

"Yeah, and I know where that path goes."

"Where Brin? Enlighten me."

"How 'bout disappointment? Despair? Helplessness? Emasculation?"

"Really? You don't seem emasculated at all. Actually, you're downright arrogant and self-righteous, even more than our Bible-wielding mini-youth pastor!"

"OMG, says the woman who's constantly whining 'Why Me?' How would you know?"

We are standing in the CVS parking lot, arguing like an old married couple who can't find their car. Brin is still ranting, her winged blouse flailing as if she might take flight at any moment. "You're so goddamned busy taking notes like a high school cheerleader, and yet you don't engage anything or anybody. You never open yourself up unless you're shit-faced. You mock everything. You don't want to work at becoming evolved, you just want the three easy steps to happiness. You don't hear what people are telling you ..."

"What do ..." I try and interject, but there is no stopping her now.

"You're so busy chasing the 'thing,' you wouldn't know it if it hit you in the face. You're always after the next new answer ... and shit, you haven't even found the first question!"

"Wow, Brin, first Jason and now me. We're all just lost souls waiting for Brin to show us the way."

"I'll show you the way, alright. I'll give you a million-dollar seminar right now." She's totally in my face, hands on hips. "You, my dear Sara, can't be real because you are afraid of real. You're afraid of authenticity and vulnerability. You're afraid of what might happen if you expose yourself. You want to hold on tightly to your trauma. You want to dress it up and wear it out on the town, put lipstick on it and hope no one notices you hide behind your sarcasm and your wit. And I suspect those biting words of yours bite you the most."

She points to the lit cigarette in my hand and my bag full of cheap wine and Advil. "None of that crap will take the pain away. Not the drugs, legal or illegal, not the sex, not money or success or love. Nothing will take the pain away except facing it, living it, feeling it. You're right, I'm angry. I hurt. Sometimes I'm not nice. But at least I'm not trying to be something I'm not."

She draws a deep breath and looks me in the eye. "Screw you, Sara Wells. I thought you might actually be ready to be real. I thought after your meltdown in the desert you'd be ready to do something amazing with your life and yourself. I guess I was mistaken. You're just as shallow as the rest of them." And with that she walks away, stopping to turn around for one last shot. "I'll send you a link to a few one-day courses that should set you right. After all, you're not interested in real growth, just the weekend special."

I'm left paralyzed, thinking maybe I should follow her. But I don't. I have chased this experience before and it's only ever ended with me apologizing for being who I am. I need to process everything she just said because I honestly don't know what was truth and what was her projecting a ton of shit onto me that has nothing to do with me.

Honestly, it's weird to feel this way. Because normally I would try and fix it, right here and now. I'd chase her down and we'd have it out because if I didn't, it would be like a hanging chad desperate to be fully plucked from its perforated paper. I have always had a need to fix conversations, apologize for my shortcomings and failure, all to make it better. And yet in this moment every ounce of my being says, "Let it hang," because I know she's right. Maybe she could have been nicer about it ... ironic that I want her to be nice and loving and kind like I expect a teacher or guru to be. I have a lot of expectations and I don't often hold myself to the same standard. And so I watch her walk away.

Maybe that's growth?

CHAPTER 18

I make it home thanks to a dude named José—a really nice guy who drives for Uber while also working construction and selling pot. All of which he pitched me. I don't smoke pot and I don't own my apartment, so I wasn't any help in his version of the gig economy, but he was chill and played good music. I sort of half wondered if this is what I was about to become, a trifecta of trades. Like, was this how I would make money in the near future? He appeared happy and at ease in his situation with a hint of a dream but without the grandeur of a man who thought it might actually happen. *Maybe I should learn to lower my expectations and just be happy with what I have, like José?*

So far on my journey to enlightenment I've interviewed many of the Who's Who in the New Thought game, been to the birthplace of it all and still have no idea what I'm looking for or what will bring me happiness and peace. I've encountered a ton of people ready for that big manifestation, people with just a little bit more work to do and then "it" will come. What "it" they were waiting for I'm still unsure.

I have always thought there was more. More of something not quite tangible or explainable, just different—a feeling that I was always missing something. I think my more is about wanting truth, connection, and love. Ironically, one thing I've learned from Brin is that I don't know how to give or receive any of this. What I have is a solid stash of coping mechanisms, which ultimately keep everyone at arm's length because I can't trust anyone, especially myself.

My apartment feels empty and unwelcoming. No dog, no lover, odd spaces where something used to be but isn't anymore. Brin was right. I am a shallow being. In the past, on a night like this when I was feeling the way I do now, I'd reach out for a booty call. There is no shortage of men who want to get laid, no strings attached. Hell, they'll even cuddle with you after if you've got good beer. Sex is the only time I feel connected to a man, the only time I allow myself to feel even slightly vulnerable. The rest of the time, I could cut them with a butter knife if necessary.

Look, I don't hate men. I just don't have faith in them. And I know exactly where my distrust comes from. Even as a child of nine I knew exactly what they wanted. Once, on a commercial shoot, I was in my dressing room with the wardrobe woman. The male director walked in to check my outfit. He didn't like it and picked out a new shirt from the rack. He told me to put it on. I took the shirt from him and looked at him.

So, here's the thing, dressing rooms on film shoots for not famous people are called honey wagons—

trailers with usually six to eight tiny little rooms with bathrooms at the end. So the wardrobe woman, me and the director were all standing in this barely 4x4 room and he wants me to change my shirt. I'm not wearing a bra. I'm nine, with no undershirt either. So I stand there and look over at the wardrobe woman, confused. And the director gets annoyed. "We don't have all day!" he says.

I look back to the wardrobe woman and she sort of nod/nudges at me like, "Just put on the shirt," which means I have to bear my naked little nine-year-old body for this man. So I take off my shirt and he doesn't turn away. He doesn't avert his eyes. He just stares at me. I try and do it quickly, but it's a button-down shirt, so I have to unbutton it and then pull it off and then pull on the other one and then button it up. We do this five times with five different shirts and he never took his eyes off me.

I told my mom about what happened, and she said, "He didn't mean anything by it. He's a busy man, you shouldn't have made him wait."

I ended up working with that director about fifteen more times. I never had to audition for him, he just booked me. And on every shoot he would come into the dressing room and watch me try on all the clothes. Eventually it didn't matter. He gave me work, he made my parents happy and in turn I felt loved … even by him.

These thoughts are not helping me sleep. I reach over to check my phone and knock the nightstand. Out of my drawer falls one of my very best friends

on nights like this when no one answered the call—
Ryan Gosling, my vibrator. *I can't even right now.* I roll
over and remember one of the tips from a recent
book I read, a mantra to help you sleep, and I start
repeating the words "love, peace, abundance, joy,
perfect radiant health." Nothing like monotony to
make you bored enough to crash,

I wake up to a text from Dana. "Let's have
breakfast, my treat. Sloan's, 9 a.m." I realize it's 8
a.m. and to go to Sloan's one must show up ready to
be seen. *I don't want to be seen.* I remember Ryan and
the drawer and I look over the side of my bed and
he's still there, in the very spot he fell, begging me
to receive him, calling to that place in me that just
wants a release, because that's just what always used
to make me feel better before all of this happened.

I lie back in bed and close my eyes and I cry
because I slept really well and I did it without
alcohol, and I did it without Ryan or Tom or all the
other Dicks and Henrys. Maybe I'm getting some of
this after all. I guess maybe the mantra worked.

I'm late to meet Dana and I'm not ready to be
"seen" and I really don't give a damn. I'm dressed. I
brushed my hair and, let's face it, there was no time
for a quick jaunt over to Neiman's. *This is me. Deal
with it bitches.*

"Dana!" I call out as I find her on the patio.

"Jesus, Sara, I've been waiting for half an
hour." She literally eyes me up and down like I'm
auditioning for Playmate of the Year, which I'm
clearly never going to achieve.

"Damn, Dana, I just got home from a shoot and you call me late at night and leave me a message that I don't get until eight a.m. Lighten up!"

"Sara, I called you at nine p.m. and you are never asleep at nine. You're usually just opening your second bottle of wine by then."

"Nice, well, I haven't been drinking. I actually meditated myself to sleep."

"Meditated? You meditated yourself to sleep." She's laughing one of those, 'Can you believe she just said that?' kind of laughs and it's annoying the hell out of me. *Why does everybody refuse to believe I really want to change? That I need to change?* I start to explain the process of putting yourself into a meditative state to experience better sleep, calming the breath, repeating a mantra … and she slaps her hand down on the table so loud I think everyone is going to take cover under their tables.

"Sara, you got so drunk four days ago, you'll probably keep Ardent in business for twenty more years undoing the trauma you caused. So, let's not kid anyone here."

I immediately get defensive. "Look, things are going fine. Ardent is fine and I'm fine."

"No, you're not fine. Everyone in town knows about your merry little fire-walking trip. Listen to me—if you screw this up, you need to understand that I will have nothing left for you."

"Wow, now that's a pep talk. I'd like to see you as the keynote for Ardent's next conference." Damn, that was bitchy says my inner voice. *Why are you always so mean?*

"You're my friend, Sara, no matter how pissed I am at you. You might not realize it, but I'm doing my best to help you not wholly mess up your life. Because if you do, I have nothing for you. I will always love you, but I will not be an enabler for you anymore."

She says 'enabler' like I'm addicted to opioids. Wow. The waitress finally arrives. "Can I take your order?"

Dana pushes back her chair. "Nope, I'm leaving. Sorry, Sara, you should have been on time. Love you bunches." And with an air kiss and a wink, which is impressive because she keeps one eye in a mortal death stare the entire time, she walks away.

The waitress gazes at me, like "Whatever honey, are you going to eat?" I feel stupid and guilty, so I order the Eggs Benedict and have to remind her three times I want real bacon on the side. But when my food comes, I'm not hungry. Dana's outburst has gotten to me. I'm pissed, actually. Pissed and guilty. Yeah, I screwed up with Joao and yeah, I blew my reputation. And now I'm still screwing things up. But what about all those years I didn't screw up? What about two decades of Sara being totally "on it," sticking to the normal program, making everybody a shit ton of money?

She says she's supportive but is she really? I know she loves me. But maybe there's a part of her vested in me staying the same old productive, predictable Sara. I'm also realizing I am kind of an asshole. (Thus, the guilt.)

I leave my food and the restaurant and spend a few hours walking around the very trendy Melrose District, which has hit hard times and is now on its way back up. I can't wait to see the first "Body Shop" on the block. Then full gentrification will be in effect. I buy nothing, even though my bank account says I can. I go home and am reminded I have no dog, no friends, no boyfriend and nothing to eat—and now I'm hungry for real. There is a fun little Mexican fusion place around the corner. I used to stop there on my walks with Zak, have a margarita, a shot of tequila and some amazing taquitos, and yak with a bartender named Jeff. I decide to stop by for the taquitos at least. It's about 5:30 and still happy hour. I walk in and, yep, there's Jeff.

"Sara! Hey, where have you been? Where's Zak?"

I swear people would never remember me if it weren't for Zak. He really is an awesome dog. "I've been away on a shoot, so he's been staying with Tom." Jeff raises an eyebrow and looks at me sideways. "Yeah, I know ... but he loves Zak and, well, they did bond. I'm trying on that I'm such an amazing ex-girlfriend we can share our pets and talk about our new lovers. I haven't made it to the new lover part yet—I'm still trying to get over the last one."

I find my favorite spot at the bar. Within moments, without my asking, Jeff has a large top shelf margarita, over ice, no salt, waiting for me with my usual side of tequila. I take a deep breath and am about to explain I'm not drinking when he offers,

"I'm so glad you're still drinking. All of my usuals seem to be going 'sober'." He does air quotes and winks. "I haven't seen Jamal or Sandy in months, and Tony comes in. But now he orders the vegan tacos and the kombucha that tastes like a margarita, but seriously isn't."

I feel bad because I think Jeff is lonely and reaching out and I need to show up as a compassionate listener. So I figure I'll just sit there and nurse the drink, skip the tequila and enjoy my taquitos and get out of there as fast as I can.

You knew that was a lie, didn't you? You already know me so well. You know it's not going to go like that. And it doesn't.

Turns out Jeff and El Pecado will be changing directions in a month, new menu, all vegan, and the bar is being replaced with a kombucha counter and juicery and will now be called La Abadia. The irony that it's going from "Sin" to "The Abbey" forces me to finish my first drink and order another from poor Jeff who is struggling in the "retraining of the American worker." And here I'd had my bets on AI replacing the workforce or maybe the evangelicals making everything illegal again. I never thought it would be the vegans.

I sit there for a good hour listening to Jeff's struggle with his existential crisis as he transitions from Sam Malone to a sous chef to Tal Ronnen. Who are we kidding? He's basically going to be cutting up cucumbers and being a nursemaid to a family of SCOBY. (SCOBY, BTW, are the living bacteria that make kombucha what it is.) Somewhere in there I drank the shot of tequila he so lovingly and co-dependently poured for me and, as it slid down my esophagus, instantly my foot burned. I admit it—I felt that pang of shame in my heart, like heartburn. But it's not heartburn. It's really a piece of my soul bursting into instant flames as I betray myself and my own best intentions. And after the initial eruption of flames, it becomes like a tiki torch out of fuel, smoke billowing, obscuring my inner truth.

It tastes terrible and feels like metal in my mouth and yet the burn is good. It's familiar. When you experience shame, there's nothing better than feeling the "not shameful" alcohol can eventually give you as it helps you remember you're actually a good person, funny, sexy, all of it, even if you don't really believe you are. There is always a moment of doubt when you wonder if you should go home or drink more. But you need the flame and the smoke again and there is only one way to get it. So you take another drink because it's like BDSM—it hurts in a good way.

So I am now two shots in, and Jeff has never let my "one margarita" empty. He had a pitcher ready for the night. Damn, he really is a good bartender.

At one point we discuss him becoming a budtender, which is a bartender for pot. And then he does it. He asks about Tom. Of course, shot number three is ready for the "?" to that sentence and I take a good long look at it and I'm faced with a choice. I can drink that shot of tequila and be free of the shame and failure for the rest of the night, or I can face what I am.

I look around the bar. It's basically empty. Sam isn't hanging out at the foot of my stool. I'm going to go home to an empty apartment and sleep alone and I already know I'm a shitty person—everyone in my life is currently reminding me of that. At this point I have nothing. So, I figure "What the hell?" One more shot isn't going to change any of that. I can quietly go home and sleep it off and wake up tomorrow, visit my dog, and see the man who broke that last bit of heart I had left. If nothing else, I can buy a car and drive for Uber—in a different city of course, or maybe even a different country.

Two hours go by. The bar is technically closed, and Jeff is cleaning up. I'm drunk, but not sloppy—or so I tell myself. I've been scrolling Facebook. Everyone looks so happy, out with their friends or on a date night with their man, babies and cats everywhere. And then I see it, a picture of Tom with Zak at the dog park. "Me and my boy," he has captioned it.

My heart wrenches and I try and breathe to calm my stomach. Damn he is hot, and so is Tom. Look at them, so happy, playful, and perfect.

The other thing alcohol does is offer you the truth in sort of a brightly colored, comic book Pow! Smack! kind of way. Think "Joker," but more like the Juaquin Phoenix Joker, not the Jared Leto one. The décor in El Pecado is Mexican, of course, with a focus on *Day of the Dead* colorful skeleton masks and hearts with burning flames made out of tin. Christmas lights hang twinkling from the ceiling, which flicker against the shiny red tin hearts of flame bringing the fire to life in my eyes and my mind. *I really have set my life ablaze, haven't I?*

The truth that has been revealed—or at least the truth I'm ready to accept—*kapows* me and my entire soul takes the hit. I was an asshole—to Tom, to Dana, to Joao … okay maybe not Joao. But to Tom for sure, even though he cheated. Of course, he cheated. I set him up to cheat. How can anyone stay if I don't make room for them to stay? I owe them all an apology. I should call Tom and apologize right now. I look up his number and I take it in, gazing at his little circular image, a picture I took of him on our trip to Mexico. I actually thought he was going to propose, and for the entire trip I kept bursting into tears when he would start to ask me a question until I realized he wanted to know if I wanted green or red salsa. I think I actually brought home one of those tin flaming hearts since my heart was burning up with disappointment over not getting a diamond. My finger hovers over the little phone icon.

I should have been better for him—patient, more understanding of his needs and not just wrapped up in my own patterns. That's what they call it right? Your patterns. I can see now that I was never really there for Tom. I was there so I could live out my patterns over and over again. Okay. I see it. I'm getting it. I can fix this and then move on to the "I love myself" part! I heard that in AA you have to

make amends before you can change. I may not be
sober, but I can still make amends. Fuck it.

I hit the call button and it rings exactly once
when I hear him answer. "Sara?" His voice is like
chocolate and wine, like a windy road in a sports car.
His voice is better than Ryan Goslings. I manage a
sob "Tooom … gasp, gasp, gasp."\

"Where are you?" he asks..

"I'm at El Pecado, which is becoming La Abadia
in like a week or something and Jeff is freaking out
and Zak is missing and I'm sorry …" There is silence
and I think maybe I lost him and am about to do my
best Verizon, or is it the Sprint guy, "Can you hear
me?" when he says, "I'll be there in five minutes."

Jeff waits out front with me and in exactly five
minutes Tom pulls up in his Prius and I get in. There
is an awkward silence, which I just can't handle and
so I launch into my apology for being me, which
I have been rehearsing since I called him. "I'm
so sorry! I really screwed things up. I'm a terrible,
selfish, person. I make it hard to love me. I have trust
issues and I should have talked with you about how
stressed I was and tired. You and Dana are right,
I should have just taken a vacation. I'm just really
impulsive and, you know, not very well educated and
so I don't always make the best choices for myself."

He kisses me, and it's like the post-canoe, rain
kiss in The Notebook and the next thing I know we
are at his apartment, in his bed, him on top of me,
pounding it out, and I literally leave my body. I see
myself. And instead of feeling relieved and happy

to be back in his arms, well, in his bed anyway, I'm disgusted. The tequila has entirely stopped doing its job, and I'm very present to the fact that I'm sad … and angry.

I try to do the old Sara routine of justifying what's happening. Maybe this is his way of telling me he loves me? Maybe instead of listening to my apology, taking it in, listening and nodding like someone who's really hearing me—like the gurus do when you talk to them, like someone who really loves you listens even when you suck—maybe instead of responding with his own heartfelt truth, this is how he does it? Maybe I should enjoy this and appreciate his way and then maybe later we'll talk?

.   And in that moment, I realize I've always been willing to wait to be heard—to accept whatever form of love is thrown my way, to replace intimacy with sex, to apologize, to make excuses. I also realize I haven't been truly open to receiving the love I want because I feel I don't deserve it. I think I'm not worth the effort to hear and really love. I realize I don't give love either. *It's all just me going round and round in my head playing a story line out. Do this, get love, give love … when none of it is love.*

The part of me floating up above the bed that sees me there—hand bracing myself so my head doesn't make contact with the wall, moaning and groaning and encouraging this being on top of me to finally orgasm so it can all be over—feels so much pain it hurts like a knife wound. And I can't take the pain anymore. I can't do this to myself any longer. I am unable to check myself out and play the role for another instant.

Suddenly, I feel rage.

I feel the fire burning within me. It doesn't puff out, it builds, and I let out a scream like a woman watching her child die. I am dying! I am going to die unless I save myself! I throw Tom off of me and jump out of bed, naked, tears of rage streaming down my face. He is stunned and confused and I really don't care. I turn to him and scream, "I don't want this! I don't want to die! I don't want to live this life anymore! I hate you! I hate what you did to me! I hate myself and what I did to me!"

I am screaming incoherently, crying, pounding my fists against my thighs, and Tom and now Zak are standing there, panting, frightened. "My God, Sara, what are you doing?" he cries, shocked.

I slump to the floor in a heap. And suddenly I know the answer. "Anger therapy!"

CHAPTER 19

After about twenty minutes, I stop crying. Tom has just been sitting on the end of his bed, staring at me, unable to move, unable, I think, to process "Real Sara," angry Sara, in pain Sara. Of course, he can't. Very few people ever learn how to do this—to be present with someone else's suffering without trying to fix them, judge them, make them wrong, or defend themselves from their failure. I suppose I should give Tom points for shutting up and doing nothing, even if it is probably out of shock. Zak on the other hand, is nestled in my lap, one paw knowingly pressed up against my heart. I look up at Tom from the floor and I feel nothing for him. I don't know if it's because I have nothing left to feel or if I ever really felt anything for anyone or anything to begin with. Besides Zak, of course.

I am learning that disappointment in the world builds up, like plaque on unbrushed teeth.

When I was small, I thought I was a fairy. In my mind I could fly and the garden gnomes around my house could talk and my stuffed animals came alive when only I was looking. They showed me a world where I could think of anything and it would be true. My kindergarten teacher told my parents how creative I was, but that I needed to be "grounded." This is a big word in the spiritual movement, grounded. As a child I didn't want to be grounded. I wanted to fly, and so one day I dragged a dining room chair into the kitchen and climbed onto the counter because I knew I could fly, in real life, not just in my imagination. I climbed up on the kitchen counter and, with every ounce of energy I had, threw myself into the air. And for a moment, I did, in fact, fly. Until I didn't. Until this reality we exist in, the slowest of all frequencies, caught hold of my dream and dragged it kicking and screaming to the floor.

I landed with the weight of a million little lies onto the linoleum and my mother came running into the room as I shrieked in pain and shock. "Are you hurt?" she asked in a panic. I wasn't physically hurt. But I guess you could say this was one of those moments that imprinted onto my soul story, my brain, and my belief system. Prior to this horrible moment I believed what the story books told me: that I could be anything, do anything. Evidently, I could not. And when my mom laughed when I told her I thought I could fly, in that moment I felt shame. I felt stupid, like there was an inside joke I wasn't a part of, like I'd been left out of the secret that everyone knew except me.

I could not fly, my gnomes did not actually speak to me, and everything I thought was true wasn't. Eventually, I realized that this was just one of the many lies we tell our kids—like Santa Claus. Once I figured out that everything my father said about all I

could be was a lie, grounded is what I finally became.
I accepted that I needed to dream in a "normal" way
like everyone else. Dream to find a man to marry
and care for me. Dream of the house with the picket
fence, two point five kids and the dog. And like a
good girl, I dreamt those dreams, believing that in
those dreams lay the happiness, the connection, the
approval, the love that I was looking for and was told
I could expect. But each time I get close enough to
taste the lusciousness, I broke a tooth and needed a
root canal.

I stand up and start to get dressed. Tom looks up.
"Where are you going?"

"That's a great question," I reply as I sort of
chuckle to myself. *That is the ultimate question isn't it?*
Along with "Who am I?" Quietly I tell him, "Home, for
now, and then back at it on Tuesday." Isn't that what
we do? Be calm and carry on?" I'm dressed and bend
down to hug Zak goodbye. "I'll see you soon buddy."
Zak whines a little. He knows, he sees, he hears. How
is it that humans became masters on Earth without
managing to do any of that? Arrogance, I think, and
opposable thumbs. Other than that, we really have
no business being in charge.

My Uber is waiting outside. It's early and the sky
is grey-blue, and the roads are filled with busy people
going places or coming from places, and I wonder if
any of them actually know where they are or where
they are going and why. Maybe we are all just here,
doing what needs to be done so we can finish this life
believing we actually accomplished something.

We stop at a red light and next to me sits a guy driving an older Subaru with tons of bumper stickers, aging and faded like the driver himself. *Look at this guy,* I think. *Like he's really got something to say about it all, doesn't he?* I wonder if he knows who he is and, as he pulls forward, I notice one sticker that stands out: "The Truth will set you free, but first it will make you miserable."

No kidding, dude. No kidding.

I arrive home and spend the rest of Sunday and Monday lying on my couch, trying to sleep. I barely eat. I barely move. I can't even watch TV. I sold that months ago and don't have the energy to replace it. Scrolling Facebook is a soul killer. The only food in my house is Top Raman and tomato soup, the foods you find in the cupboard of college students and people on the bottom rung of their career ladder, not the food of a successful human. I lie on my couch, staring at my stack of self-help books, my white board with my magical list that was going to fix everything in my life, my bag of swag from the expo with brochures and cards from people all willing to help me become better, wiser, more spiritual, happy, quit smoking, quit drinking, eat vegan. Two of the pamphlets catch my eye. One has this beautiful picture of green mountains and waterfalls with an invitation to come to Peru, the other has a picture of an alien with the words, "The truth is out there."

What Truth? I've spent almost 20 years building a career and all I've got to show for it is a bag of processed noodles and a can of Campbells soup.

"Mmmmm-mmmm good" is not what I'm up to.

Who am I? What am I? What do I want? I stare at the brochures and drift off into a dream state and now I see a second version of me crying, "I don't know! How am I supposed to know?"

I can't handle two of me, pissed at each other. One "me" mad at my lack of understanding of even myself and the other "me" mad for asking a question I clearly don't have the answer for.

Suddenly, the room morphs into a steel box with bright lights hanging from the ceiling. I am strapped to a table, wearing a white hospital gown. My eyes dart around the room and from above I see large, egg-shaped, black eyes peering down at me. My brain is trying to connect the neurons to what I am seeing and, like a bolt of lightning, it hits me: It's an alien. I have been abducted by aliens! Or maybe it's a really weird dream? People say that dreams are actually different dimensions of reality. Either way, it's frightening!

There is now a second alien standing there and some sort of automatic strap wraps around my forehead and clamps my head to the table. "Wait, wait, what are you doing?!" I beg for an answer as another automatic lever moves towards my mouth— there are levers on both sides of the table with some sort of leather strap in the middle, and I'm recalling this contraption from one of Joao's movies, except that one had a ball and all I can think of is the Anal Princess—and the mouth thingy lowers, pressing past my lips, and I am now muted, silenced, save for muffled screams and moans. How fitting.

Alien # 1: "Well, it's female, mid-thirties. She smokes too much and is bordering on alcoholic, and that will probably kill her. Make a note that so far one hundred percent of our human subjects are afflicted with addictions, chemical and emotional. Hm. Her eggs look good, but her prospects for procreating at this late stage are low."

Are you kidding me? I'm still in my prime and I don't smoke that much! Okay, I do. But who are *they* to judge? I try to respond, but everything coming out of me is unintelligible.

Alien #2 raises its skinny, rubbery comic book-drawn hand and pulls down a large metal arm with a laser gun on it with a bright red light pulsing from it. He begins to scan my body slowly. It doesn't actually hurt and I'm grateful he doesn't shove it up my ass. Then I hear Alien #1 speak again.

Alien #1: "Let's do the brain."

Out of nowhere a large cone-shaped helmet appears with long wires leading into a dark abyss. Alien #2 attaches it to my head and I'm waiting for the electric shock therapy to start. Alien # 1 goes back to reporting his findings like he's Bill Nye the Science Guy. "Arrested Development. Stuck at age fifteen. Brain usage 5.6 percent, capable of complex thought, but without desire to think beyond basic concepts. Anxiety levels are abnormally high. Hmmm."

Hmmm? What's the hmmm? I want to know!

"High levels of endorphins and enkephalins, and

yet also extremely high levels of adrenaline. The limbic system shows high levels of fear, anxiety and stress, which is suppressing the needed oxytocin levels to promote love and peace, cutting off the endorphins ability to reach the brain. She has potential, intelligence, empathy and kindness, and yet it's all blocked up by fear of failure and abandonment. Oh, she does experience a lot of sexual pleasure. And yet, as we find in most humans, sexual pleasure has been confused with love. Pity, she has much potential."

Oh nice, I get laid a lot, but that isn't enough. *I could have told you that without the leather mouth gag.* And with that I am blinded by a flash of light and my eyes pop open and I am in my living room, on my couch, clutching a pamphlet picture of my new alien boyfriend. *At least he gets me.*

I ponder the meaning of this latest installment of "Sara dreams" and combine it with all the brain lectures and literature I've been reading, and here's what I get: Humans are essentially bags of chemicals that control us. We become addicted to those chemicals—usually not the good ones—because of early childhood trauma which bombards us with fear, doubt and "WTF is happening?" chemicals which take over, not leaving much room for the love chemicals to get through.

We think we're happy because our society is filled with stuff like wine, chocolate, sex and Gucci which still deliver oxytocin, but it's like fake oxytocin. It's generic oxytocin, which is always cut with the cheap stuff. Either we're adrenaline junkies or addicted to knock-off oxytocin. To transcend this predicament, we have to be spiritual ninjas or go to rehab, which is why the Mind Body Spirit/self-help industry is worth about $500 billion dollars and addiction recovery is big business. The truth that I find miserable, lying there on the sofa, reeling with the sad truth of it all, is that most of the time none of this actually works. It just replaces one addiction for another—just like Brin snapped at Jason the other day in the parking lot. Because despite all the talk about finding God and becoming empowered and spreading the Light and Love around, most people just don't change. Our habits and patterns are too ingrained in our brains to actually change. This is who I am. There is no "new Sara." There is just "Sara."

We're sold this hyped-up image of ourselves as Spiritual Masters and Light Workers and told we can fly. And just like when I was a little kid, I bought it. And where did it get me? Drunk out of my mind yet again on tequila, fucking an old boyfriend who obviously doesn't really even know me or care to know me. Once again, I thought I could fly. I thought I could change. And now, this time, I find myself splayed out on the living room couch at age 36, believing there is no hope for humanity.

Fuck it! I quit.

I quit everything—trying to be something, loving anyone, doing anything for anyone else. I am going to be in it for me for a change. I'll finish this damn movie and, well, I'm not sure what I'm going to do after this movie. Maybe I'll go back to Joao, ya know?

At least I knew where I stood with him. There were no pretenses about what we were up to. We weren't trying to change the world, and I could afford shoes and a filet mignon and a nice bottle of wine and I should have just been happy with that.

I send a group text reminding everyone of our studio call time for Tuesday and go to bed.

CHAPTER 20

The next day we interview three of the world's most famous thought leaders on set in LA. When I arrive, I am a changed woman. I am not weak, lost or hoping for anything. I have left all that behind me at home along with all my drama. I am "grounded" in who I am—a bad-ass producer, a cynic who is not interested in any more pseudo-psychology or spiritual science. I've spent enough money on therapy and I'm still unhappy, so maybe that's just how I roll. I am Sara Fucking Wells, unhappy, unchanging, yet grounded. Acceptance. *That's a big buzz word in all the personal growth books.* I'm just going to accept myself as I am and screw you if you don't like it.

My expectations are made clear to each and every one of my crew. "Fabio, please do not interrupt another interview with dead batteries. Jason, if you look at your phone one more time during an interview, I'm going to confiscate it like your mother did when you were a teenager. And Michele, make sure lunch is on time, hot and edible." When Brin asks me if I want to talk about the upcoming interviews, I respond "Nope," with a new sense of conviction. I'm not an idiot and this isn't brain surgery.

Everyone snaps to it and I can tell they are a bit confused as to who this person is who showed looking like Sara. Good. It'll keep them on their toes.

INTERVIEW TRANSCRIPT #1

Sara Wells: Who are we, really?

Interview Subject #1: When you sit in stillness, you can connect with your formless self. Each of us has a formless self. One must see beyond the story we tell ourselves about who we are so that we may connect with the soul.

Sara Wells: What is the soul?

Interview Subject #1: The soul is your truest self.

Sara Wells: Who is that?

Interview Subject #1: Y.O.U.

They literally spell it out as if that's going to make it actually make sense.

Sara Wells: I'm sorry that doesn't make any sense to me.

Interview Subject #1: Then you need to meditate more.

Interview #1 over … WTF?

INTERVIEW TRANSCRIPT #2

Sara Wells: What is oneness?

Interview Subject #2: We are all connected because we are all energy emanating from one source, the infinite source of all knowing. We are a part of that source, manifesting into this reality to experience life.

Sara Wells: Why?

Interview Subject #2: Why not? You are the source, think of yourself as a single beam of light emanating from one source, to expand outwards as far as your light can reach, to expand endlessly and to make known the unknown

Sara Wells: Why would an infinite being of all knowingness need to make known anything if it already knows everything?

Interview Subject #2: That's a great question, the ultimate question if you think about it. What does your heart tell you?

Sara Wells: My heart and I aren't on speaking terms right now.

The interview subject laughs as if I am joking. I'm not.

INTERVIEW TRANSCRIPT #3

Sara Wells: What do you mean by "follow your heart?"

Interview Subject #3: The light will give you the gifts of this life, the darkness will make way for the light. Your heart is the light; it illuminates your path and all you have to do is follow that path to your bliss.

Sara Wells: What if your heart is lying to you?

Interview Subject #3: Your heart never lies. It's your beliefs that can trip you off your true path. Your fears can convince you to make choices that seem to protect you, but are, in fact, taking you away from your bliss.

Sara Wells: What is the difference between bliss and pleasure?

Interview Subject #3: Pleasure is sensual, it's physical. It brings us into our bodies. We experience pleasure because of something, an experience, a kiss, a taste, a smell. Bliss, on the other hand, is a state of being regardless of the external situation. Humans can become addicted to pleasure without ever experiencing true bliss. Bliss exists if we are willing to receive it, even if we are experiencing suffering. Bliss is when you are connected to the totality of

all that is, all that you are. To be in bliss one must
be awakened to their heart and have awareness of
every breath, every cell, every particle of life, known
or unknown. Bliss is connected to everything.

Sara Wells: Is bliss even possible? True bliss?

Interview Subject #3: When you are ready to let
go of all the beliefs that are holding you in a space
of fear and doubt, when you are ready to close
your eyes and see how much more there is than the
thoughts of fear running through your mind, when
you are ready to quiet the mind and hear the truth,
you will find bliss.

All I can think of when I close my eyes is aliens,
demons, and fire. I think I'll just keep my eyes open
and focused on the end game.

And the LA shoot is a wrap.

Shockingly, no one got injured, no one got up and
stormed out of an interview. Surprisingly uneventful,
exactly the way it should be. I'm back on track. I'm
home and in bed early. The van leaves at 5 a.m. for
Arizona and the ranch of the crystal skull whisperer
Michele is still involved with. I don't want to dream.
I don't want to think about anything. Thinking,
analyzing, and contemplating is what led me down a
dark rabbit hole and I've spent enough time chasing
that damn rabbit.

I get comfy in bed, turn off the lights, ready to sleep and my inner voice asks, "What do *YOU* believe, Sara?"

Fuck.

CHAPTER 21

The team and I meet up Wednesday morning. The van is packed, and we hit the road, heading into the rising sun. The ride out of California is quiet and boring, long endless miles of the I-10 freeway bordered by an unending sea of tract homes built for the ever-expanding populous that works in LA or the surrounding areas but who can't afford the real estate. Like a virus, humans spread out into the vast deserts, dry and brown, and the homes try and blend in. One tract ends and another begins on the outskirts, the next batch of homes waiting to be filled by people just wanting to survive.

I wonder what it would be like to live in a beige house, surrounded by other beige houses, anonymously existing, driving for hours each day to work and then home to eat, sleep and do it all over again the next day. I see beige schools. The only green around are the fields kids play sports on, possibly their only hope out of the drabness of the life their parents created. Maybe I'm judging them too harshly, maybe my desire for something more is what causes me to be unhappy. Maybe they are actually really happy with the simplicity of beige. Maybe they have actually figured out the key to life. Maybe they have balanced out their chemical make-up and found enough love juice. Maybe that's what life is about, figuring out the chemistry so that you can exist.

We cross the border into Arizona, and if it weren't for the sign telling us so, one wouldn't know we had crossed anything. It's more of the same, towns, brown houses, roads, desert, repeat.

Deep into Arizona we take an off-ramp and head further into the desert toward the mountains. Lawrence, the skull guy, has a ranch somewhere near Prescott and we've taken a side road. The landscape is filled with large rocky peaks and more desert. The colors are as warm as it is hot outside, and I'm grateful for our air conditioning. The road is quiet with not many travelers, and our GPS indicates a road closure ahead, suggesting an alternate route. Jason dutifully obliges, and we enter what seems to be another reality, one that is usually reserved for locals. I decide to scroll my phone and find that even the internet isn't welcome here. Everyone else in the van is asleep, hypnotized into unconsciousness by the monotony.

I scan the desert, counting cacti, almost dozing, when there is deafening *BOOM!* and Jason practically leaps from the driver's seat, wrestling the wheel as the van careens left then right, tires screeching, smoke billowing from under the van. Jason gains control, and everyone in the van is now wide awake, performing their own version of one of those wild Chinese operas, "Wa, Woo, Whaaaaa," as we're tossed about like little rag dolls.

Jason comes to a halt on the side of the road and flies out of the van first as everyone else, still trying to find their way back into reality, crawl out slowly with the expected chorus of "What happened? What's going on?" The loud boom was, of course, a blown tire. I check my phone and there's no service. *Of course, no service, of course a blown tire.* Jason checks for *a spare and … no spare.* Of course, there's no spare. All was good when I left my desire for knowing at home. But the minute I try and understand the nature of reality, questioning people and their little beige existences, I'm slapped upside the head like a kid who just dropped the F bomb in front of their grandparents.

Damn it's hot. I scour the van and find we have four bottles water which I distribute as I scan the horizon hoping for another wayward traveler who listened to Siri when she offered up this alternate path. (I wonder if Siri is in on the secret that there is no "right path," just a series of long, deserted roads peppered with pretty things to distract you, triggering a false sense of pleasure which makes you think all is right in the world until you eventually discover upset and disappointment, which come as a surprise because your guide's directions were spoken in such a softly gentle, yet convincing voice with a slight English accent that makes her sound like she knows exactly what she's talking about.)

Someone else besides us has to have been suckered into taking the detour, and I assume it won't be long before that someone passes by. Of course, assumptions usually end up turning everyone into assholes. Which means, after about two hours of assuming, out of water, baking in what must be 110-degree temperatures, everyone is getting pissy. We're arguing over who's going to try to walk to the nearest gas station, who's going to stay with the van, and who's going to die first so we can eat them. Brin and Jason have been going at it, arguing the concept of chaos theory versus the hand of God, with Brin wondering where the hell God is now and what sin did Jason engage in on his days off that brought God's wrath down upon us, because obviously it was his fault since he was the one driving.

Fabio, gentlemanly as always, has taken some of the gear out of the truck and built a make-shift shade spot which only one person can fit under, which, of course, is Michele. Me? I've just been staring off into the horizon. It's true that when heat rises off the pavement it creates a highway mirage and this must be what people are referring to when they talk about a crack in the hologram. It's as if reality isn't stable. It moves, warbling in and out of focus. There are moments when I am sure I see another car and then it's gone, replaced by a blur of possibilities. I wish I could just imagine what could be there and it would appear. Isn't that what all the books say, that we create our reality? Why doesn't it work like that?

"God has nothing to do with this!"

It's Brin, shouting at Jason. "Do you really think there is some dude up in the sky who's sitting around on a cloud, bored and says, 'Hey, I'm going to screw with those people right now.' Shit happens, Jason. It just happens, because there are millions of events occurring simultaneously and sometimes they crash into each other. They're not guided by anything. And then we get to decide how we want to react. We get to choose our response. It's called free will! Maybe you should put down your Bible and start listening to some of the people we interview!"

I'm done. I've had it with her shitting on everyone else just because she's trying to find some peace in this fucked-up world. "Leave him alone Brin!" I shout. "Stop it! Stop acting as if you have somehow figured it all out and are the Bringer of Truth. There is no truth. And each and every one of us is just trying to find a way to survive the pain, the fear, and the hurt we all heap onto one another."

I walk toward them, the sun pounding down on my head, the heat radiating off the pavement. It's so damn hot I can't even sweat. "Look," I tell her, "if God works for him, who the fuck are you to take that away from him. How about you? Are you happy? Are you living in bliss? Have you found the yellow brick road to nirvana? No, you haven't. Your life sucks just as much as everyone else's. So shut your damn pie hole."

Everyone is silent and staring at me … actually, staring past me. I turn and out of the hazy, heat-distorted distance, it looks as if something is arriving through a portal from another dimension—an old red pick-up truck. It's big, and as it approaches it takes over both lanes of the road as if it owns it. The truck, which turns out to be an old Chevy Silverado, slows then comes to a halt beside our van. The driver's side window rolls down and an older woman pops her head out. "Looks like you need some help getting back on the journey."

Ha! She has no idea. About twenty minutes later we're packed into the king cab like sardines, our gear is loaded in the truck bed, and we're heading toward Lawrence the great crystal skull communicator's residence. Turns out our Florence Nightingale knows Lawrence and will take us all the way. In addition to Florence and me in the front seat, there is an older man I'm guessing is Native American by the black hair, turquoise and feather jewelry he's wearing. I think she called him Ed. We are about an hour's drive from the only town with anything of use, and Florence's real name is Gayle. How perfect. She's probably early 70s, a former Hollywood actress and a Vegas Go Go girl who is retired out here and knows everyone—which isn't saying much. According to her there aren't many people to "know" out here, which is why she likes it. I'm relieved to have found someone who understands the "biz."

"Thank you so much for saving us from certain death in the desert," I bubble. "Wow, what luck! We haven't had much luck on this gig." I ramble on. "I don't usually do documentaries. I produce for Joao Salvadore, do you know him?"

Gayle cocks her head as if she's really thinking about it and then looks me right in the eyes. "Nope."

"Yeah, well, I don't know why I asked you that.

I doubt his type of movies are the ones you'd be watching. Anyway, this gig came up and I thought I'd try something different, ya know? Shake it up a bit—sort of like you, moving out into the middle of nowhere." I'm riding shotgun, sandwiched between Ed and Gayle, in the middle seat, no seat belt and Gayle likes to run this baby hard and fast. Ed hasn't said a word, he just stares at me, curious, like I'm a ship and he's a ancient Native Indian who is trying to figure out what the disturbance in the force is.

Gayle speaks, her voice deep and raspy, sort of like Katherine Hepburn. She sort of looks like her too, except a redhead, like her truck. "I wasn't looking to shake it up. I was ready to silence the noise and embrace quiet and sunsets—like the one you're missing." She waves her hand in exactly the way Katherine Hepburn would, gracefully, as if her hand held a brush and she was painting the scene.

I get the hint and shut up and take in the sunset she painted. It is magnificent. And just as I feel a tiny bit more settled, my reverie is interrupted by a succession of dings from my phone. We've landed in cell tower range, which means all of my texts have now been sent. Soon, I start getting pinged back. One of those texts is from the rental van company informing me that we broke our contract by driving our van across state lines and thus our rental insurance will not cover the costs related to towing and repairs. It'll all be on us to cover.

I turn around, ready to lay into Michele and I see that, for a moment at least, Fabio has his

wish. Michele's head is resting on his shoulder as
she sleeps. No wonder he was willing to take the
middle seat. Brin and Jason ride on opposite sides of
them, pouting as they face out the windows. I take a
deep breath and swallow my anger, because at this
point, yelling at Michele isn't going to accomplish
anything. I don't think she knows what a state line
is, really. She's just a kid who's desperate to get out
from under her daddy's watchful eye, or, more likely,
her mother's while still using daddy's credit card. I
can see why she fell for Indiana Jones and his crystal
skull—rich, handsome, older, wiser. At her age I did
that too, although my sugar daddy didn't come with
an occult following and a glass-shaped skull in his
briefcase.

I call the rental company and ask them to drop a
new van at the Temple of Doom the next day, then
find a tow truck to take the van to the repair shop
they have set up through their national division.
When we arrive at skull central, Lawrence and
Company is waiting to greet us in a grand driveway
in front of a grand house designed as if it were in the
midst of the Italian countryside, not the middle of
the Arizona desert. He and his staff stand in line as
if we are the English delegation carrying the Queen
of England herself. Turns out he was really there to
love up on Gayle and thank her for our rescue. As
I watch, I'm pretty sure these two have had a little
fun in the Temple of the Chachapoyan Warriors.
Michele stands by, not so patiently, eyeing them both
as well, while Jason and Fabio unload the truck.

We are escorted into this behemoth that is part residence, part retreat center. As we enter the main house, Lawrence disappears and what I assume is a butler greets us and shows us around, proudly pointing out the meeting space behind the house where we will be shooting. It looks like an old horse-riding arena transformed into a large meeting space than can hold up to 1000 people. Off to the side is a huge dirt parking lot where people are literally pitching tents and parking RV's, some of which look as if they will barely make the last 100 feet to their spot. Others are modern and grand with pop-outs bigger than my apartment.

The boys, with the gear, are ushered toward the retreat space. Brin, Michele and I climb the grand staircase that's so grand it makes me wonder if Trump had anything to do with the place. It's marble. It's gold leaf. It's grand—like overly grand in a way that says, "I have money … now." As we reach the top of the stairs, a woman appears out of nowhere and whispers something to Michele. "Oh!" she exclaims … like really, she *exclaims*. "Sara, you and Brin get settled. I made sure Lawrence gave you both the best rooms. I'm off to do a private meditation with him and the skull and some of the V.I.P.s."

Brin and I look at each other because apparently, we aren't V.I.P.s. Strangely, she actually notices. "These people don't want to be filmed," she non-explains hastily. "I'll be back for dinner. It's at 7 p.m. And dress appropriately."

I'm left wondering what I packed in my carry-on

size go bag that would be considered appropriate for dinner at the mansion. "Michele, we're on a shoot, not a state visit. But I'll do the best I can."

"Yes, of course," she mutters, and disappears behind a wall of gold velvet curtains. I'm tempted to peak behind them, wondering if I'll find a little old man pulling levers and speaking into a large microphone. Jeeves motions for us to continue down a long hallway and, yes, I'm sorry, but it has me hearing "Red rum… red rum" in my head. I can't help myself. I know it's annoying, even for me, this incessant need to make pop culture, movie, or historic references. It's the product of an over-active mind and keeps me distracted from myself and all my issues.

We pass several doors until we reach the end of the hallway and Brin is shown to the left and I to the right. Jeeves opens my door and I walk into a suite which is literally the size of my apartment, decorated in a modern mid-something century Italian style, but not quite right. Think Paolo Buffa meets Wayfair or Overstock.com. It's like Lawrence wanted to show up in the right style, chic and temperament, but didn't want to blow the bank. I wonder if I pick up one of the cheesy gold balls on the coffee tables, will the price tag still be on it? My door is still open, and I look across the hall and see Brin. Her room may be smaller, but she is already splayed across a gigantic bed which requires a stepstool to get into. On her back, shoes still on, hands behind her head, she lifts her head in a nod-and-smirk that clearly says, "This is revolting and so tacky!" that only Brin can pull off, which is made even more irritating because I'm still mad at her. And with that, Jeeves exits the room and closes the door.

It's weird in here. It's quiet and it feels like one of those museums where they place furniture in a way that the original owners used to live but are dead now. No one lives this way in real life. Of course, the walls have paintings of dead people on them, perhaps the same dead people who once graced these halls. Oh, wait, we're in Prescott, Arizona, not 1930's Italy. I check my phone. It's 4:30, which means I have two and half hours to chill and then come up with something to wear that is suitable for this costume party. I lie down on the bed and all I can think about is Rocky Horror Picture Show—like are we about to be sacrificed? Does anyone know I am here? Anyone who cares? What character am I? Of course, you know where this leads.

It's a dark and stormy night …

Okay, I won't. I'll spare you, just trust me. I am sincerely wondering if I'm going to make it out of here alive and am considering my options. Hell, we don't even have a getaway car … van. Everything in this room is round, no sharp edges. Who in the party is Meatloaf, because I kinda liked him.

I sleep for a bit, stare at the ceiling, sleep, etc. It's 6 p.m. and I have an hour to prepare for dinner. One thing I'll say is that I agree with Brin's obvious disgust. Lawrence is basically rich because he has convinced thousands of people to pay thousands of dollars to pitch a tent in his back field and then meditate in front of a Spirit of Halloween special edition $19.99 glass skull. I mean, I am all for the power of thought, attitude, positivity and all, but to pay upwards of five thousand dollars to spend two nights sleeping in a tent or on the floor of a former horse arena just to stare at a piece of glass is nuts. People really are gullible, especially when happiness, love, self-empowerment and money are the prize you supposedly win for playing. I wonder if the ancient wisdom schools of pre-history offered early-bird pricing and a fast track if you paid extra? Like could you skip the den of snakes test if you paid more?

It's annoying that right now I can find agreement with Brin. But least I'm surrounded in faux luxury and there is a bathtub. Calgon is taking me away…

After I bathe in a ridiculously large tub—as if there are four people in this room all wanting to have a bath together—I settle on a pair of black pencil slacks and a black blouse and pearls. Why I brought pearls, I'll never know. But hey, spirit must have been speaking to me and somehow prepared me to dress for tonight's ritual. Maybe I have angels after all? I slip on my little black ballerina flats, which are actually really comfy. I'm in all black, which seems fitting. *Here's hoping I'm not the sacrifice.* I head down the long, horror movie hallway with carpet that reminds me of a Sheraton I once stayed in, down the stairs, and find the butler who I'm now calling Riff Raff instead of Jeeves because we've moved on to *Rocky Horror Picture Show* and the metaphor needs to be complete.

He points me towards a room off of the main entrance hall. There I find Michele, who has somehow managed to pull off a Stella McCartney cocktail dress, emeralds and some really nice strappy black heels. (I don't know yet what expensive Italian showroom they come from, but I will.) The boys are down in what the boys always wear when they shoot, Fabio in black shorts and a t-shirt, clearly feeling underdressed. I have a feeling that boy cleans up well. Jason is wearing clean jeans and a t-shirt, which is what Jason always wears. Brin—damn, okay, I need to learn this from Brin. She has an endless supply of black flowy pants and matching flowy blouses, with amazing chunky jewelry and she looks like she just walked off the Johnny Was runway—classy, bohemian chic, rich enough to afford sustainable, indigenous and authentic. Nothing is ever wrinkled, she doesn't need an iron and she can pair them with Uggs or her favorite strappy crocs, which still look more chic than my best INC. business casual. Another reason to hate on Brin. I am usually the best-dressed person on set, and she has, hands down, beat me on that every day.

Lawrence stands next to a gorgeous mid-century modern bar replete with crystal carafes filled with the elixirs of the Gods themselves. "Ahh Sara, would you like a drink?" He asks me as if he knows what road that will lead us down.

"No thank you, I don't drink while I'm working."

"Of course you don't. Then let's move on to dinner, shall we?"

Okay, we are definitely in *Rocky Horror Picture Show*. I'm still not sure if I'm Janet, but Lawrence is definitely Frank, Michele is Columbia, Fabio is Eddie, Jason is Rocky, and Brin is most certainly Dr. Scott. So far all of my team is accounted for, so we are not eating any of them tonight. *OMG, I need to stop. This is serious and I need to be present and get a good interview…*

We enter a large dining room with, yep, you guessed it, a mahogany mid-century oval dining table that could probably seat thirty but for now it's been reduced down to a size ten—our gang plus some people I haven't met who seem to be Frank's sidekicks. We sit. Rif Raf and Magenta serve and I'm waiting for Eddie's head to show up on a platter. (Even though that's Fabio. Stay with me here. He's still in the room, so I have no idea who we are eating.)

Interior: Dining Room: Evening

LAWRENCE/ FRANK
I hope you have found your rooms accommodating.

SARA/JANET
Why yes, they are lovely, you seem to be a fan of Paolo Buffa.

Lawrence/Frank looks baffled at Sara

SARA/JANET (Cont)
The famous Italian furniture designer … mid-century.

LAWRENCE/ FRANK
(Interrupting)
Yes, yes, of course, well my designer knows what I like.

I figure this is a good time to rescue him and to lock down our schedule.

SARA/JANET
So, we are filming the meditation with the skull tonight?
When can we get the one-on-one interview with you?

LAWRENCE/ FRANK
How about now?

Wait we haven't even eaten yet and I'm starving. Touché Frank. Touché

SARA/JANET
Well, I suspect we're all hungry, so how about we eat and then the boys can set up and I can review my notes.

LAWRENCE/ FRANK
(Not really prepared for this "Janet")

Okay then. Although who needs to prepare for the truth?!

Everyone at the table laughs one of those, "We're all laughing because we don't want to be served in the next course" kind of laughs, awkward, nervous, all sycophant-like and creepy. Yeah dude, whatever. Just whip out the garters and the cabaret number and let's do this.

END SCENE

We eat an amazing meal. I'll give it to old Lawrence, he may have cheap knockoffs for décor, but the food is the real deal. I really wish I could have enjoyed the cabernet he's pouring. I'm sure it would have gone well with the filet. At one point I say I am surprised that he serves meat, at which he retorts, "I knew you'd like it." Do I scream carnivore? Freaky bastard.

By the end of the meal it's 8:30 and the meditation starts at ten. We have just an hour and a half to get to the bottom of Frank's mad scientist secrets, raise the dead, and lift this rocket ship up into the air.

CHAPTER 22

We are all set up in Lawrence's/Frank's study. The room is dark, with walls lined with books and again I wonder if they are real or just really realistic-looking wallpaper. A massive amethyst crystal stands in one corner and another massive rose quartz crystal in another. Those must have set him back a pretty penny. Once again I am reminded that everything this man has, he has because he is charming and convincing and who knows what else?

Do not get sucked in by his charm Sara. You know his type. Charming, with a knack for poetic prose that lulls you into a false sense of intimacy until his forked tongue is halfway down your throat and he's locked you in his red room.

Lawrence/Crystal Skull Interview

Sara: As a spiritual person, can you justify how you make so much money off the skull?
Michele gasps!

Michele: Sara!
Michele slaps her hand to her mouth and reddens as Brin crosses her arms and Fabio gives her a cold stare.

Lawrence: It's okay. Let's get something straight. The term "spiritual person" is an oxymoron.

Fabio: (blurts out) A what?

Lawrence (to Fabio): A contradiction in terms. (To Sara) Spirit is spirit. Human is human, and never the twain shall meet.
Brin starts to object but Lawrence puts his hand up, practically in her face. She narrows her eyes. I'm actually offended for her.

Lawrence: Yes, I know, unseen spiritual energies underlie the physical realm. Of course. But as physical human beings, are we privy to the workings of spirit? No. Do we understand it? No. If we did there wouldn't be any confusion about our identity in the first place and all this "seeking answers about who we are" would never occur.
He takes a sip of wine, gloating.

Sara: You charge five grand for two nights. Per person. So, is it that the wisdom you offer is only for the rich? Is it just for an elite few? Wouldn't it be better if all people understood it?

Lawrence: Some of the proceeds go to support further research, some to archaeological digs, some to me. Money is just energy Miss Wells. Work with the skull long enough and you'll transcend your lack consciousness and concern for such things. Those

who are pulled to the skull come from all walks of
life and find a way to get here. For them, money isn't
a block to their higher consciousness.

I am suddenly aware of Brin, her childhood, or her
lack of a childhood so her parents could pay the likes
of Lawrence to unlock the magic kingdom for them.
Now I am even more offended he put his hand in her
face and I forgive her … a little.

Sara: So, where did you find this skull, exactly?

Lawrence: I am unable to identify the exact
location of where I came to be the steward of this
particular skull. I have made a promise to the beings
that allowed me to share it with the world we exist
in. Just so you know, many of the funds I derive from
these events go to support them, protect them and
their way of life. They hold other skulls and were
instructed to send this one out into the world to
expand the wisdom, the gift, because if this world is
going to survive, then we need more people to have
the knowledge the skull imparts. That is my mission.
That is what I was called to do.

I lived a very simple life before I came upon this
calling. And despite what you think, it isn't easy. I
live mostly in isolation, and so now I am allowed the
creature comforts humans desire. I have a nice house,
and yet, do I get to hang out with friends, travel the
world frivolously? No. All of my work is around

protecting this unimaginable gift to humanity. I am constantly doubted, attacked, and called a charlatan by those better than you Miss Sara Wells. Look at my property. It is filled with people who desire the wisdom the skull carries. Before every event the land must be prepared, toilets provided, water provided, electrical hook-ups provided, permits, insurance handled. Afterwards it all has to be cleaned. And then there is the fact that the government has one geo-stationary satellite permanently affixed to my location at all times. I am followed, audited, harassed, and I pay for a team of lawyers and CPA's to handle the attacks. Do you think awakening humanity to its greatness is easy or cheap?! Here's the thing … crawling on this planet's face are some insects called the human race, lost in time and lost in space, searching for meaning, They need me. They need the skull!"

Okay, that just happened. Lawrence literally just quoted Frank-N-Furter with an impassioned crescendo as if he were a fire and brimstone, evangelical, southern Baptist preacher calling his flock into the fold. And I can't say that he is wrong. I am lost in time and space, clearly without my Brad. The thing about used car salesmen is that you really can't beat them in a straight up verbal debate. They have all the lines, all the angles. You have to come at them all stealth-like, by surprise. And I don't have the element of surprise, yet.

"Okay, I think we have it."

The camera stops rolling and Michele moves

giddily over to Lawrence, fawning over him.

"Oh, that was so great. You looked amazing and sounded so powerful and commanding and spoke with such authenticity."

Excuse me while I vomit.

Brin shoots out of the room without a word, which, I guess, is how she's dealing with what just happened. What did just happen? We got slimed, that's what happened. This isn't Cynical Sara or Angry Brin. Again, I really do see the value in the concept that attitude is everything and that humanity can be better. But I can buy a pair of Nikes for that wisdom. I have yet to see what $5000 and my own tent will get me.

I look up to say "Thank you" to Lawrence, but he's surrounded by Michele and the others who were at dinner. The boys are packing up and getting ready to head to the arena. I figure I'll change quick and meet them there.

As I walk back to my room it feels even more like I'm on a movie set. Maybe if I look on the back side of the walls they will be held up with sandbags and stands like we're on a soundstage somewhere. I hate the fakeness of it all. I'm mad that I didn't push him harder. I'm mad that Brin is still mad at me even though what I said was true. I feel a little shitty I was so rough on her, but hey, you reap what you sow. Right?

I am often told I am too blunt, like I need to become more PC and softer in my delivery. One of the issues I thought I might deal with on this journey is my "meanness." Even my mother told me I was too "masculine." I have always been driven, mostly because I was taught if you have a dream you need to go after it. Much of what I've heard so far on this journey is that the dream should just magically fall into your lap, like if I meditate long enough a Mercedes will suddenly pop out of my ass. (Okay, I did make a list and got a movie—although I'm not sure this one's gonna make me rich or help anyone.) The gurus are constantly saying that the Universe is always trying to give us what we want and that we are always screwing up the Universe's plans. (Wow, it's kind of amazing to think I am more powerful than the Universe!)

I switch out the slacks for leggings and a long black shirt, sneakers and ankle socks. I suspect we'll have to be barefoot and my feet get cold. As I am about to leave my room, I feel a cold chill run up my spine and I look around this fake place and realize I can't remember the last time I was real. *Who am I to judge Lawrence for making a buck off other people's dreams and desires and need to hide from reality?* Shit, I made tons of bucks providing a fantasy escape room for people in exactly the same position as the seekers showing up here. If I'm honest, I did it bigger. Joao's films make millions and millions of dollars worldwide.

The only difference between Joao and me and Lawrence is our shtick was socially acceptable. Porn, sex, schlock, drugs and alcohol—they're all totally okay. Going broke in a desperate search for the doorway out of this hell house of mirrors by meditating with a crystal skull? Crazy town.

Suddenly I feel a little less judgmental and a lot shittier about myself. *Yay!*

I head back out of my room and back down the hallway. Did I mention this hallway is sort of weirdly long, like it should be in one of those Las Vegas Hotels that seems almost normal on the outside, but endless on the inside? Like they are totally messing with the space-time continuum? But it's not. It's a house—well, it's a *mansion* in the middle of nowhere. I have too much time to think walking this hallway and I recall some of the interviews I've done so far and some of the spiritual "truths" I've been exposed to.

"There is nothing that has happened to you that should not have happened."

"The Universe always has your back. Are you paying attention?"

"When you are in alignment with your soul's desire, life flows with ease."

"Your heart never lies. It's your beliefs that trip you off your true path. Your fears can convince you to make choices that seem to protect you but are, in fact, taking you away from your bliss."

The thing about gurus is that they seem to have the whole speaking in tongues, human-whisperer thing down where everything sounds so amazing and loving and all lit up like a damn Christmas tree, and yet no one has been able to explain to me what the heck they are actually talking about.

My entire life I have been going after what I

thought my soul wanted, even when I didn't even know I had a soul. Love, money, success, happiness— all these things are the things we are all taught to seek. Right? I'm not alone in this quest, am I? Isn't that what we're all trying to find? Can't someone just spell it out? What are the three easy steps? Seriously. What is the meaning of life? How can I be happy and blissful?

I make my way out of the house to the old horse arena which has a been rejiggered into a large open meeting space in which, I kid you not, about one thousand people are packed. At five K each for two nights, tonight this dude is making 2.5 million easily. The dirt floor has been covered with sheet plywood, taped down for safety, all totally insurance worthy. There are sections cordoned off with numbers which must align to what people paid. Lawrence has asked that we set up close to the skull and, as Jason is locking down the camera, I spy a reunion. *Weird*, I know this girl running up to Jason, but I can't place her.

"Hey you?!" she cries.

Jason looks up confused—until he realizes who is standing in front of him. It's none other than the mistress of the firewalk herself, Morgaine, actual name Lyra.

"Wait, hey, what are you doing a here?" he asks. A reasonable question from a guy like Jason who hasn't guru-shopped. He's gone from heroin to halleluiah and stuck with it.

She hugs Jason like he is her long-lost brother. He hugs her like he hasn't been held in years. They finally break apart as I make my entrance, almost sorry to interrupt because this may be the only action Jason has seen in a while.

"Hi, I'm Sara. We haven't met."

"Oh, yeah. I saw you do the firewalk!" she says. "I'm Lyra."

I wince a little, but Lyra is hasn't taken her eyes off of Jason and he hasn't even acknowledged my existence.

"So, what happened?" he asks. "I thought Ardent was your guy, and now you're here..."

She shrugs. "Ardent WAS my thing but I've so evolved from that space. I was a total mess before the skull came into my life.

"Really?"

"Sometimes the meditations last all night. But it's worth it. It's really tuning me into myself, you know?

I take a moment to watch Jason. He's confused, he's attracted, she's nuts and I'm judgmental. A perfect threesome.

"But of course, you know," she gushes. "You're making a movie to uplift the consciousness of humanity! You understand the power of the Universe and how it speaks to us!" She looks at us like we're U2 and she's backstage. I'm totally The Edge and Jason is Adam Clayton ... kind of the soul of the band but totally underrated. "You really live this stuff!"

Both Jason and I have no idea how to respond because, truth be told, neither one of us is living our "truth." We're just trying to survive this disaster without causing more irreparable harm to ourselves and others than necessary. Suddenly, a loud gong-like sound echoes throughout the arena. Lyra gasps with excitement, hugs Jason again and dashes off. Everyone settles in their assigned position on the floor.

It's show time. Fabio has shown up with a second, more mobile camera and has placed a microphone on the stage. A small black platform silently rises from beneath the stage floor lit by a white laser light. The crystal skull rests on top.

A collective "Ahhhhh" fills the vastness of the cavernous space. I point to our open area by the front of the stage and out of nowhere Brin pops up behind me. She shouts/whispers, "Once you're down there you're gonna have to stay for the whole meditation, you know."

I shrug, I'm down. Let's see what this skull baby can do. I bet most of these East coast liberals with money will crash out in an hour. Jesus, look at them. The crowd is mostly 50 somethings with a smidgen of 20 somethings. What's Lawrence going to do when his audience ages out? Does medical cover this shit? I settle into my spot. This isn't going to last all night and I can roll.

One hour later everyone is still sitting motionless in front of the skull, meditating. Okay, maybe they are a two-hour group. It can't be much longer than that. Everyone's into it. Lyra, wow, she's so still. Michele is next to her in the front row. Fabio shuts his camera off, having been handheld for over an hour shooting a lot of nothing. He comes over to me and whispers, "How long is this going to last?"

I have no idea, but I tell him to grab the monopod (a single leg camera tripod) out of the bag next to me.

At three hours I'm struggling to stay awake. I'm reminded of going to see Hamlet, the longest damn play you'll ever see live. Everyone dies, BTW— hate to ruin the ending, but pretty much in all Shakespeare's plays everyone dies or suffers or is betrayed or is sleeping with who they shouldn't be. You really only need to see one live. I liked *Rosencrantz and Guildenstern Are Dead*, but that's not technically Shakespeare. Or when they make them into musicals. But the only music rockin' this theater is this weird, droning *hummmmm*, not even really an *ohmmmmmm*; it's a lower frequency than that, which makes it really hard to stay awake. *This is what they must play to hypnotize us,* I think.

Okay, we're four hours in and nothing. Everyone is in a trance-like state. Poor Fabio is struggling to keep his camera upright. Jason is out like a light, but his red light is still on which means his camera is still rolling. That's good, although this shit is gonna suck in the editing room—hours upon hours of nothing is boring to wade through. Truth be told I am vacillating between sleep and that "I'm awake" state which means you aren't but you're trying to convince those around you that you are.

In a moment of "I'm awake" I make eye contact with the skull, and it's as if they suddenly changed the lighting. Of course they have effects—one must go all the way when millions are on the line. Right? I think we're about six hours in… *damn it's been a long day.* No one would notice if I closed my eyes. I could stay sitting up. I turn my focus to the stage, staring at the skull, because if I'm looking that way, no one will notice I'm sleeping, right?

I make eye contact again, okay. It's not really eye contact because the skull doesn't have eyes, just sunken holes where eyes should be, but wow, the light coming from those suckers is bright. I prefer total darkness when I sleep, and this light is like that annoying cellphone flashlight people use at a sleepover—blinding and disorientating. And then it speaks … like no shit… the skull's mouth is moving and sound, recognizable sound is emanating from it.

CRYSTAL SKULL

So, you've returned to the mystery rites you left so long ago in another life.

SARA

Great. You don't even have a tongue and you're speaking in tongues. If you've got something to say, just say it.

CRYSTAL SKULL

Always the impatient one. You want the three easy steps, do you?

Well, I'm going to give you the real secret, there's only one step:

Follow the light within your own heart.

Suddenly a bright beam of light emits from the skull's mouth, and as it reaches me it's penetrating. It's blinding. It blasts me with a light so bright it's like a police light beaming into the car where you and your boyfriend are trying to figure out how to get to second base. *That's uncool dude!*

The skull's laser beam eyes pierce right into my heart and I feel it, like I really physically feel like I'm being shot. I think I've been hit by something. I need to move! I need to get out of the way, fast! Someone is shooting at me! Maybe the FBI has shown up and is finally coming after Lawrence for tax evasion?! Maybe there are underage girls kept in a dungeon somewhere. Maybe there's a cache of guns! All of this is possible and must be why I am being attacked. The light burns! It hurts every part of my existence! Why did I sit up front? I'm a sitting duck for the apocalypse that is raining down upon this space. And suddenly I'm standing, I'm running, looking for cover and I hit something or something hits me …

CRASH!

The podium falls over, the skull soars into the air, bounces onto the carpet and rolls down the aisle as chaos ensues.

AUDIENCE
The skull! Oh my God! The skull!

Spotlights illuminate me as my eyes pop open and I take in what I have done. What have I done? I was injured. I was shot with a laser! Like in *Star Trek!* There should be blood! I look down at my chest and there is no blood, but people are still running and screaming and the stage is moving up and down as if it's caught in a loop, the lights are strobing and there is no blood and the light is still pouring from the eyes of the skull even as it lies on the floor in the aisle, staring up at me.

I faint. Or I die. I'm not actually sure which.

CHAPTER 23

I wake up in my room with Brin staring down at me.

"Jesus girlfriend. That was wild."

I hear the words. I see her lips move, but I don't even know where I am or how I feel. I'm not sure I'm alive. Is this my last moment of consciousness? Or is this the in-between state between life and death where someone leads you towards the light? And if it is, I sure didn't expect my guide to be Brin.

I hear the skull again in my head: *Always the impatient one. You want the three easy steps, do you? Well, I'm going to give you the real secret, there's only one step: Follow the light within your own heart.*

I still have no idea what that means. What fucking light? What fucking light am I supposed to follow, for fucks sake? *WHAT FUCKING LIGHT?!*

Brin grabs me and shakes me and suddenly I realize I'm shouting this in the real world and I stare at her wildly and for a moment I see her, like I really see her. And I can feel with every ounce of my being that she is asking the same question.

Everyone is.

A few people have the truth revealed to them, somehow. Some people pretend to have it figured out. A lot of people think they have it figured out and don't. But mostly, we are all lost in a dark tunnel searching for the light like a dog hunting a squirrel. And every time we see even a little shred of light, we're chasing that sucker down.

But what light are we supposed to follow? It's damn confusing down here. There are too many lights. Pleasure has been confused with bliss. Wisdom confused with intellectual knowledge. We are conditioned from day one to believe things about the world, about ourselves, that really don't serve us— things that aren't true and that pretty much cause every ounce of suffering we experience. Why do we do that to each other?

Wow, that's a weird thought, like where did that come from?

I repeat it out loud. "Pleasure has been confused with bliss and nirvana and truth has been replaced with memes," I say to Brin. And then I vomit onto the probably fake Bellino linens on the bed. At least I hope they are fake because I suspect I'll be replacing them. My guess is even if they are fake, I'll still get a bill for the real ones.

And yet the sentence stays with me ... *pleasure, bliss, belief, truth.* Brin has ahold of me and is staring intently into my eyes. "Listen, I need to know if you can walk out of here on your own. They've asked us to leave."

Of course, they have. It's like my early twenties all over again, except this isn't the Troubadour on Sunset and it's Riff Raff standing at the door instead of The Rock. I snap my head toward him and I gaze into his eyes and he smiles at me and slowly nods his head like he knows … he heard it too. Michele arrives at my bedside with a bottle of water.

"Sara, what happened? Why did you freak out like that? You didn't even have any wine at dinner."

I look at her, because I think maybe she'll understand. "Michele, the skull spoke to me. I'm not sure what he meant. I mean I think it was a "he." It had a dude voice, for sure, and light, light blasting out of every damn hole on that head!"

She smiles. "Yes, I know, it happened to me too. I just didn't try and tear the place down. Lawrence was very calming."

Ugh … Lawrence, yeah, I'll bet he was calming. Well, he sure wasn't calming for me. None of this is calming. This is about the least calming experience I've had in my life. I quit drinking. I quit smoking. (Okay, I'm trying.) I kept my eye on the prize, stayed focused and bam! I get whacked by the light.

But isn't that what you're looking for? something whispers in my head. I push the thought aside. "Okay, let me get up and we'll go. Everyone be at the van in fifteen minutes." I stop and shoot a questioning look at Brin. "The new van is here, right?"

She nods and I feel a sense of relief. I don't really know what else to do except retreat. I feel weird, lightheaded and my body is tingling, like my nerves are pinched. But I have to get everyone out of here. I have to get out of here. Gingerly I ease out from beneath the vomit-soaked duvet.

As I stand up, Brin heads toward her room. Michele lingers "The boys are already packing the van, and um, I'm not coming with you."

Brin stops just before she hits the door and slowly turns. She's about to go into one of her "I am Brin knower of everything" rants and I catch her eye and shake my head "no." She stops, mouth open.

"Michele, are you sure this is what you want? School starts in about three weeks. We're almost done filming. What about your dad?"

"I've already called him and told him I'm staying and taking a gap year. I know this is where I need to be. Lawrence loves me."

Okay, everyone stop with the eye rolls. She's basically a teenager experiencing her first love beyond her father. Give the girl a break.

I understand. I *feel* her, like I physically feel her. Have you ever had the experience where you just understand someone? Even if you disagree with them with every ounce of your being, you just know that they have to walk the path they're walking, and you just need to love them and let them be? Yeah, well, I usually don't. So it's weird, because usually I would go all Brin on her. But I don't. I look her in the eyes, and I see her and that's all I can do. That's all I need to do.

"Okay, I get it. You feel this very strongly and I get it. Just take care of yourself, okay? At some point this might be very painful and that's okay too. No matter what, you're going to be okay. And I am always just a phone call away."

She hugs me and it's a real hug, heart to heart, and my tingling arms take her in and I know this is what real connection must feel like. And in that instant I understand why so many of us use drugs and alcohol to try to get here. I feel genuine love for her. And I like it. I like feeling this way, even if it also feels like I'm not quite here. Have you ever had those moments where you see little floaters in your eyes but there isn't anything in your eyes? Or like you've been crying as you're driving home from a horrible date and the lights go all fuzzy? This is how the world is looking to me right now. *Whoa, maybe we're all in The Matrix after all.*

I am the last person to make my way to the van, and there is no one there to see us off. It's as if the entire place has gone silent and abandoned. The sun is just coming up and the parking lot is still full of tents and RV's, but no one is out and about. We're being ghosted by the ghosts.

Fabio is driving the new van. It's obvious he knows about Michele's decision by the tightness of his jaw and his fists clenched whitely on the steering wheel ... and his silence. Jason and Brin each take a seat in the back and I take the front passenger side. As we begin to pull out of the driveway Brin leans forward with her phone towards Fabio. "We're going to Colorado." Fabio looks at the address and I look at Brin, confused.

"We need to see someone. I'm pretty sure you had a kundalini awakening, an unprepared and uninitiated and definitely not-guided kundalini awakening, which can be really dangerous if not handled properly. We're going to go see a yogi. I met him once when I was a kid. He actually wasn't creepy, and I know he can help you."

"Wait, you think the skull and I had sex and the orgasm literally blew my mind?" I think I'm confusing kundalini with tantra, which are very very different as Brin is about to explain...

"Not tantra, Sara, Jesus. Kundalini." She sees my blank look and sighs. "Okay, so basically each of us has a powerful force, an energy, life energy, safely sitting in the base of our spine. Through practice and initiation, you can be taught to awaken this energy and move it up through your body. The force of it can connect you to the unseen and open you to the divine truths. Or it can be cracked open like an unsuspecting egg and dropped into a frying pan. That's what I think just happened to you."

Wow, that's actually a really good metaphor. Cracked and burning is a good way to describe how I feel. Broken, empty and yet full of something hot. It's like a snake has crawled up inside of my soul and lit a fuse. I take a very long and very deep breath and I am silent. I have no words. I can't disagree with Brin. Something really fucked up or really great is happening to me. I'm not sure how I feel about it. I vacillate between warm and fuzzy and feeling nauseous. I have no argument left in me, especially with Brin. My phone dings and it's a quote from Madame Ling. "You are a livingness, a verb. What is arising in you, at this moment, is the great realization." - Christopher Zenn Loren

Well, at least this time she gave an attribute.

Madam Ling is growing on me. Maybe she really is connected to me somehow. Or is it that I find meaning in everything she sends? Does it matter which came first, the prophecy or it's fulfilment? There's no such thing as time. Right?

I can see the drive time from Prescott to Cortez, Colorado is six hours. Not that far. *What is it with these gurus? Can't they choose a location with a Starbucks close by?* I'm tired and slump in my seat. It seems as if everyone left in the van is too, and we drive in silence. By silent agreement nobody is talking about Michele's decision. Fabio, however, is in charge of the playlist, which, if my basic Spanish is still intact, is all about a woman breaking a man's heart. And I just don't have it in me to talk to him even though I can see he is obviously upset.

I close my eyes as a new wave of nausea sets in. Did you ever watch that TV show *Stranger Things?* It's all retro 80's about the underworld, sort of a Dungeons and Dragons spin on sci-fi/horror. The girl with all the powers blindfolds herself and ends up in this black space with water on the floor—I guess because water is a conduit to move energy. Anyway, when I close my eyes, I'm in that black space too.

In the show the heroine goes into this void to find people she's looking for. Me? Right now, I'm looking for my Dad. I don't know why, because my dad really didn't help me in my life, but he loved me. He made me feel safe in a world that often wanted to pull the rug out from underneath me. He always persevered. He always found a way out of the darkness and into the light and was an optimist right up until the moment he died. I am searching, but I can't find him in this black room. But I hear his voice, and it takes me back to the night he died.

I was out of state on a shoot. Dad had been in and out of the hospital for years, suffering from complications due to diabetes. I lost count of how many times I took a call from my mother, who, convinced he was dying, forced me to grab a plane to come and say goodbye. He would always come through, though, get out of the hospital and be the epitome of life, refusing to do whatever the doctors and my mother told him to do. That man had Snickers bars hidden all over the place—his glovebox, desk drawers, tucked in his underwear drawer and in shoes stored way in the back of his closet—shoes he couldn't wear anymore because his feet were so swollen. Near the end of his life, he bought a 1970 Cadillac Deville hard top and I used to call him Boss Hog. My mother hated that car.

He also insisted on moving to New Orleans with my mother because he loved the music. In every club we went to all the old players called him "The doctor." (As a side note there is nothing more unique than clubbing with your dad. He drank straight up Coca Cola. I drank rum and Coke.) There he found a modicum of success selling university degrees to foreigners. It seems everyone wanted a degree from an American university, and he found a way to sell them to people. He traveled a lot, seeing the world, which is what he loved. To keep Mom happy, he bought her all the antiques she wanted for the house that she had dreamed of having her whole life. My favorite picture is him, sitting on a camel on the Great Wall of China. Why there was a camel there I have no idea. But he looked so happy, like he had finally done what he came here to do, which, I guess, was ride a camel on the Great Wall of China. I've never felt the way he looked in that picture—at peace—happy, joyful even.

He called me the night he died. My phone rang as I sat in my hotel room in some city I didn't know, and I will never forget that conversation. Each word is embedded in my brain and my heart.

"Hi Dad," I chirped. "how are you? Mom says you're about to die but I can't get on a plane until the morning. Will you wait for me?" This was a sort of joke he and I had come up with. "Hey dad, are you going to die today?" Weird, I know, but humans find ways of coping with the things they aren't ready to deal with. And I was not ready for my father to die. He was always there, ready to go out for ice cream or to the arcade. He didn't often say "I love you." But I felt it from him in a way I have never felt from anyone else. He was my first love, my champion, my knight, and I hadn't found his replacement yet, so I needed him.

"Oh, Hippo," he sighed (My nickname was Hippo … and now you know why I have body issues.) "I'm not going anywhere, but in case I do, I want you to know you're loved."

"Aww Dad, I know you love me."

"No, Sara … of course I love you, but that's not what I mean. What I mean is you are loved. It's okay to accept that, to accept love, to accept the light you are offered, because in that light you will find what you are looking for."

My dad did love to wax poetic, but even this was sort of odd for him. As he spoke those words the "Song For Someone" by U2 was playing in my hotel room and the last line was, "If there is a light, you can't …" And I couldn't keep myself from crying. "I love you dad!" (I wouldn't accept the fact that he was going to die and the only light I ever knew in my life was about to go out.) "I'll be there in the morning dad, hang on for me!"

"Sara, sweetheart, I will never leave you."

It's weird because he sounds just like the skull, same voice in my head, same tone, tenor, frequency, same penetrating stare right into my soul like when he knew I was lying about being happy and fulfilled. But back then he just smiled at me and offered me some chocolate.

What is love? What is it really? Are there words to fully describe that feeling of total safety, acceptance and peace? I hear the sound of water being displaced and the grunt of some kind of animal and I turn around and I see my dad, perched upon his camel, smiling the widest, biggest grin I ever saw—light, bright warm light, emanating from him. And for the first time in my entire life, I feel it.

Love.

CHAPTER 24

I open my eyes and notice Brin is now driving. We must have stopped along the way. It's now about 3 p.m. and the sun is making its way towards the west, casting great shadows upon the surrounding magnificent rock formations known as the Great Ancients. *To think we were once a simple tribe of humans focused solely on food and shelter and now we're a complex society that is still mainly focused on food and shelter.* You would have thought we'd make that quest easier on ourselves, but all we've done is overcomplicate it.

We make our way along deserted, bumpy, unkempt, off-the-beaten-path roads, untraveled by those who exist in the normal world. Finally, we arrive at the ashram and Brin pulls up in front of an adobe home at the base of a rock formation. It's modest and yet somehow it feels majestic—like what Lawrence so wanted to create but disguised in opulence, putting on a show. This place is … it just is here, right where it should be.

A small man is standing in the doorway. He wears the orange robes of a monk. Brin stops in the circular driveway and exits first and hugs him. They clearly have history. The boys exit the van, and he greets them with a small bow, hands placed in prayer position at his heart. Straightening, he turns his gaze, searching … for me. And I'm not sure I want to be found.

Reluctantly, I finally exit the van. He stands for a long moment, eyes unfathomable, peering, apparently, into my soul. Then he smiles, turns and winks at Brin, then takes my hands. I feel awkward and in that moment I have two options, melt or retreat into what I know. I retreat.

Shocking, I know. Fear lingers in me like the smell of fish cooked in a small unventilated kitchen. I am unsure of what I am supposed to do. On one hand I feel a sense of release from the vision … dream … whatever I had in the van with my father. I am loved and my father was proud of me! Despite this new and profound realization, despite this new safe feeling I just woke up with, nothing outwardly has changed. I still have a film to finish, one that is probably not going to live up to the expectations of the people who want it made. My career is most likely over. I'm alone in this world. My kundalini is cracked, and I'm still lost … loved or not. What am I supposed to do now?

I do what I know. I take a deep breath, smile brilliantly and say, "So, I guess we're doing an interview?"

The monk smiles gently at me. "Yes, if you say so."

I look around at everyone just standing there and motion to the van and the gear waiting inside it. Everyone snaps to it. The monk bows to me and Brin and ushers us into his home. It's beautiful, sparse, yet warm, with windows open to the sun. I see a few other people in the shadows, not fully present, but there, ready as needed. The monk tries to look into my eyes, my soul. I won't let him. I'm not yet ready for that level of truth with a stranger and turn to business. "So, where would you like us filming you?"

He leads us into a living room that, while actually small, seems as vast as the universe we are surrounded by. The walls are fully glass, allowing for a view of the rock formations so massive and breathtaking they seem uncapturable. And yet his windows seem to frame them perfectly—like gods standing in his home waiting to be greeted.

The boys set up and the monk sits on a large, cushioned dais on the floor. Jason frames the shot perfectly with the amazing ancient monuments in the background. As soon as everyone is ready, I take my usual place in a chair next to Jason's camera.

Sara: Who should pursue a spiritual life?

Monk: Spirituality is not for people who are incapable of taking responsibility for life. Spirituality is not about sitting around in saffron robes having everything handed to you. You have to want truth more than you desire breath itself. You have to be willing to do anything to attain it.

Sara: Most people in the West don't seem all that interested in truth.

Monk: In the West, people think spirituality is about personal growth and evolution. But the truth is, spirituality is the gradual lessening of identification with everything personal, including your ideas about spirituality.

Sara: So, what you're saying is ...

Brin (bursts out): But if I don't desire personal growth how will I change?

I turn to look at her, surprised by her sudden outburst. Brin claps a hand over her mouth and then quickly removes it mouthing a silent "sorry."

Sara: Sorry about that. So, you're ...

Monk (to Brin): Nothing is wrong with desiring personal growth. Desire is the only thing that will bring change into your life. But there is nothing personal about spirituality. The ego, however, doesn't realize that. It thinks it's going to become enlightened.

The monk bursts out laughing at this and we all sort of giggle even if we are unsure about what is so funny.

Monk (cont): The ego can never become enlightened. Absence of the ego and enlightenment are the same thing.

I feel the frustration beginning to boil up in me. I have grown exhausted from the constant talking in circles without these gurus ever fully expressing what they mean. I have nothing to lose at this point, so I speak up.

Sara: I'm sorry, I just don't understand what you mean. What are we supposed to be seeking if not enlightenment?

The monk's eyes brighten with humor.

Monk: First, humans are seeking peace, safety and security. We haven't evolved much beyond that. Even with our new technologies, we're still just trying to survive, and it's actually become harder. Life is hard. There is much misery and suffering, mostly because we live a life trying to attain things—money, homes, respect, love. But we don't know what love truly is. We have been taught to be loved we must achieve a certain status, and so we spend our lives working at achieving these things. We are constantly seeking to fill the empty space inside us, and enlightenment is now something that's in vogue to seek as well. But not very many people actually understand what it is they seek.

He pauses, looking me squarely in the eyes, and I know his next words are directly meant for me.

Monk (cont): There is an old Zen saying, "If you meet the Buddha along the road, kill him or you will follow him your whole life." What does this mean? There are many interpretations. Most simply it means you must kill that which you seek, that which you worship, or it will kill you.

Sara: What are we supposed to do then? My whole life has been about seeking success, money, fame, approval.

Monk: And in many ways, it has been slowly killing you. You must live, of course, and make a living. Not everyone can spend their lives hiding in a cave, meditating all day and night. But you must live with non-attachment to desired outcomes. Live life in joy, acceptance and a knowing that this life isn't everything, that everything you achieve here is only temporary. Have the experience of it all, but don't become attached to it. As my favorite rapper MC Hammer said, "It's all good."

Okay, a monk just quoted MC Hammer. The brief pause is broken by a cell phone ringing. Pissed, I look around the room and realize its mine.

Sara: Sorry! I thought I had it on vibrate, so sorry, so ...

As I grab my phone to turn it off, I notice it's Michele. I'm about to send to her to voicemail when

I suddenly get this pang in my gut and my body shivers, I feel compelled to answer it.

Sara: Shit. I mean ... um ... this is totally unprofessional, but I have an emergency. Can we take a break?

The monk nods graciously and I get up and walk to the living room door, phone to my ear. At the doorway I pause and glance back. Brin is now sitting at the feet of the monk, listening intently, like a child hearing their favorite bedtime story. Normally she would probably have something snarky to say about a devotee prostrating at the feet of a guru, but this isn't that at all. This feels more like a genuine surrender, a metanoia, if you will, a transformative change of heart, a releasing of all the anger and rage and hurt and betrayal Brin has carried her whole life. She is earnestly open. I can see it.

I hear what sounds like crying in my ear and realize it's Michele. And now there are two scenes playing out simultaneously. Two souls are about to come face to face, in vastly different ways, with their choices and paths.

MONK:
Brin, you're okay. You have done such wonderful things in your life. You are here, you have all that you need and more.
It's time to forgive and say goodbye to the past and be who you are now.

They both begin to laugh.

SARA
(into phone)
Michele, What's up? … You're what?

Fabio, who has been trying to keep filming the monk, looks over.

SARA
Pregnant?! Are you sure?

Brin's laughter turns to sobbing as the monk pats her shoulder.

BRIN
(Sobbing)
I have held on to so much anger for so long.

MONK
And it's time to leave it behind. Only surrender leads to the bliss you seek.

SARA
Calm down. Oh, sweetie. It's okay. Stop crying for a second
and … He said *what?*

BRIN
Bliss seems so far away.

MONK

Bliss is all you truly are, once you shed the story of

your anger, your resentment at what hasn't happened or what did happen. It's all in the past. Where are you now?

That is all that matters.

Fabio stops shooting and gets as close to me as he can, listening in.

SARA

Can you get to Phoenix and catch a plane? We'll be back in LA tomorrow and ...

MONK

And it can happen in a moment ...

Brin's face is naked. Tears spill down her cheeks.

FABIO

Is Michele okay?

I wave him away impatiently.

SARA

Michele you can't stay there. Just rent a car. Put it on the

company card and ...

Loud wrenching sobs break out and I whirl back around to see Brin dissolve at the monk's feet.

SARA

What the fu... fudge?

Brin is on the floor. The monk gets up and kneels beside her quietly whispering into her ear. I walk back in the room to Jason who's standing there, mouth open in shock.

SARA

What the hell happened?

JASON

Beats me. One minute they're talking and the next ...

FABIO

What's with Michele?

Oh yeah, Michele. Jesus! What the hell is happening?

SARA

Crap! Michele, are you still there? Okay, okay... listen to me ... no, stop crying and listen.

All I hear is loud sobbing, on the phone, in the room. We seem to be dropping like flies here.

FABIO

Let me talk to her.

SARA

Not now Fabio. (Back into phone): get out of there.
Get a flight back to L.A. and call me as soon as ...

Fabio grabs the cell out of my hand. Brin wails anew.

FABIO
(into phone)
Michele, it's Fabio. Whatever happened, it's okay.
I'm on the next flight coming to get you!

He runs off still talking.

SARA

Hey! My phone!

Fabio runs back.

FABIO

I'll call you right back on my cell. Michele! I love you!

He shoves the phone into my hand and runs off. I stare at it, hold it to my ear. Nothing. Brin's sobs are the only thing shattering the quiet of the room.

JASON
What the hell's going on?

SARA

Beats me. I'm just the director on this rocket ride.

We stand there, silently watching the monk and Brin. Tears streaming, face soft and filled with light, Brin is transformed. Jason looks on in wonder.

JASON
(softly, reverently)
Amen, sister.

Suddenly my phone buzzes and a text all in caps from Dana comes through marked urgent: YOU NEED TO COME TO MY OFFICE AS SOON AS YOU GET BACK TO LA.
Of course, I do.
So much for fixing my broken kundalini.

CHAPTER 25

It's almost dark by the time we pack up the van. Brin walks out to say goodbye. I never even asked her if she was going to stay at the ashram for a bit. It just seemed obvious. "Thanks for understanding," she says. Then she *hugs* me. Like really hugs me. Then she hugs Fabio. "Go get her. And don't let her get away. Okay?" Jason, looking nervous, escapes around the front of the van, gets in the driver's seat and guns the engine. I open the passenger door and Brin's hand on my arm stops me. "Hey. Master Dechen says you're okay. You had a powerful awakening. But he says your energies are aligning. You're good to go."

Uncertain what I would have said or done if they weren't, I just nod and say, "Thanks."

We drive the van to Durango and the nearest airport, fifty miles away, so that Fabio can catch a plane to Phoenix and go back for Michele. I knew that guy would come through. I take a flight back to L.A. to meet with Dana. Jason agrees to drive the van and gear back to LA on his own. I think he was actually really happy about that. Some peace and quiet would do us all good.

Fifteen hours after her text, I arrive at Dana's office. She is waiting for me and there she informs me that I have been fired. Fired for negligence,

for incompetence and, the piéce de résistance—
for exposing the financier's daughter to a cult and
getting her knocked up. The way Dana is raging
you'd think I'd been the one to inseminate her.

Turns out this was Michele's dad's project all
along. *Un-fucking-believable.*

As I leave Dana's office, I feel numb, lost and
completely alone. Why didn't Brin tell me he was
behind the film? I mean, she obviously knew, and
I'm trustworthy, right? Sure, we had our fights. But
we were friends. Weren't we? I don't know how I feel.
But betrayed is in there somewhere.

And how can Michele's dad blame me for her
getting knocked up by a charlatan snake oil salesman?
It was his fault for putting her on this movie, not
mine. It's true that at the time we met Lawrence
I was pretty self-absorbed in my own drama and
probably should have taken better care of her. Hell,
if I'm being honest, I've always been self-absorbed
in my own drama. My own success, my own dreams.

I walk down Fairfax avenue, descending into a
rabbit-hole vision filled with memories of all the
times the truth was right there in front of me and I
missed it because I was too busy looking for "it"—
making life all about me. *Dana is right about everything.
She called it even before I left on this gig.* All I had to do was
listen to her. She spelled it all out for me right before
that yoga class.

I'm still wearing the same clothes I was in at
the monk's ashram. I feel sticky and grimy and I
need a shower. I decide to cut through a back alley

toward my street. Up ahead, coming toward me is a homeless person pushing a shopping cart. I can't tell if it's a woman or a man, and I put my head down to walk past. Suddenly, I hear a woman giggle knowingly.

"Ahh … the walk of shame. I've been there."

I love how she assumes I'm coming back from getting laid. Ha! If she only knew the source of my current shame maybe she wouldn't laugh. I try and sneak past her, but there is no way around her without being rude. Plus, she clearly has something to say.

"When are you going to stop walking around feeling ashamed?" she says, hands on lumpy hips, dark eyes probing mine. "You have nothing to be ashamed of. You have to stop blaming yourself for other people's choices. There is no end game and no trophy at the end of your life or special achievement award. Success is a lie. It's not success you're truly after anyway, it's wisdom. And you gain wisdom by having experiences on the journey. Sometimes the experiences are fun. Sometimes they're brutal. Either way, you hopefully learn something about yourself and grow. And that's the reward."

She cackles. "And no one can tell you what you need to learn. *No one.* You have to experience it. That's what this world is, after all, the plane of experience. This is why you are here—to go on your journey, yours and no one else's, with all the good times and screw ups, the right choices and the wrong ones. That's it honey, that's why you're here. So stop taking on everyone else's crap and deal with your own."

Okay, things definitely just got weird. And yet why not? Why not meet a homeless woman in an alley who finally explains everything I've been struggling to understand in language I can understand? I look into her eyes. They are clear and bright. They are present, more present than anyone I have ever experienced being with except for maybe Brin's monk. She has the warmest smile and there is almost a glow emanating from her. I examine her cart—extra shoes, a sweater, a blanket and pillow (all scrupulously clean), and a box of Bliss Bars. (I kid you not!) Riding shotgun on the cart's handle are three bobble-head dolls: Jesus, Buddha and Einstein.

I don't know what to say, so I just smile at her. *I guess the saying, 'When the student is ready the teacher appears' is true.* Who knows? Maybe my homeless teacher is the reincarnation of the Pythia, the ancient Oracle of Delphi. Stranger things than that have already happened to me. I wonder what people would do if Jesus showed up homeless too?

The woman giggles as I move past her. "I hate to ruin the ending for you my dear, but everything is going to be okay. I know it." And with that she moseys on down the alley—slowly, intentionally. And even though she appears homeless, she looks at peace.

As I make my way back to my apartment, the world around me is in morning mode. People are rushing to their cars, and the streets are busy. Yet I don't feel a part of it. I'm moving slow. Time doesn't seem to exist for me. Why should it? I don't have a job, a career, a partner or even a dog at this point. I am completely alone. And I still have a dysfunctional kundalini. Amazingly, I'm not currently broke. Michele's dad didn't ask for a refund. He actually told Dana to tell me to keep the money. And I did film a ton of footage for them, so he'll probably find something useful to do with it.

I let myself in the house and lie down on my couch and once again survey the white board leaning up against the fireplace, the starting point of this leg of my journey on this "plane of existence." I like the homeless woman's description of this world, like a level of a video game. *I've always sucked at video games.* Sighing, I read the familiar words:

MEANINGFUL LIFE-CHANGING MOVIE, LOVE, MONEY

It's all there, my pathway to success. Apparently, I just don't have what it takes to get to the finish line. And yet … *Ha!* According to my back-alley oracle, there is no finish line. Life is just an endless maze of experiences. Hopefully, we learn something about ourselves from them. And then what? Wisdom was what she said. Then wisdom.

I close my eyes and I'm back in my black box. No one is there. I'm alone. I sit, crisscross applesauce in the silence and slowly, as if coming from another dimension, I hear a cacophony of voices, both men and women. It's hard at first to make out what they are saying. I see words floating above me appearing from the void and I reach up and grab them. And as I do, the full sentences come into view and I hear the voice behind them.

To know yourself as the Being underneath the thinker, the stillness underneath the mental noise, the love and joy underneath the pain, is freedom, salvation, enlightenment. - Eckhart Tolle

And then another:

No one saves us but ourselves. No one can and no one may. We ourselves must walk the path. -Buddha

And another:

You're just suffering from the belief that there's something missing from your life. In reality, you always have what you need. - Byron Katie

Suddenly the quotes begin to form one after another. Eyes closed, I listen to the words to feel their vibration.
Not all those who wander are lost. - J.R.R. Tolkien, *The Fellowship of the Ring*

Though the road's been rocky, it sure feels good to me. - Bob Marley (Ok, I'm glad these voices have a sense of humor.)

We don't see things as they are, we see them as we are. -
Anaïs Nin

*You are what your deep, driving desire is. As your desire is, so
is your will. As your will is, so is your deed. As your deed is,
so is your destiny.* - Brihadaranyaka Upanishad

Finally, as the voices and words and images fade
away, one last sentence remains, luminescent in the
darkness:

*Embrace nothing: if you meet the Buddha, kill the Buddha,
live your life as it is, not bound to anything* - Linji-
Founder of Chan Buddhism

The last quote echoes in my mind and I see before
me a moment at the very beginning of the journey,
when I was in the elevator at the expo, leaning on
the back rail feeling dizzy and disorientated. Michele
leans over to me as the others are fully engaged in
their battle of the quotes about god and spirituality.
"Are you okay?" she asks. It was a simple question, yet
really sweet and thoughtful. And now I remember all
the times Michele had my back—at the firewalk, even
at Fran-N-Furters, she still cared for me. It wasn't
until the very end, in our last moment together, that
I ever repaid her with the same presence she gave
me...

Now I see myself at the firewalk and I'm being
carried. I thought it was Brin who dragged me to
my room but, as I see it now, it was Fabio and Jason

who carried me, Michele running ahead to open the doors and Brin is carrying my stuff.

Another vison … me riding in the van, trying to sleep in the front seat, my head hanging in the most awkward way and Brin, ever so gently, lifts my head and then scrunches my sweatshirt into a pillow and rests my head on it.

Okay, this is totally cheesy, but I'm seriously having a full-blown Ebenezer Scrooge moment right now. Then the memories shift and I'm no longer watching myself. I see Brin standing in a moment of trance-like peace in the middle of the labyrinth at the expo with Jason in the background, shooting. I see Michele sitting next to Lyra at Skull Ranch, back straight, focused and attentive and sincere. Fabio— sweet Fabio in a hotel lobby, Macchiato in hand, waiting for Michele to come down off the elevator at morning crew call. Jason …

My eyes pop open and I sit up so fast I surprise myself. *I can finish the film!* I know exactly what to do and how to do it. I just need Jason to be willing to help me. I fish out my phone from my bag and call him.

"Jason, where are you? Are you back in LA yet?"

"Yeah, I got in a couple hours ago. Just caught some z's in a rest stop and …"

"Do you still have all the raw footage?" I can tell he's hesitating. Does he know yet?

"Yes, I have it. Why?"

"I know you were making a blooper reel of all the dumb shit I did. I know you had it all organized."

Jason sputters defensively but I ignore him. "Do you still have it?"

Silence.

"Look, I don't know or care what you planned to do with it. It's okay. Really. I just need to know if you've still got it all."

Finally, "I didn't think you knew. Yeah, I still have it. Why?"

"I'm coming over. Are you home?"

"Yeah."

"Alright! We have about 48 hours to do something that I think will save the film—save all of us."

I hang up and call for an Uber. I don't bother changing. No one is going to care what I'm wearing. I grab my house keys, run out the door, and direct the driver to Jason's place, which is near downtown. As I walk inside, I notice it's a cool but downright total dude's apartment—clean, with dark brown furniture and some nice black and white photography on the walls. He looks wary and confused as I barge into the living area. "Where's your computer? You do have editing software, right?"

I must look like a strung-out crazy woman right now and I really don't give a shit. He points toward a large desk by a picture window. The blinds are drawn, which is why it's so dark. A single lamp gives the room a seedy glow, which is kind of perfect as we are technically about to commit a crime. Okay, maybe not a crime. But I'm fired and technically barred from doing anything further with the film. I'm not sure what Jason knows or doesn't know.

"So, what do you know?" I figure I should probably just ask him.

"I know that you were fired. I know that on Monday I'm supposed to drop all the footage at some office in Beverly Hills."

"Okay, then we have the weekend," I say as I push past him, drop my bag and keys and pull up a chair from his kitchen table and sit down behind his desk.

He's just standing there, looking baffled.

"Jason, I know how to make this film awesome, ground-breaking, funny and, most importantly, transformational for anyone who sees it." He sort of nods as if to say go on. "This movie isn't about the people we interviewed, it's about us, *our* journeys. I'm sure in addition to filming all of my own crazy antics, there's footage of all of us. Right? You weren't the only one with a camera."

He nods.

"So, what if we took all that footage and used the interviews to guide the audience on their own journey with us? What if we could show them, through our own struggles and battles with our demons and each other and, okay, my total hot messes, that that's the whole point. That enlightenment—okay, maybe forget enlightenment, like ya know, ascending into the ethers like a damn master on a violet flame of awesomeness—but that love, peace, kindness and friendship are all possible in spite of our fucked-upness. That's what people need to know about."

I am literally spitting as I talk. Jason paces a

little. "I'm not supposed to even be talking to you," he mutters. "No one is. You are persona non grata."

I can tell he's conflicted. Years of AA and Bible thumping make it hard to break the rules. "Jason, listen to me, if after Sunday it's terrible and doesn't work, I'll leave, and you can throw out what we did and turn in everything just like you're supposed to. I won't tell a soul. I promise!"

He's standing still now, frozen between two choices.

"Jason, you have nothing to lose and we have everything to gain. Why did we do all of this—just so it can be shelved? We didn't go on this journey for it to end like this. Each of us learned something. Each one of us grew and had a transformation."

He seems unconvinced. "I don't know that any of us had anything other than a lot of chaos, drama and upset," he mumbles. "We're all kind of a mess, actually."

"Really, Jason, are we? Brin has finally found her teacher, her place. Michele and Fabio are finding each other and the strength to stand up for what they want. I … I found peace. Yeah, I might not look very peaceful right now. But I tell you I've found it. And you—you were like the damn baby Jesus, Buddha, and baby Yoda throughout the whole thing. You were steadfast in your faith and that is so powerful to see someone stand in their faith against so many obstacles, so many challenges and so much hurtful crap. You never wavered, even when we were assholes, and it taught me so much."

He likes this part, I think. He's contemplative and I'm begging. "Jason, come on, what have you got to lose?" He stands there for what seems like an eternity and finally he pulls out his chair and sits down.

We don't sleep—well, Jason catnaps here and there. It was a long drive back from Durango. We order Korean and Chinese take-out and together Jason and I make a film in 48 hours. He's as good an editor as he is a cameraman, and I am gleefully amazed that we have almost everything I was hoping for on camera—moments neither of us knew existed, pieces of our story caught in secret—moments of pure struggle, joy, pain, connection, anger, fear, betrayal, grief, confusion, hot mess Sara. All of it is there. It's as if the film is making itself and we are unwittingly participating … little mice dropped into a maze and set free to do our thing … being watched the whole time—which I could also say is kind of creepy, but you know … it's actually perfect.

Monday, at four in the morning, we finish. I send out a group text to meet me at a screening room I know in West Hollywood. I booked it Sunday afternoon when I knew we had the film. I leave Jason's to head home, get some sleep, shower and be ready to present at ten. I'm not sure who will show up, if anyone, but I know Jason has to have the footage back to Beverly Hills by noon, so if no one shows, then he can still live up to his agreement. If nothing else, he and I will know what had been possible.

I arrive early, as does Jason. He meets with the

projectionist and I wait in the lobby. Michele and Fabio arrive right on time, holding hands, excited to see me and to see what we created. I'm not sure they know what happened, but if they do, they aren't letting on. At 9:59 Brin walks through the door. She smiles at me. There is hope in her eyes and a bit of a wink and I know she's on my side.

Everyone is seated and it's 10:05. I'm not sure if I should start the film or wait. We are all in the screening room when I hear the creak of the door and I brace myself for my official first meeting with our Executive Producer, Michele's dad.

He enters the screening room and takes a seat in the back row closest to the door and nods at me. With that the lights go out and the film begins.

Black Screen:

Slowly the following words emerge from the void, soft gentle music in the background: *Embrace nothing. If you meet the Buddha, kill the Buddha, live your life as it is, not bound to anything* - Linji- Founder of Chan Buddhism

Epilogue

I am sitting in an audience full of celebrities, wearing a Vintage Valentino dress. (You remember, THE DRESS, but for real this time.) It's short in the front to show off my legs, which are short, but damn sexy. The dress has a long train and is black with tiny but sparkling adornments. A simple yet brilliant

emerald-in-the-raw necklace is around my neck,
because we're sustainable dammit. (Which is why I
wore vintage—no need to kill any children to make
a new dress. Let's honor the ones who already died.)
My shoes are Salvatore Ferragamo, black as well,
strappy and FYI, the same ones Michele was wearing
for our infamous dinner at Frank-N-Furter's. (I told
you I'd find out who she was wearing.)

Where are we? Okay, it's not exactly the Academy
Awards, and yet it's still something. A very large
and very cool Indie film awards night. Brin is there,
looking stunning in something she probably pulled
out of her closet at the last minute. *Damn, how does she
do that?* Fabio and a very pregnant Michele, looking
like the couple of the damn year, sit next to us. And
look at Jason—turns out he cleans up well and is
looking rather dashing in a Sabyasachi Mukherjee
(famous Indian designer), waist coat, black with tiny
gold thread inlay.

Why is Jason wearing a famous Indian designer?

So, here's the scoop, Brin and Jason are now
a thing. After our screening in West Hollywood,
where everyone laughed and cried and clapped
(even Quincy—ya know, Michele's dad) as we each
had an opportunity to watch our story from the
outside, the sexual tension between Brin and Jason
finally showed itself so palpably, so alive, that after
our raucous celebratory lunch of wine and decadent
food (all paid for by Quincy), Brin and Jason ended
up getting it on and they've been a couple ever since.
She took him to India. He took her to meet his

parents in Indiana.

Oh, the irony.

Fabio and Michele? Here's the kicker in that story. Turns out early on in our adventure Fabio did, in fact, bed Michele. We caught the beginning of their rendezvous on camera. After our first crew meeting, the kids (Jason, Fabio and Michele) all decided to have a drink to get to know each other. (Bummer, I wasn't invited.) Michele can't handle her liquor, (we'll skip the part that she wasn't even legal) and even though Fabio isn't that kind of guy, I honestly think—and if you watch the footage, which, of course, Jason filmed in the bar—it really looked like she liked him. Which she must have because they had a hook-up, which Michele felt utterly ashamed of afterwards and then tried to cock block Fabio for the rest of the trip. Then in comes Fran-N-Furter and she thinks she's found her way out. And guess what? That baby isn't Lawrence the skull wranglers. It was Fabio's all along.

Of course, it is. Damn, that kid is going to be gorgeous.

So, finally, how did we all really end up on this bizarre imitation Fellini flick? Well, here's the back story. Once upon a time, Brin dated a cinematographer who would sometimes show her the dailies from films he was working on. One of those contained my Extravaganza of Rage in the Desert epic short film, and while he laughed, she told me that she saw something, someone— herself—in me, and all the rage and pain she herself felt at the unjustness of the world. A month or so later she went to India and met Quincy.

A hugely successful venture capitalist, Quincy figured out that no one was investing in black-owned business, so he did. He ended up making millions managing one of the largest black-owned investment firms in the US. After a mild heart attack, he did what so many lost souls are doing and took up yoga, found Paulo Coelho's book *The Alchemist*, (which is sort of like finding God and being born again) and went on his own spiritual journey ending up in an ashram India. The experience changed his life, and it was there that he met Brin.

These days everybody wants to make a movie about their spiritual awakening, and he happened to have the resources. His daughter wanted to be in the movie business, and he hoped to imbue a little spirituality in her at the same time. (Although I don't think he expected her to be impregnated with it.)

Brin took on the project and called her ex when she got back to the States. He hooked her up with Jeremy, who said he knew my agent and would reach out. Her ex also connected her with a few other film industry people, which is how she ended up finding Jason and Fabio. Pretty impressive for someone who isn't technically a film producer.

Another divine move by Brin was she told both Fabio and Jason to film everything they could, including the crew, and to keep it on the down-low. My flash of insight on the couch that awful day I got fired was in total alignment with her plan, even if she didn't know what that plan actually was. I asked her why she made that call, and she said she didn't really understand it herself. She had been meditating and got the message to film everything, even the crew. And when she saw the film Jason and I cut, it all made sense. *Afterwards.*

Sometimes you just gotta let go and let the divine Universe do its thing. Sort of like my going to a yoga class (unlikely!) and ending up making that list, or when I took that call from Michele, or probably millions of other moments when I got signs from the Universe. Since the film, I've started to pay way more attention to my heart and my gut and the signs. (I've named the Universe Bob, because we gotta call it something. Some people call it God, or Source or the Universe. It's all the same thing and so I just call it Bob.)

That's important. Source, the Universe, God—it is all the same thing—the thing we're all trying to connect to. Something filled with peace and love and safety and it's everywhere and within all of us, even when we don't know it. Even when we're assholes, Bob is always there.

Like my goddess of the alley predicted: "I hate to ruin the ending, but it's all going to be okay."

That night as I walked out on stage in my Valentino gown to receive an award for Best Documentary Film, no blood spewed from the trophy, ruining my dress. No one stood up to call me out as a fraud. I humbly said, "Thank you," took my trophy, honored my comrades and walked off the stage. It was entirely uneventful and entirely fulfilling. Because I finally did it. I found success (or rather it found me). I found love. Not with anyone in particular, but with myself and the journey I am on.

FYI, I did not go back to Tom. I did, however, pick up Zak. Today, I am happily single, sober, smokeless and going to yoga with Dana three times a week. I still eat meat and really enjoy hanging out with Jeff at the new and improved La Abadia. He actually makes a mean Margarita-tasting Kombucha. As I write this, today's message from Madame Ling is: *Love your life, every detail of it.* - Jack Kerouac

Damn, that woman is good.

My final takeaway from my own version of the Camino De Santiago (except without the need for a passport and hot Spaniards) is this: The stories I once told myself about life and about myself, the beliefs and goals I was attached to, no longer serve me. I've overturned the shrine and my blind belief in material goals as "the only answer." And I've given up on gurus. I've given up thinking anybody can lead me to the life experiences I need except me.

I've killed my Buddhas. Okay, well, some of them are dead. Others are gasping their last breath, and I'm sure there is an army of Zombie strippers writhing in the shadows somewhere. But it's a start.

What would happen if we killed them, all of them? What would our lives be like then? Maybe, someday, I'll find out.

THE END

Author's postscript:

*People often ask me why I titled this book "Killing Buddha."
Many years ago I read the Linji quote.* ("Embrace Nothing:
If you meet the Buddha, kill the Buddha. Live your
life as it is, not bound to anything.") *Afterwards, I had
a dream. In it, much like in this book, I became aware of how
many Buddhas, or beliefs, I had accepted as absolute truths,
only to find out that, in fact, there was nothing absolute about
them. Things my parents told me, friends, books, gurus and
teachers. Ultimately, I discovered, it's up to me to choose what
to believe.*

*As I enter into my 50th decade, I have understood that beliefs
shift and change as do the seasons of one's life. Greater
awareness happens when we are open to it, and from it we get
to expand, change and grow if we want to. But to continue to
grow we have to be willing to let die the beliefs and ideas that
no longer serve our true hearts, our most authentic values and
selves. To me, that is what this journey called life is about. I
don't know if we ever get to the end of the road, or if we're
supposed to. I do know that I am humbly grateful for every step
along the path.*

Betsy Chasse

-

ACKNOWLEDGMENTS

It took a long time and a lot of killing my own Buddhas to come to a place of humble gratitude for each and every person I have encountered on this journey. Some brought gifts of roses and chocolates, others, well, let's just say, at the time, I wasn't seeing the beauty in their offerings.

As I am now 50+, I am most grateful for my family and the friendships that have persisted throughout all of the wild adventures my life has taken me on. My dearest and most wise friend Cate Montana, who spent years (literally) on this journey with me and supported me in countless ways in telling this story. Steadfast, honest and the utter embodiment of BFF.

My big sister, Suzette. Who has always shown up for me, guided me and offered a loving kick in the ass when I truly needed it.

My kids Max and Elora. Who push every button I have and are my "why," for everything I do. you two are the best chaos and mayhem a mom could want.

And to my wonderful coven of GF's, Kirsten, Teresa,

Rebecca, Debbie, Anna, Teri, Marla (and I'll add her hubby Jami who isn't a GF but an awesome dude) … thank you for being there, listening, taking my late-night calls, drinking wine with me, reading this book so many times and finding my typos. You have made my life rich and full of laughter and love.

To my delightful sommeliers at The Stonehaus, Lexi and Jeremy – Thank you for welcoming me into a new home in a new town with a sumptuous glass of wine, a warm smile and a feeling that I somehow always belonged on your portico surrounded by grapevines. I don't think I would have finished this book without you.

And lastly to my Dad, who did teach me to dream big, who, as we drove around Hollywood ogling the mansions, told me wild stories about the famous people who lived there, assuring me that one day I would be just like them. Well Dad, I don't live in a Hollywood Mansion, but because of your inspiration to live out loud and outside of the box and to always follow my heart and to have fun, I am rich beyond my wildest dreams.